CHAINS OF AIR, WEB OF AETHER

Philip K. Dick

McVane, content in his isolation, forced himself to help the woman who lay dying in the neighboring dome. His support was all that kept her alive—but, even terminally ill, she had strengths he couldn't imagine . . .

☆

ALL THAT GLITTERS

G. C. Edmondson

Old Frank took the stranger who showed up near his deep-woods cabin for a wandering prospector. And maybe he was—but what was he after if he was throwing away all that gold?

☆

THE NOBEL LAUREATE

Robert E. Curtis

Mankind had learned a lot from its thousands of years of war, famine, and pestilence—but not enough. It was time, the Teachers felt, for a final exam . . .

☆

CORPUS CRYPTIC

Lee Killough

As a coroner, Dr. Dallas March wa
But the dead physics prof
to every last cell anc
cause. Faced with two i
the only logical answer:

GRIM... LAW

L. Neil Smith

The Temporal Academy's strictest rule was against letting its existence be known to anyone in the past—so how come the time-jockey was entertaining his bar companion with top-secret anecdotes of the future?

Also edited by Judy-Lynn del Rey:

STELLAR #1

STELLAR SCIENCE-FICTION STORIES #2

STELLAR SCIENCE-FICTION STORIES #3

STELLAR SCIENCE-FICTION STORIES #4

STELLAR SHORT NOVELS

SCIENCE-FICTION STORIES

EDITED BY

Judy-Lynn del Rey

A Del Rey Book

BALLANTINE BOOKS • NEW YORK

A Del Rey Book
Published by Ballantine Books

Library of Congress Catalog Card Number: 75-34193

ISBN 0-345-28065-2

Printed in Canada

First Edition: May 1980

Cover art by Darrell K. Sweet

"But retrospect is fond to say:
I have had help along the way . . ."

TO

Selma Gore
Leonard Albert
The Family Ladar
Vera and Jay Stolar
Robert M. Guinn
Mavis Fisher
Frederik Pohl
Ian and Betty Ballantine
Ron Busch
Robert L. Bernstein & Company
Richard A. Krinsley

WITH THANKS

Contents

The Sword of Damocles

James P. Hogan

For some reason the object escaped detection by Earth's long-range radars and astronomical instruments until it had gotten within a million miles or so of the Moon. This could have been due to its unusual geometry, which made it a poor reflector of radar waves, or maybe it was because the object was constructed from materials with high absorptivity; possibly the reason was a combination of both factors. In any event, suddenly it was just *there*—falling gently inward toward the Earth from somewhere in the direction of the outer solar system.

It first appeared as a set of echo-coordinates and trajectory data included in the inventory of space-borne objects maintained by the computers of the NORAD near-Earth surveillance network. The computers decided that it oughtn't to be there and flagged its entry with a query, which was about as much as they could say about it. The echo signals were weak and confused, enabling little to be reconstructed of the object's shape and surface contours apart from that they were irregular and complex; they showed none of the familiar characteristics of a naturally occurring wanderer such as a large meteor or stray asteroid. Terrestrial and orbiting telescopes trained on the point indicated by the electronic fingers revealed something that looked like an indistinct, low-albedo, six-faceted strawberry, tumbling sedately at two revolutions per minute as it closed in on a path that would set it into a high-Earth orbit in a matter of days. Once its motion had been determined accurately, its size was estimated by measuring the times for which it eclipsed background stars; apparently it was about a mile across.

As the days passed by, the object, by this time christened *Nomad* by the intrigued scientific teams following its progress, gradually resolved itself into the form of six, one-mile-diameter, circular constructions arranged to lie in mutually perpendicular planes that formed the faces of an imaginary bounding cube, rather like six dinner-plates fastened to the surfaces of a large box. Instead of a solid box, however, the interior space enclosed by the "plates" contained a confusion of structural members of some kind which couldn't be resolved with certainty because of the moving, ever-present shadows cast by the outer surfaces. The "plates" were concave outward like shallow parabolic dishes, and their surfaces absorbed radiation strongly, appearing almost black-body to the probe beams directed at them from installations on the lunar surface and from orbiting laboratories. Furthermore they were electromagnetically passive, emitting no detectable energy in any part of the spectrum, apart from a thermal background consistent with the temperature of interplanetary space. The only other thing that could be said for sure at that stage was that *Nomad* bore no resemblance whatever to anything that had ever been put into space by any nation of Earth.

A week later, *Nomad* had settled into orbit above the Earth and was still showing no signs of activity. Nothing more happened nor, after a while, seemed likely to. NASA and the Air Force began hasty preparations to send a team of scientists and other experts aloft to investigate the mysterious intruder at closer quarters.

The soft, melancholic notes of Beethoven's *Moonlight Sonata* trickled around the apartment like the tinkling of a mountain stream reduced to slow motion. The face of the woman sitting at the grand piano by the large bay window of the spacious and elegantly furnished living room betrayed no emotion as she played, but the lines in her skin beneath its layer of powder, and the wrinkles beginning to form around her eyes and neck, hinted of the premature aging that comes with years of solitude and loneliness. While her fingers danced smoothly over the keyboard, assembling the notes into shape and form without need of any conscious intervention of mind, her eyes stared distantly from beneath her mantle of graying hair, replaying their own themes and variations of memories.

"Ah, excuse me." The voice of the apartment's computer interrupted suddenly from one of the grilles concealed as part of the decor of the room. It was a bright, cheerful, female voice, emulating a girl in her early twenties and synthesized with a trace of a South Carolina accent; the tenants could specify things like that to suit personal perferences.

Doreen Waverley stopped in mid bar and returned to the present. "What is it, Naomi?" she asked in a tone that was firm, clear, and carefully cultivated.

"The visitors you were expecting have arrived—your daughter and granddaughter. They're in the lobby now. Shall I bring them up?"

"Of course!" Doreen's face broke into a smile of relief and anticipation. "Let me say hello to them first though."

"Sure."

The flat-panel screen of the living-room viset by the far wall pivoted around on its flexible support-arm to face Doreen. An image formed immediately of a tall, slim, good-looking woman of thirty with shoulder-length fair hair, standing framed by the background of the main entrance lobby below. Accompanying her was a girl of ten, also fair-haired, deeply suntanned after the sweltering summer, and wearing a yellow dress with white polka dots. They were both smiling.

The girl was jumping up and down excitedly and trying, not very successfully, to conceal a brightly wrapped package behind her back.

"Carol!" Doreen rose from the piano stool and approached the screen, at the same time throwing out her hands. "It seems like such a long time. I'm so glad nothing went wrong at the last minute. And Amanda, you're so brown! You've certainly been making the most of the weather we've been having."

"Hi, Mother," the woman answered, laughing. "Happy birthday. You haven't been worrying again, have you? I told you nothing would stop us from coming today of all days, not even the Air Force."

"Happy fifty-fourth birthday, Grandma," the girl chipped in.

The two figures moved forward out of the viewing angle, and the screen went blank. "Make some coffee for us, Naomi," Doreen said, addressing her words to no point in particular in the room. "And fix whatever it was Amanda liked when she was here last. I can't remember . . ."

"Coke and cookies," Naomi supplied after a couple of milliseconds access delay. "Everything will be ready when they get here. Do you want me to turn the air-conditioner down a little too? Carol said it was cold the last time she was here."

"Oh, yes, so she did. Yes, do that would you?"

"I have a question," Naomi said as unseen circuits shuttled binary digits to and fro, and hidden motors whirred spasmodically.

"Oh, what?"

"Why was your granddaughter trying to hide the parcel she was carrying?"

Doreen sighed. "It's to do with an old custom connected with birthdays. I'll tell you about it after they're gone, when there's more time. For now, we have to pretend that we haven't seen it, so don't mention it."

"I see." Naomi's voice was concurring, but at the same time managed to convey just the right shade of mystification.

Two hours later, after a dinner of crab-and-lobster salad followed by ice cream and a cake that Carol had brought, the two women were sitting talking over coffee in the lounge while Amanda was in the bedroom engaged in emptying her grandmother's jewelry boxes and arranging the contents into patterns on the dressing table.

"So, how much leave have you got left to go?" Doreen asked.

"Another two days," Carol told her. "Then I'll be going straight back into space."

"Oh. What for this time?"

Carol smiled apologetically. "I can't tell you I'm afraid, Mother. It's a classified mission."

"Oh." Doreen looked around to change the subject, and her eyes came to rest again on the set of hand-sculpted Dresden-china figurines arranged on the top shelf of the recess between the bookcase and the door leading through to the kitchen. They blended perfectly with the room and added just the finishing touch that it had needed. "They really are beautiful, Carol," she murmured. "I really do appreciate them. Did you say they came all the way from Europe?"

"I thought you'd like them," Carol said. "I know how you like anything German, and I've always said that that place up there needed something to fill it."

"You certainly picked the ideal thing," Doreen told her. "But where did you find them? I've never come across anything as fine and detailed as those over here. They're craftsman-made . . . not imitation at all."

"I planned it," Carol confessed, smiling mischievously. "One of the other officers from our wing—Tom Fairburn, I've told you about him before—went to Germany a few weeks ago on some equipment trials. I asked him to look out for something like that, and he came back with exactly what I had in mind. They are beautiful, aren't they."

"Do you . . . see a lot of him?" Doreen asked. She

tried to sound casual, but there was a serious undertone in her voice that she couldn't disguise.

Carol shot her a reproachful glance. "Oh, Mother! He's just a good friend. Don't sound as if you're trying to get me married. This is supposed to be a party."

Doreen nodded, but Carol already knew that motherly concern was not going to let the subject rest at that. "I don't want to interfere or anything like that," Doreen said. "Your life is your own affair. But . . . oh, I don't know . . . sometimes I can't help thinking that perhaps for Amanda's sake if nothing else . . ." She shrugged and sat back in her chair, apparently having thought better of finishing the sentence. Then, after wrestling with her thoughts for a few seconds she continued, "I can't imagine why you never married Amanda's father. Don't get me wrong; I'm not trying to preach morals or anything like that. But you were both young and intelligent, both with exciting futures ahead of you . . . and you seemed to think the world of each other. It seemed as if it should have been the natural thing to do, baby or no baby." She looked up and confronted Carol with a direct stare. "He wanted to, didn't he?"

"Yes," Carol replied simply. She didn't feel offended or that her mother was being meddlesome. Doreen led a lonely life, and apart from her career as a concert pianist, had little in the way of personal matters to concern herself with other than Carol and Amanda. Her concern was only natural, and in a way Carol found it touching.

"So?" Doreen implored, shaking her head in the effort to comprehend. "I know the Air Force can be demanding at times, but the two aren't irreconcilable. Lots of people manage to mix careers and marriage quite happily."

"Oh, it's not that, and you know it, Mother," Carol replied. "It's . . ." She shrugged and tossed her hands up in front of her. "We've been through this before. I *like* being independent. The thought of being shut up in a box with the same person full-time, not being able to do anything without agreeing on this and compromising on that . . . it's just not *me*. I'd be stifled." She smiled and shook her head despairingly as if Doreen were making hard work for herself by seeing everything but the obvious. "You should understand if anybody can, Mother."

Doreen fell silent as she heard the words that confirmed what she feared deep down inside. She blamed herself for Carol and Amanda being on their own, even though it never seemed to bother either of them. In fact they seemed to thrive on each other's company, and Amanda had never shown signs of being deprived of anything that mattered. Nonetheless, Doreen worried, and she blamed herself.

Thirty years had gone by since her own husband, Phillip, was killed. It had happened within a month of Carol's birth, and he never saw his daughter. Perhaps that was the part of it that had affected Doreen so deeply. She had never remarried, but instead devoted the years to a life that divided itself between music and bringing up her daughter single-handed. So Carol had never known a household with a man as part of it. When Amanda was born twenty years later, after one of those all-cares-to-the-winds encounters that had taken place while she was at university, Carol stubbornly chose to continue the self-reliant life that her mother had taught her. Or was it in fact the opposite—an unconscious fear of a style of living that she had never been conditioned to deal with? And now Amanda was ten years old, and perhaps already on her way toward carrying the tradition forward into another generation. The thought troubled Doreen.

Amanda's father had been a physics graduate—brilliant, competent, and ambitious—the kind of young man for whom everybody had predicted a dazzling career studded with great accomplishments. In earlier years he had done about as much as could be expected from a father from long-range. For a long time, it seemed to Doreen, he never quite lost hope that one day Carol might have second thoughts about the situation. But Carol's obstinacy had persisted, and after a while his appearances became less frequent.

"Do you still see him?" Doreen asked at last.

"Who, Don?"

"Yes."

"Not so much these days," Carol admitted. "I hear about him though. He's taken an executive position with the government, something to do with the Distant Solar Relay Program. It sounds good. He'll do fine, I'm sure."

Doreen's brows knitted slightly. "Isn't that something to do with the colonies they've been talking about for years?"

Carol nodded. "The colonies will be built from materials processed from lunar rock in plants constructed on the Moon. The plants will be powered from enormous solar collectors—miles across—in orbit around the Moon, beaming it down as microwaves. The first six are almost finished now, and Don will be involved with the program to get them up and running." Exhilaration was burning in her eyes. "It'll mark the beginnings of the next phase of human evolution—outward from the solar system. Don't you think it's exciting? It's what Don always dreamed of."

But Doreen's thoughts were a long way from orbiting relays, lunar construction plants, and the next phase of evolution of the human species. "It's all such a shame," she said, shaking her head sadly.

At that moment Amanda reappeared from the bedroom carrying a framed picture of a handsome, keen-eyed man wearing a uniform jacket that bore the insignia of an Air Force colonel. Carol stared for a moment at the familiar features of her father and then raised her eyes to take in Amanda's inquiring stare.

"That's your grandfather," Carol said before Amanda could voice any question. "You've seen that picture before. He was the spaceman who never came home."

"I know," Amanda replied. "But I've never noticed

this before." She pointed at a badge stitched to Phillip Waverley's upper sleeve a few inches below the epaulette. It bore a simple design of a red sword against a black background. "See. There's a sword on Grandpa's sleeve." She turned to look at Doreen. "Why did Grandpa have a sword on his sleeve?"

Carol stiffened for an instant and glanced at Doreen before turning back to face Amanda. "You shouldn't bother your grandmother with things like that on her birth—" she began, but Doreen cut her off with a wave of her hand.

"It's all right. It's not as if it happened yesterday." She took the picture from Amanda's hand and gazed at it fondly for a moment. "You see, before spacemen go away to do something very important—on a special job that they call a mission—they sometimes choose a sign. Everybody who goes on the mission wears the sign, and then afterwards other people will know that they were part of it."

"You mean like the badge we get when we finish summer camp," Amanda said. "We all wear the same badge, and when we get home everybody can see where we've been."

"Something like that," Doreen said, nodding.

Amanda thought for a second. "Was the sword-badge mission that Grandpa was part of an important one?"

"Very important."

"Why?"

Doreen sighed, and then smiled as she saw Carol starting to get anxious. "You tell her, Carol," she suggested. "You know far more about that kind of thing than I ever will." Amanda shifted her eyes toward her mother.

"You know what planets are, don't you?" Carol asked. Amanda nodded. "Well, there are lots of great big rocks out in space too, as well as planets. Some of them are bigger than whole cities. Most of them move round the sun in nice, steady circles like the planets do, but some move about all over the place so that you can never be exactly sure where they're going to go next."

"Do they jiggle about like flies?"

"Not quite as much, but you've got the idea." Carol paused. When Amanda said nothing, Carol continued. "Anyway, a long time ago, when your grandfather was a spaceman—"

"How long ago?"

"Just about thirty years ago. It was in 1993."

Amanda's eyes widened. "That's a *long* time. It's even longer than before I was born."

"Yes," Carol agreed. "Anyhow, one of the biggest of these rocks—they're called meteors, before you ask—was coming nearer from a long way away in space, and it looked as if it would crash into the Earth. If it did, lots and lots of people might have been killed."

The message didn't really register, and Amanda just nodded. "Did it crash into the Earth, or did somebody stop it?" she asked.

"That was why Grandfather's mission was sent off," Carol told her. "They went out a long way from Earth in a big spaceship and met the giant rock while it was still farther away than Mars. They fixed some big, powerful motors to it to drive it away into space again so that it wouldn't come anywhere near Earth at all. Everything worked the way they planned it, and lots of people who might have been killed were saved."

"Why did they make the badge a picture of a sword?" Amanda asked, gazing at the photograph with a new respect.

"Because the name of the mission was *Damocles,* and that's also the name of an old, old story about a sword."

"What kind of a story? Did it have wizards and dragons in it?"

"Oh dear," Carol sighed wearily. "It's too long a story to tell now. Why don't you ask our computer to tell it to you when we get home? He'll tell you all the details; I've forgotten most of them." She sat back in her chair to try to close the subject. "We'll have to be going soon, you know. Now how about putting that picture back where it came from and tidying Grandma's jewelry."

But Amanda was not to be put off. "Did Grandpa go on more important missions after that one?" she asked.

"That's enough, Amanda." Carol's voice caught as she spoke and took on a sharpness that she hadn't intended. Amanda pulled a quick face and went back into the bedroom. "I'm sorry," Carol said to Doreen. "She didn't mean anything."

"It's all right," Doreen replied quietly. But her eyes had gone suddenly misty.

The *Damocles* mission had gone down as one of the most tragic unexplained mysteries in the history of space exploration. Communications with the mission ship were lost when the vessel was a few weeks short of its scheduled rendezvous with the approaching meteor. Presumably the members of the mission pressed on regardless and accomplished their objective, for the threat to Earth never materialized. But nobody ever found out why the communications system had failed or what exactly happened after that. The ship exploded suddenly and violently on the first leg of its return trip home; there were no survivors.

Two hours after the last shuttle from Vandenberg had made its rendezvous, transferred across its load of personnel and equipment, and detached, the fleet carrier *Guam* fired its main drives and began climbing out of low orbit toward where *Nomad* was riding fifteen thousand miles farther up. The *Guam* was less than five years old and had been built in orbit as a mother ship for satellite hunter-killers and orbital interceptors, and a mobile base for surface-bombardment operations. It was designed to exist permanently in space, destined never to enter a planetary atmosphere or touch down on a solid surface. For over thirty hours it climbed upward until at last it was in a parallel orbit standing twenty miles off from the strange alien construction. For a while it waited; nothing happened. Eventually the time came for the *Guam* to assume a more active role.

Major Carol Waverley, U.S.A.F. Communications Service, attached to the 2nd Tactical Wing of Orbital Command, watched the main display-screen from her post on the control deck of the *Guam* while the robot probes that had been dispatched earlier sent back the first views of *Nomad* to be obtained from close-up. Around her the atmosphere was tense as the rest of the control deck's duty-officers and crew watched silently from monitor consoles and control stations around the room. From the raised bridge overlooking the control deck from one end, General George Medford, commanding officer of the *Guam* and acting director of local operations around *Nomad,* brooded from the center of a huddle of aides and advisors.

Each of the six dishes that formed *Nomad*'s external geometry was supported from the rear by an enormous pylon almost half a mile long and in the form of a slender cone with a slight concave sweep from base to tip. The six pylons projected outward from the structure's central nucleus in a three-dimensional cruciform pattern, thus establishing the cube-face relationship between the dishes. The nucleus itself consisted of six broad, flat, cylindrical housings to support the bases of the pylons, disappearing into a bewildering tangle of huge torroids wreathing the core at various angles, curving and merging surfaces of metal, gigantic windings, and interwoven structural members, all of which encased a central form that seemed to be basically spherical, although no part of any continuous spherical shape was actually visible. The nucleus was not a symmetrical arrangement, but comprised all manner of strange projections and ancillary constructions, the purpose of most of which was far from obvious. Among them, however, was a squat turret emerging from the confluence of three of the cylindrical bases. It was capped by an elaborate system of terraces and ridges which culminated in a flattened dome. The dome housed what appeared to be a cavernous docking-bay, two hundred feet or more across, situated behind a pair of gaping doors, which were open. The view on the screen was one being transmitted back from a probe that had passed between the rims of the dishes and penetrated through to the nucleus and was now scanning the inside of the docking-bay with a powerful searchlight from a point fifty feet outside the doors. So far no response had been evoked from *Nomad* by radar beams, lasers, optical beacons, radio, infrared, or X-rays.

"The bay goes back in for about fifty feet," the voice of the operations controller recited from his console below and to one side of the bridge. "There are tiers of platforms around the sides, with doors leading through to the inside. They could be airlocks. There are what look like three large, oval locks along the rear wall, possibly docking ports. Above the— Just a second . . ." The voice paused for a moment. "Probe Four, back up your beam and let's see that center lock again." Computers elsewhere on the *Guam* responded to the command, translated it into binary, and flashed it out to the probe. On the screen the pool of light at the back of the bay halted, then retraced its path to settle on the middle one of the three docking ports. "I thought so," the commentator's voice said. "Look. That center door's open."

Murmurs of excitement rippled round the control deck. On the bridge, Medford leaned forward to talk to one of the screens in front of him to confer with the Mission Director and his team, who were following the proceedings from inside the Pentagon. Then he sat back to exchange a few words with members of the group immediately around him; a couple of heads nodded. A few seconds later, Medford's voice sounded from the room's overhead speakers.

"Take the probe on into the bay. Try and get a beam on whatever's inside that door."

The periphery of the bay, brightly lit up by arc lamps positioned back behind the probe, yawned wider as the probe approached and then slipped suddenly off the edges of the screen. The scene darkened, leaving only the open port standing ghostly bright amid the gloom. The port expanded to fill the screen, and details of the inside started to become visible.

"It looks like an airlock chamber," the same voice as before resumed. "There's an inner door, also open. Impossible to make out what's on the other side of it."

"Can the probe get inside the outer door?" Medford's voice inquired.

"Negative, sir."

A short pause ensued while Medford, his advisors on the bridge, and the watchers in Washington went into conference again. Then Medford announced, "We're sending in the boarding party. All units engaged in operations in this sector can stand down. Maintain surveillance and monitoring functions only until further notice."

At different places around the control deck, mutterings of voices and stretchings of cramped limbs signaled the release of tensions that had been building up over several hours. Meanwhile, in another part of the *Guam,* a line of figures who had been standing by suited up were already hauling themselves smoothly and effortlessly along handlines into the transporter vessel that would carry them inside *Nomad.*

At her own station, Carol was following the progress of Probe Two as it nosed its way outward along one of the immense, sweeping metal surfaces that formed the outside of one of the pylons. It was one of five other probes being controlled by Carol's team of operators, deployed around *Nomad* to collect pictures and data for consumption by the *Guam*'s computers and copying down to Earth.

She watched with a feeling of awe that she had still not gotten used to as the strange configurations of line and curve flowed slowly through the probe's viewing field. Everything about *Nomad* seemed to embody concepts of shape, form, and function that were utterly unlike anything that had ever formed in the mind of a designer from Planet Earth. It wasn't so much the sheer scale of the contours dwarfing the probe from every side that produced this feeling, but the essence of the beings that had conceived them which they seemed to project. The fundamental geometric elements from which *Nomad* was formed, and the ascending progressions of greater wholes that they flowed together to create, suggested more an abstract art form rendered in engineering than a functional theme designed according to any principles that she was conditioned to recognize. And yet it *was* engineering; clearly it had a purpose. But at the same time it was such an . . . *alien* . . . version of engineering. What kind of alien purpose, Carol wondered, had it been built to serve?

She returned her attention to the screen in front of her as she realized that something had registered unconsciously while her mind was wandering. Whatever it was had gone. The probe was looking outward along the pylon toward its tip, where it narrowed and blended into a dense cluster of raised structures projecting from the rear of the dish that the pylon supported. Something in there had caught her eye, in among the shadows a quarter of a mile from where the probe was hovering. It had lasted for only a second or two, when the patterns of blackness that marched endlessly around behind the dishes as *Nomad* rotated parted to allow a thin shaft of sunlight in to where the dish and the pylon joined. Then it had disappeared back into shadow again.

She leaned forward a fraction and spoke into a microphone projecting from one end of the console fascia. "Probe Two, replay the last ten seconds of video on channel three." The image on the screen reset itself and began rolling again. Carol watched intently, waiting for the shadows to open up. When the precise moment came she called, "Freeze it."

It was something long and yellow, lying across the pylon right up underneath the mounting supports of the dish. It must have been the color that had caught her eye; everything else on *Nomad* was either black or metallic gray. "Magnify," she said. The smear of yellow expanded into an object that seemed to be a cylinder, crossing the tapering outline of the pylon as if it had collided with it at a random angle and somehow stuck. Carol estimated the object to be perhaps fifteen feet in diameter and about four times that in length. The probe had captured the original view at coarse resolution only, and no additional detail could be extracted from its stored record.

"Connect me to Probe Two control," she directed.

A few seconds later an audio grille below the screen acknowledged, "Probe Two control here."

"Move it out nearer the tip," Carol said. "There's something out there I want to get a better look at. Narrow the scan by factor four."

"Roger."

"Computers, unfreeze Probe Two image and resume real-time transmission," Carol instructed.

The view changed to show the object beginning to grow almost imperceptibly as the probe moved. Then the image jumped out suddenly as the intensifiers switched to a narrower scan, higher resolution mode.

The cylinder was surrounded at its center by a collar of short, dome-ended tanks and a web of supporting struts attaching the whole assembly to the pylon. There was something else that was unusual about it apart from its color, Carol realized. For a moment she couldn't put her finger on what. And then it came to her: what was so unusual was that it wasn't unusual at all.

It looked the way a piece of purpose-designed engineering should. Everything else about *Nomad* looked and felt 'alien'. The yellow cylinder didn't. It somehow looked "normal", and that was what made it seem out of place.

The view enlarged further and marched slowly across the screen to reveal lines of rivets along the cylinder's sides, tangles of pipes that looked the way pipes should and were woven into structural latticeworks that were designed the way lattices should be, and spouting valves that looked like valves. After the rest of *Nomad,* this cylinder seemed almost homely.

And then, suddenly, Carol gasped out loud and brought her hand involuntarily up to her mouth. The heads nearest her turned instinctively at the sound. Her face had turned pale.

Moving slowly into the center of the view being shown on the screen in front of her was a painted emblem of a red sword shown against a black background. Above it, stencilled clearly on the yellow surface of the cylinder, were the letters, *U.S.A.F.* And below the sword, standing out in red against the same black backdrop, was the single word *DAMOCLES.*

"There can be no doubt. We've checked everything against archived records beamed up from Washington. Those are the plasma motors that were sent out with the *Damocles* mission of 1993 to divert a rogue meteor that was supposed to be heading for Earth from the vicinity of the Asteroid Belt." Lieutenant-General Calvin Chalmers, officer in charge of computers and communications aboard the *Guam,* paused in his address at the officers' briefing for his words to take effect. The yellow cylinder had turned out to be just the first of a total of eight that were later discovered attached to different parts of *Nomad.* They were all from the *Damocles* mission of thirty years before.

After a short silence, Carol spoke from among the small group facing Chalmers in the *D* Deck mess. "The only thing that can mean is that there never was any meteor. It must have been *Nomad* that showed up in the Belt thirty years ago. The whole story about the meteor was some kind of cover-up."

Chalmers nodded. "That's what we figure too."

"But why?" somebody else demanded. "Why did they divert it off into space? And why all the secrecy?"

"That I can't answer," Chalmers replied. "All we can conclude for now is that the powers-that-were thirty years ago found a good reason to want to send it away.

Whether they meant it to come back again after thirty years or whether it was just a freak occurrence, we can't say." He paused for a moment and tweaked his moustache, then added in a more confidential tone, "In my own opinion, it seems highly likely that they intended to happen exactly what has happened. The set of motors is controlled by a sophisticated, highly reliable navigation and course-correction system that seems to have been designed for failproof operation for much longer than thirty years. In other words it's almost certainly been functioning exactly the way it was meant to, which means that *Nomad* reappeared because it was supposed to, when it was supposed to." He raised his hand to forestall the obvious question.

"No, we don't know why. We can only assume that our predecessors of thirty years ago were able to study *Nomad* for longer than we have so far had an opportunity to, and that therefore they managed to deduce more of its nature. Clearly it's important for us to waste no time in finding out whatever they knew, and the first phase of doing so will involve everybody in this room." A murmur of heightened interest surged around the circle of listeners.

"The detachment landed on *Nomad* has penetrated through to what seems to be the control center of the small section intended for occupation by whatever kind of beings built it. The equipment in there is as screwy as everything else about the place, but nevertheless it's probably the best place to start looking for answers. Clearly that's a job for computer-communications and instrumentation specialists, which means us. We'll be assisting the civilian team shipped up from Washington in a preliminary survey scheduled for oh-two-hundred hours tomorrow." Chalmers shifted his eyes to single out Carol.

"Major Waverley, since you have the honor of being the first person on the *Guam* to identify *Nomad*'s connection with *Damocles,* I'd like you to take charge of our half of the team. Would you stay behind after the briefing, please, to discuss objectives and procedures."

He raised his head to address the rest of the group. "Thank you. That's all for now."

Everything about *Nomad*'s control center, if that was indeed what the place was, was so . . . alien. What made it even more so was that it was completely dead, with no lighting, no sign of life from any of the peculiar devices which seemed intended as controls and indicators around the room, and none of the subtle vibrations in the floor and walls to signal the humming of unseen machinery as was omnipresent in the *Guam*.

Carol was floating among a collection of strangely angled and sculpted objects that could have been consoles or furnishings, or maybe some obscure combination of both, forming a cluster on the highest level of a series of tiered, irregularly curved platforms that ascended in complicated, interpenetrating steps and terraces toward the center of the room. They were glowing softly in the makeshift lighting installed by the *Guam's* engineers, appearing predominantly white but with subtle undertones of rainbow hues that seemed to shift and play in an elusive dance that the eye could never quite catch. A raised walkway connected one of the intermediate levels to the low, wide doorway leading into the room from one side; the rest of the area was bounded by intersecting segments of circles and curves to produce a floor-plan in the form of an asymmetric, many-leaved clover, with the large terraced dais taking up most of the central area, and the lowermost extremities forming the tips of what would be the leaves. These descending sections around the periphery formed miniature amphitheaters of semicircular steps, facing outward and downward toward a number of small black archways recessed into the walls, which led nowhere. Several partly enclosed galleries looked down over the room from the blending of curves, vaulted surfaces, and chiseled angles that enclosed the space from above; there was nothing obvious to distinguish anything that could be called a "ceiling" from anything that were clearly "walls".

There was thus an evident sense of *up* and *down* inherent in the general layout, although no force was in evidence to serve as gravity. Because of the room's orientation with respect to the rest of *Nomad*'s structure, the possibility of gravity being simulated by rotation had been ruled out—there was simply no conceivable axis about which *Nomad* could have been spun to generate a *down* in the direction where the floor lay. The team from the *Guam,* together with the equipment they had brought with them and the tangles of cables running back through the doorway to connect them via relays to the *Guam*'s control deck, were hanging and drifting in all manner of attitudes and gyrations amid a mesh of anchor ties and safety lines. The *Guam*'s engineers had also constructed a temporary airlock across the open port in the docking-bay and filled *Nomad*'s living quarters with air hosed through from the supply tanks of a transporter, so at least the team had the consolation of not having to work in helmets. They were wearing suits as a precaution, however, with helmets back-slung to be always within instant reach.

For a control center, the place was distinctly lacking in the profusions of panels, consoles, screens, buttons, and lamps that would have been normal in the corresponding part of a terrestrial vessel. This observation had led Carol and Chalmers to suspect that the aliens had used remote, probably portable devices of some kind to communicate with *Nomad*'s computer system, or whatever else it employed. If so, they had reasoned, the room ought to contain sensors somewhere to complete the links. Accordingly, for the last two hours the team had been scanning the interior of the room methodically with narrow electronic beams of all frequencies and signal patterns and measuring reflections in a search for any sudden changes in absorption ratios. They had found one spot, immediately above the middle of the main dais over which Carol was hanging, that seemed exceptionally sensitive, and were subjecting it to a systematic barrage of every kind of photonic ammunition contained in their arsenal.

"It dipped sharply at fifty-four-point-two," Dr. Hap Pearson, one of the scientists from Washington, announced as he interrogated a monitor display floating beside him a few yards to Carol's left. "Take it back through the decade again and ramp the form-factor at an increment of ten." Farther across the room, an Air Force operator keyed instructions into the panel of a portable field-computer while others round about went through their routines in silence, by now oblivious of the scores of eyes watching every move from inside the *Guam*, the Pentagon, and a few other select places. The arrival of *Nomad* had been followed by too many observatories for NASA to be able to deny that an alien object was orbiting Earth; statements had been issued to the effect that the object was being investigated, but so far details of the investigation were not being made public.

Suddenly Carol looked around sharply. Just as before, something had caught her attention from the corner of her eye. She ran a puzzled gaze over the collection of strange shapes and projections from where she thought the something had been, but nothing had changed. Or had it? She hesitated for a second and then activated her throat-mike. "Hold everything. Douse the lights for a moment, Echo Three. I think something's happened." A few frowns were exchanged around the room, and then the lights dimmed. Excited murmurings and a few whistles of excitement broke out in the gloom.

A curved, concave surface that formed a sloping projection from one of the white shapes was glowing with an array of studs, symbols, and geometric designs that had appeared seemingly embossed where a minute ago there had been nothing. They were radiating a fairyland mixture of subdued reds, blues, greens, yellows, purples, and silver, like a display of jewelry that had come to life with an inner light of its own. "Brighten it up a little," Carol said. The lights came on again but steadied at a level low enough for the colors to remain visible. Carol looked around the astonished faces turned toward her from all parts of the room, then shrugged and hauled herself over to the glowing pattern. Hap Pearson joined her a few seconds later while a sergeant floating above the access walkway followed their movements with a hand-held camera.

"What is it, some kind of control panel?" Pearson asked.

"Search me. Could be anything in a place like this." Carol stretched out a hand cautiously and touched a bead of amber. The bead vanished. It didn't just go out; the surface where the bead had been a moment before was now smooth and featureless. Other jewels in the array had also disappeared, others had materialized in other places, and some had altered their shapes and colors to yield a new overall pattern.

Carol stared helplessly at the meaningless presentation. "I hardly touched it," she said. "The thing seemed to respond to proximity." She touched a slender triangle of emerald green. The pattern reconfigured again, but nothing else obvious happened. A pale blue crescent, a yellow oval, and a row of small red circles produced similar results. Carol became bolder and tried touching pairs of symbols simultaneously. Suddenly a three-dimensional, incandescent image of light appeared from nowhere above one of the central plinths. It was about two feet across and was clearly a representation of *Nomad,* visually transparent with what could have been various internal compartments and functional systems differentiated into contrasting colors. As she tried different combinations, the model altered itself, some sections vanishing and others forming as if *Nomad* were being dismantled and reassembled instantaneously in different sequences. The image expanded, contracted, turned itself over first this way and then that, and then vanished. Carol was unable to recreate it.

More experimenting produced lighting in the room that seemed to emanate evenly from the inside of the materials of the structure and fittings rather than being concentrated in particular places. Carol felt a surge of elation and studied the latest version of the pattern in front of her with more interest. On one side, a large purple rectangle had appeared, surrounded at a short distance by a thin, silver frame so that the rectangle filled about half the area enclosed by the frame. Carol stared at the figure for a moment, and then brushed her fingers lightly across it.

The whole pattern came up at her and hit her jaw . . . solidly. An instant later the floor slammed into her feet and buckled her legs. In the same split second the sounds of crashing equipment, thudding bodies, and sudden shouts of alarm came from all around her. Hap Pearson was clinging desperately to the curved panel that held the array, bracing himself with one leg to a projection behind him. The sergeant who had been recording the proceedings was lying on the walkway entangled in relay cables, with his camera on the floor where it had fallen a few feet away; everywhere else, prone and bruised bodies were starting to stir among the wreckage of what, a few seconds before, had been a neat and orderly military operation. Carol had, it seemed, discovered *Nomad*'s source of gravity.

She began pulling herself back onto her feet, but even as she made her first moves she realized something was wrong. She found herself sliding back down the splayed column that supported the panel; her legs were refusing to straighten. The force was becoming stronger! The gravity, or whatever she had unleashed, was increasing moment by moment, dragging her irresistibly back toward the floor. Around the room, the figures that had started to stand up were slowly being crushed down again. She concentrated all the strength she could muster and forced an arm that was turning to lead to drive itself upward inch by inch toward the panel. Her fingers found the edge, clung there hopelessly for a moment, and then fell away.

A few feet above Carol, Pearson, still clinging on grimly with his arms wrapped around the panel, could feel his grip being torn open and his body beginning to slide down across the concave surface. In the pattern in front of his face, the purple rectangle was growing steadily outward toward the silver bounding frame. He braced his leg more firmly, freed one hand, and began jabbing frantically at the rectangle and at any other symbol that looked even remotely associated with it. What he did right he never discovered, but the rectangle stopped growing; the force-field stopped increasing. Perspiration poured down his face as his other hand started to slip. He stabbed again at what he hoped were the same symbols, and the rectangle shrunk a fraction. He repeated the procedure, and the rectangle shrunk some more. After a few more repetitions, the pressure that had seemed about to snap his leg had relaxed, and his fingers no longer felt on the verge of coming out of their sockets. He sucked in a deep lungful of air, let go of the panel, and dropped lightly on his feet. The forms around the room straightened up slowly, and Carol pulled herself up from below.

"Jesus!" she gasped shakily. "That'll teach me not to fool around. I'm sorry. I guess I got kind of carried away." She felt the swelling that was already becoming visible on her chin. "It was lucky you just happened to be where you were."

Pearson had turned white and clammy with a mild case of delayed shock. He swallowed hard, put a hand out to steady himself against the panel, and closed his eyes for a second or two. "Just . . . don't make a habit of things like that, Major," he whispered. Then he pulled himself together quickly and asked in an almost normal voice, "Are you okay? How's the jaw?"

"It'll be stiff for a day or two, I guess, but that's about all. Thanks." She looked up and surveyed the room. "Was anybody hurt?" she called. Luckily nobody had been. "Check equipment for damage, and report." She turned her head to talk to Pearson again. "I want to get a replay of everything we did before we even look at anything else. Let's see if the channels to the *Guam* are still working okay."

As they turned and began walking across the dais to where the relay operator was re-erecting his monitoring station from a mess of packs and boxes strewn around the floor, a loud peal of laughter from somewhere behind them stopped them in their tracks. They wheeled about, puzzled. The other heads around the room jerked up sharply.

The laughter seemed to be coming from one of the recessed archways that lay at the feet of the sets of curved steps around the periphery of the room. The surround of the arch was glowing with nested lines of colors, and on a projection emerging from the facing ledges, more rainbow symbols had appeared. In the arch itself, framed where previously there had been just blackness, there was now a face—a solid image that looked real enough to touch.

Carol stood stunned in speechless disbelief at what she saw. Beside her, Pearson had also become petrified to the spot, his mouth frozen open in silent protest. After the effect that the rest of *Nomad* had already had on her, she would have been prepared for just about any grotesque or bizzare composition of an alien countenance that the imagination could devise, or even for something that imagination in its wildest convulsions would never be capable of concocting. But what she saw was just about the last thing she would have been prepared for.

For the face in the archway was as human as any in the room.

"I see you've located the gravity synthesizer. Actually you weren't in any real danger. After a few more seconds we'd have turned it down from our end." Whoever it was, was speaking in a normal American voice.

The first word that came into Carol's mind to describe the face was "gnomish." It was the face of a man in his late fifties, with a shock of unruly dark hair sprouting above a pair of darting eyes encased in wrinkles and peering out over a rounded, bulbous nose. His mouth was twisted crookedly with a mirth that he still couldn't suppress, and revealed a set of uneven, not very white teeth. "That was pretty quick work," he went on in a tone of mocking approval. "According to our calculations, the *Servochron* should have entered orbit just under two weeks ago. You sure didn't waste any time."

Servochron? That had to be *Nomad*. Carol moved a level downward toward the arch, at the same time struggling inwardly to collect her reeling thoughts into something sufficiently coherent to put into words. In the end she asked lamely, "Who are you . . . ? Where are you?" The face creased into another spasm of amusement but made no reply. It looked at her challengingly, as if waiting for something obvious to register.

As she looked, bewildered, Carol realized that there was something vaguely strange about the figure. The face had receded a little to show more of the person to whom it belonged, as if a camera had moved back, revealing the upper part of a jacket worn over a shirt and necktie. The clothes were different somehow in cut and style from the trends of men's fashions over the most recent decades; they seemed quaint, in a way —stiff, over formal, and constraining—in a word, "old." And there was surely something familiar about the face itself. Carol had the feeling that she had seen it before somewhere—in a photograph, maybe, an old movie, or a television documentary—something like that. She racked her brain, but she couldn't place it.

Suddenly Hap Pearson emitted an audible exclamation, moved past Carol and down a couple more levels, and peered at the image closely. The face in the arch began nodding encouragingly. "Garfax!" Pearson whispered. "You're Lambert Garfax, former President of the United States!"

"Correct;" the face confirmed gleefully. "Ten out of ten. Except for one small detail—the word 'former'. I *am* President of the United States."

Pearson frowned. "What do you mean, *am?* You're

dead. Norfield is President. You were in office when . . . ? It must have been before the turn of the century . . ." His voice trailed away as he became aware of the absurdity of the conversation. The dialogue was interactive; the face couldn't be a recording. Pearson shook his head as if to clear it. "What is this? What's going on?"

"1992 to 1996," Garfax said. "The answer to your question is perfectly simple. You see here where, or maybe I should say *when,* I'm talking to you from, I *am* President. It *is* 1996."

For what could have been, as far as she could tell, a second or an hour, Carol's thinking processes came to a complete halt.

"What?" she heard Pearson choke from a few feet in front of her. His tone wasn't really that of a question; he had simply plucked the word at random from the confusion boiling inside his head, and tossed it out to inject something into the void until anything more meaningful came together. Maybe it was just one syllable, but at least it was more than Carol herself had been able to manage.

"That's what the *Servochron* is," Garfax informed them. "It enables communication through time, or at least that's one of its functions. Unless we are sadly mistaken, you are talking to us from seventeen thousand miles above the Earth's surface and twenty-seven years into the future from 1996. Am I right?" He paused to read the expressions on their faces. "Good. Well, at least you know who I am. Might I have the courtesy of knowing whom I am addressing?"

"Err . . . Dr. Horace Pearson, Datacommunications Advisor to N.S.F. Washington."

Carol moved down to stand next to Pearson. "Major Carol Waverley, United States Air Force, Orbital Command," she said. Her mind unjammed itself at last, and her faculty for speech returned. "This . . . 'thing' was found thirty years ago. *Your* people found it. They—"

"Yes, yes," Garfax agreed with an impatient wave

of his hand. "Let's save ourselves a lot of pointless questions. The *Servochron* was found in 1990 out near the Asteroid Belt. We've had experts studying it for years now. What it does is a long story, I'm a very busy man, and I don't intend going through the whole thing with advisory scientists and junior officers, only to have to repeat it all umpteen times over later. I would like you people, please, to arrange contact with your government at a level appropriate to my office."

"I'm not sure I . . ." Pearson began, then shook his head. "What are—"

"There are certain protocols to be observed, as I'm sure you are aware," Garfax said, beginning to sound irritable. "I want to talk to your President, of course. What did you say his name was—Norfield or something?"

"That's not possible," Pearson replied aghast. "He's not here. He's back on Earth somewhere."

"Oh, come on. You're supposed to be communications people, aren't you," Garfax answered. "Presumably you have data-links to Earth set up at this moment?"

"Yes, we have," Pearson said.

"Then it's perfectly simple. All you have to do is set up a two-way terminal down here by the communicator, tie it into your data-link, and get Norfield on the other end. I'm sure that with something like the *Servochron* showing up less than two weeks ago, he won't be far away from a network node."

"Yes . . . of course . . ." Pearson mumbled. He hesitated. "I'm not sure how long it might take though. Are you going to wait, or what?"

"Most certainly not," Garfax said. "I've a busy schedule. One of you go away and get things moving with your superiors. The other stay there; I'll put a couple of my people on the line who'll tell you how to operate the controls to call us back. No more questions until I'm through to the right people."

"I'll go," Carol said, seizing the opportunity to get away from the insane situation and think. Without waiting for Pearson to reply, she turned and climbed back across the dais to where the relay operator was posted.

The awed features of Lientenant-General Chalmers met her from one of the screens, watching from aboard the *Guam*. "General Medford is handling this," he told her before she could say anything. Carol scanned the console and found Medford's face gaping out from another screen.

"I've already beamed a message down to Washington," Medford said in an unsteady voice. "They're trying to locate the President now. Suspend further operations until somebody gets back to us."

The period of the Garfax Presidency had gone down as one of the near-disaster episodes in United States history. Garfax came into office on the crest of a wave of irrational popularity that followed a year of reckless pie-in-the-sky promises that nobody wanted to think about too seriously, and an experiment in near-evangelical public-relations campaigning. But the next four years brought an uninterrupted series of exposures of corruption, incompetence, intrigue, and mismanagement, and the tatters of the Administration were summarily dispatched into oblivion by the nation in the election of 1996.

One of the embarrassments left to posterity from this era was the Garfax Energy Plan—a vision of the energy problems being solved forever by a huge, centralized fusion complex that would be half a century at least ahead of anything conceived up until that time anywhere on Earth. At the time the plan was announced much of the nation was still intoxicated with campaign euphoria, and in a crash program that cost billions, the power grid across the country was ruthlessly taken apart and rebuilt into a radial network centered on a site near Columbus, Nebraska, which was where the fusion complex was to be built. Columbus, it was prophesied, would generate enough power to more than meet the country's projected needs for decades to come, which would relegate the status of the more conventional plants, both existing and planned, to that of mere local back-up and supplementary facilities. Construction at Columbus was begun with enthusiasm in 1993, and the various power utilities across the country began merging and rationalizing their operations and cutting back on proposed expansion programs in anticipation of the complex coming on-line.

Unfortunately, when the mess left in 1996 came to be examined by more objective parties, it turned out that the state-of-the-art of fusion technology was still a long way short of what the Garfax Plan had assumed. In short, the plan wasn't feasible, nor would it be for an estimated twenty-five years. And so the shelved expansion plans were hastily unshelved, and a large portion of the nation's technological community braced itself to the task of doing what it could to make good the loss of a lot of valuable time.

Demolishing what had been built of the Columbus complex would have been expensive without serving any useful purpose; besides, time was short and there was more than enough to be done in other areas. Work on the site simply ceased, and as the years went by, the concrete-lined excavations and steel-reinforced foundations faded away under mounds of wind-blown dust, tangles of encroaching weeds, and overlays of coarse prairie-grass. With time, saplings sprouted here and there and became small trees, until after a while only the older among the local inhabitants could remember what the straight banks and rectangular depressions had been intended for.

Back on the control deck of the *Guam,* Carol was with Chalmers, Pearson, and a group of other communications specialists gathered around one of the monitor consoles to follow the incongruous conversation between two Presidents of the United States, both in office, separated by a period of nearly thirty years. On one of the screens Garfax had been joined by two of his officials—William Josephson from the Department of Energy and Professor Nernst Kreissenbaum of the Presidential Scientific Advisory Committee—while on another, President Gregory Norfield, looking imposing and dignified with his tanned, handsome features and elegant crown of graying hair, was doing his best to handle a situation which he still felt belonged more in the realm of juvenile comic-books.

"The whole principle of what you are claiming is preposterous," Norfield was insisting. "I've discussed the matter at great length with my own people. The very notion of being able to send information into the past violates every principle of causality. Every accepted law of physics would come apart if—"

"Nevertheless it happens to be fact," Kreissenbaum interrupted from his position beside Garfax. "I do not intend launching into a lengthy elucidation of what it has taken us years to discover. Suffice it to say that past, present, and future events are all equally 'real' in a dimension of a totality that transcends the usual notions implied by the word 'universe'. They are strung out along a 'timeline', for want of a better word, which is not fixed and unalterable anywhere along its length. Causes, such as decisions and actions, at any point result in effects which manifest themselves in that point's future. If such causes are altered, for example as a consequence of information received from the future, then their effects alter also. The events reconfigure themselves instantaneously to produce a new, fully consistent, sequence. The timeline is thus somewhat plastic, and capable of remolding to accommodate changes that may occur anywhere along it."

Norfield frowned with the effort of trying to grasp the meaning of what Kreissenbaum was saying. "It doesn't make sense," he declared, shaking his head. "Are you saying that things I already remember as having happened—things that already constitute undeniable fact—could somehow be altered by what you might choose to do years in the past as a result of this conversation?" He shook his head again. "That's ridiculous. How could you affect one word of what's already written in our history books?"

"Yes, I am saying just that," Kreissenbaum replied. "You are forgetting that your memories and all your other records are just parts of the total timeline that would be reconfigured. Consequently you would retain no knowledge whatsoever that any change had taken place. Everything in the new timeline would be fully consistent." He paused to give Norfield time to digest the implications, then offered, "The concept is really quite simple. The past is shaping the future all the time, which is a perfectly familiar notion. All we're saying is that this alien technology enables a reverse-flow of causal influences to be superimposed upon that pattern. It creates, in effect, a closed, self-modifying loop —a 'feedback loop though time', if you will." He gazed inquiringly at Norfield for a moment. Then, reading the next question, he added, "We've established *what* it does. No, we don't know *how.*"

In the chair between Kreissenbaum and Josephson, Garfax was becoming visibly impatient. When a lull occurred in the exchange, he sat forward and raised his hands to cut the discussion off there. "That's enough of all this," he said. "We could talk about the logic of it all day and get nowhere. Why don't you just accept what I'm telling you for now? There's more important business to talk about."

"What kind of business?" Norfield asked. Something in Garfax's tone had made him suddenly suspicious. On the other screen, Garfax turned his head toward Josephson and motioned for him to take the question. Josephson cleared his throat and leaned forward to rest his elbows on the table in front of him.

"This communications channel that we're talking over is just an ancillary function of the *Servochron,*" he said. "The primary function is not to transmit information through time, but rather to transmit *energy.*" Norfield stared back at him nonplussed. Josephson went on, "We believe that this device was built by an alien civilization that went through an energy crisis in the course of its development, in very much the same way as we are. However, it seems that, unlike us, they made extraordinary advances in other areas—into realms of physics we haven't even begun to expect exist. They used their knowledge of the 'plasticity' of the timeline in a very ingenious way: they sent surplus energy, presumably generated at a time when cheap and abundant supplies had been harnessed, back to the earlier periods when crises existed. In doing so, they dramatically improved the circumstances of their own past, and in the process reconfigured their own situation into a far better present. So they never had to live with the consequences of past errors or problems; they could eradicate them from their universe."

Josephson sat back and regarded Norfield expectantly, as if inviting him to complete the rest for himself. Norfield's eyes widened in incredulity. For a few seconds he had to struggle to find a reply.

"My God!" Pearson whispered from where he was standing next to Carol. "That's what the dishes are. They're enormous energy-collectors. *Nomad* relays it back up the timeline."

Carol didn't seem to hear. She stared into the distance for a moment, and then turned a stunned face toward him. "I think I know why now," she breathed. "I know why they sent it out on a thirty-year orbit."

Norfield seemed to have understood too. He stared aghast out of the screen and for a few seconds his lips moved feebly without forming any sound. On the other screen, Garfax cackled with sudden mirth and began nodding his head vigorously.

"That's right, you've got it!" he exclaimed. "That was why we sent you the *Servochron* as a present. Now *you* can use it for what it was meant for—to beam your surplus back to *us*. You must remember the problems we're going through right now back here—half the Middle East is fighting over oil; Europe's almost bankrupt; the environmentalists wrecked the fission program back in the early eighties;

fusion wasn't funded early enough; solar turned out to be no solution." Garfax made a tossing-away motion with his hands. "Everything's a mess. But according to the long-range plans being drawn up right now, you should be through all that. You ought to be getting into space colonies and an expanded space program, and setting up all kinds of extraction and processing facilities on the Moon to build the hardware. And just about now, according to our forecasts here, you ought to be completing a series of large-scale, solar-to-microwave orbiters to power it all. How's that going? Is it all on schedule?"

Norfield just nodded numbly as his mouth refused to voice what was already clear in his mind.

"Splendid!" Garfax exclaimed, beaming. "So you can help us out. The collectors on the *Servochron* are designed to receive beams at microwave frequencies. All you have to do is position your orbiters in a symmetric pattern around it about fifty miles out, set it up the way we'll tell you to, then start pumping. Let's see now . . ." Garfax paused to glance down at some notes lying on the table before him. His manner became brisk and businesslike, and he rubbed his hands together like a gambler about to clean out the bank. "What's the status of the orbiters? How many have you built, what are their capacities, and what more do you have coming later?"

Norfield shook his head helplessly and directed an appealing look at somewhere off-screen. A scientific advisor who had been watching silently throughout from another screen replied. "Six virtually completed, designed to deliver two trillion watts each. Five more scheduled over the next four years at four trillion each."

"Mmm . . ." Garfax thought for a moment. "Twelve trillion available immediately, eh? We figure we could use thirty-five. Anyhow, it'll be a help to start with. But you'll have to do something about speeding up the schedule for the others." He turned an inquiring eye toward Josephson to invite comment.

"We should be able to manage on that," Josephson said. "With twelve trillion now and another twenty coming through later, the plan should go through. It sounds okay."

"This is preposterous!" Norfield shouted, suddenly finding his voice and losing his patience. "You're not seriously suggesting that we're going to allocate our entire lunar-orbiter energy production to you. You're out of your minds! What makes you think we can spare the energy? We need it—every damned kilowatt of it. Do you have any idea how many billions of dollars and man-years of effort we've put into that whole program? We'd have to shut it all down. Why should we? I don't care what problems you're having. We've solved all those problems. I'm not interested."

"I've already told you," Garfax said, evidently having expected some such outburst. "The past shapes the future. If you help us change your past, you'll be bound to create an even better present for yourselves in the process. That's what the *Servochron* was built to do. Believe me, it's a good deal we're offering."

"How's it supposed to be a good deal if we have to forget everything we've been working on for years?" Norfield demanded. "I'm not interested. I like the present we've got right now, the way it is. I'll stay with it."

"Oh, all of that will no doubt change," Garfax replied breezily. "It all gets a bit complicated. Let's just say that if you help us fix this 1996 mess, everything down the line where you are would have to end up in better shape. Maybe you'll find yourselves all over the solar system, or even out of it. Who knows?"

"Nobody *knows,*" Norfield shouted. "That's my whole point. The whole idea's madness. You'd have to be able to think like whatever lunatic aliens built that thing to want to get mixed up with it. I only *know* what I see now, and I like it. I'm not changing it."

Garfax frowned and appeared to be giving some thought to whatever he intended saying next. A silence descended. Norfield's scientific advisor, whose expression had been growing slowly more puzzled, chewed his lip pensively for a second and then spoke. "There's something crazy about this. If you've sent the . . . *'Servochron'*, as you call it, out into space on a thirty-year orbit, then it isn't where you are. So how are you going to get anything out of it? How can you take power out of it if it isn't there?"

"We only sent the transmitter part of it out into orbit," Josephson replied. "There's a receiver too, that was originally contained inside what you've got. It's very small compared to the rest. We shipped that part back here. In fact we're talking through an auxiliary communications channel contained in it."

"Where from?" Norfield's advisor asked.

"Columbus, Nebraska," Josephson told him in a surprised voice. He caught the look of astonishment on the other's face. "You haven't figured it out yet? We've started building the receiver complex already to feed into the national power grid. Officially for now, we're saying that a big fusion system will power it, but that's a lot of baloney. We're nowhere near being able to run fusion on that scale, and we know it. There are a lot of critics around who say the fusion scheme will never work, but somehow the public never gets to hear about that." He shrugged.

"We reckon that a couple of years ahead of us along the timeline as it is right now, the lid's being blown off the whole thing and a lot of fingers are being pointed. Further along from that, we're probably down in history as a not very honest bunch. In fact that's probably what it says in the books you read." Josephson grinned suddenly. "But that doesn't bother us because we don't intend to become the people who exist further down the timeline at the moment. We'll change that timeline. You see, the receiver from the *Servochron* has already been installed down at the bottom of some deep, sealed-off shafts below the Columbus complex, and pretty soon now we'll have the grid connected up to it. Then, when you start delivering, everything we've promised the country will happen. That'll create a whole, new, different timeline, and on that one we'll be good guys." Josephson cocked his head to one side as a thought occurred to him. "What's happened to the Columbus complex on your part of the existing timeline?" he asked. "Did it get shut down?"

The advisor nodded woodenly. "Yes it did. We abandoned the whole fool thing. It's all deserted and overgrown now."

"Mmm. . . . That's what we figured," Josephson said. "If you don't believe me, go see for yourselves. Dig down under the complex, open up the shafts you'll find there, and look inside. That receiver should still be there."

"No!" Norfield declared from his own screen in a decisive voice. "That is my simple and final answer. We in this decade have solved our problems satisfactorily without any of this, and shall continue to do so. President Garfax, would you kindly go to hell!"

"Oh dear." Garfax shook his head sadly, giving the impression of being forced reluctantly into having to say something that he would have preferred to leave unsaid. He clasped his hands together in front of him, sat back in his seat, and looked up.

"Mr. President," he said in an unruffled voice, "I suspect that you have not yet had time to appreciate fully the realities of this situation. My proposal to you was not so much a request as an ultimatum. If you reflect for a moment, you will see that your position really gives you no opportunity for bargaining whatsoever. In short, you have no choice but to comply."

"How so?" Norfield demanded. "What is there to bargain over? There's no reason why we should send you anything. You haven't got anything to trade."

"Possibly true," Garfax conceded. "But on the other hand, you will agree that our relationship here to you there puts us in a unique position. Whatever we choose to do now must affect your world of twenty-seven years later, but the converse does not apply. The effect is completely one-way, as it were."

Norfield rubbed his temples and looked suddenly confused. "I . . . don't understand you," he said in a faltering voice. "What are you trying to say?"

Garfax nodded and made an exaggerated show of being patient. "Let me put it to you this way: we are sitting on the planet that you will be occupying twenty-seven years from now. If you were to reject our proposals, we would be in a position to embark upon various activities—I'm sure I don't need to be specific—that could make life very . . . difficult . . . for you." Norfield emitted an outraged gasp. Garfax leered openly and nodded. "I trust, Mr. President, that I have made my point," he said.

This was the ultimate blackmail. The blackmailers could lob grenades down the timeline with impunity at their hapless successors of twenty-seven years in their future, while the victims possessed no means at all for exerting counter-pressure or effecting any kind of retaliation. It was, as Garfax had said, completely one-way.

A squad of Army engineers was sent to explore below the Columbus site, and sure enough there was the receiver installed in a deep concrete vault and showing all the signs of having lain there undisturbed for many years. The object was every bit as alien as *Nomad,* and about the size of a large industrial power transformer; it was equipped with six sets of large, supercooled, output busbars, which doubtless presented the power beamed back from the future by the rest of *Nomad.*

The connections from the busbars into the national power grid hadn't been made, which was nonsense. If Josephson had announced his intention to complete the connections within a short time of the date he had spoken from in 1966, why hadn't they been completed? If Garfax had set up the Columbus complex to feed the grid with power beamed back from almost thirty years ahead, why didn't history record it as having happened? None of this made any sense. How could the complex both be operating by 1996, which was Garfax's stated goal, and at the same time be lying abandoned and uncompleted almost thirty years later? Scientists and mathematicians in Washington tied themselves in knots wrestling with the logical impossibilities of the notion of plastic timelines, but every answer anyone suggested always seemed to pose ten fresh questions, usually all mutually contradictory. Perhaps, as Norfield had said, a peculiar, totally alien mind was needed to comprehend it—a mind possibly endowed biologically with fundamentally different instincts and schooled in a different process of conditioning concerning what made sense, what didn't, what was sane, and what was crazy.

The grenades started coming down the timeline shortly thereafter. Garfax announced that, within a month of the date from which he was speaking, an explosive mine would be planted secretly beneath the White House, fused to detonate after thirty years. The building was evacuated, and a frenzied search by a Marine Corps bomb-disposal team uncovered a dummy device bearing the sign JUST TESTING.

Garfax then announced that the next mine would be buried in a remote part of Alaska and controlled by a highly stable electronic timer set to explode at the exact moment at which Norfield was speaking. Norfield promptly made inquiries and was advised that Earth-orbiting satellites had detected an unexplained explosion only minutes previously at the precise spot that Garfax had indicated.

The next three—one buried below the Los Alamos Laboratories in New Mexico, one under the Capitol, and the third at a NASA launch facility in Texas—were all live, but Garfax gave sufficiently early warning to allow sweating teams of engineers to deactivate them before they timed out, in the last case with less than thirty minutes to spare.

The next three, Garfax said, would not be revealed in advance. The Mount Rushmore National Monument collapsed into rubble twenty-four hours later. The next three Garfax stated, would be nuclear.

It was all over.

A white-faced Gregory Norfield capitulated unconditionally, and orders went out from Washington for work on the lunar constructions to cease, and for the six completed orbiter relays to be moved away from Luna and into positions around *Nomad*. Garfax had allowed two weeks for this operation to be completed, stating that no slippage in the schedule would be tolerated. Forty tons of TNT went off under water less than a mile from the Golden Gate Bridge to emphasize the point. The schedule was not allowed to slip.

The *Guam* was the focus of all the activities going on around *Nomad,* and groups of visitors began arriving from Earth to play various parts in getting the whole operation together and running on time. Included among them was a deputation of government executives from Washington whose job had been to plan and coordinate the Distant Solar Relay Program, one of the main elements of which had been the orbiters now being maneuvered into position to feed *Nomad*'s collectors.

Carol first saw him over the top of the computer cabinet at which she was working near one end of the *Guam*'s message-exchange center. He was one of a group of men in dark business suits standing with some Air Force officers in a semicircle around one of the mural displays, discussing something being shown on it. He hadn't changed much at all in the six months or so since she last saw him. His hair was as black and as glossy as ever, his eyes were still bright and alert, and as he spoke, his mouth kept breaking into the natural, easygoing smile that had made her go fluttery inside when she was a mathematics graduate of twenty. Amanda smiled in exactly the same way.

She watched him for about twenty minutes while the discussion continued. Then somebody called for a coffee break, and the group began breaking up into ones, twos, and threes that drifted away in different directions. He stayed behind to study the screen, intermittently keying details from the display into a pocket communicator-pad he was carrying. Carol suspended the job that she was running, logged off the system, and moved quietly over to where he was standing.

"Hi," she whispered softly.

Dr. Donald Yaiger looked round automatically before the voice registered. Then his eyes widened, and his face split into a smile of recognition and delighted surprise. "Carol!" He dropped the communicator-pad into his pocket and brought his hands up to grip her shoulders. "You're here . . . on the *Guam?* I had no idea. Isn't it a small universe. I thought you were still shuttling up and down from California."

"I transferred to Orbital Command five months ago," Carol told him, smiling. "When did you arrive?"

"A day ago . . . with the D.S.R.P. delegation from Washington. We've been so tied up I've hardly seen anything of this ship. It's huge . . ." Don released her shoulders and shook his head. "It's just such a wonderful surprise . . . about the last thing I'd have expected. So, how've you been? How's Amanda?"

"She's just fine. I was just thinking how much she's got your smile."

"And your mother?"

"Oh, you know her. She never changes."

"I watched her Chopin recital from New York the other week. She was terriffic! The audience loved her. Did you see all the flowers? Did she get the birthday present I sent her—the perfume? Amanda once told me that was her favorite."

"She loved it," Carol told him. "She had a good time. We both went over to see her for the afternoon. Amanda said that people should get all their birthday presents from every year all at once, right up front; then they'd be able to get more use out of them instead of wasting all that time waiting. It's a pity

Nomad is a secret. It'd be almost the ideal thing to do it."

Don laughed. "Smart kid. She'll go a long way too, just like her mother."

"So what are you doing yourself?" Carol asked. "I hear rumors that say you're a big wheel now in the orbiter relay program. That has to be why you're on the *Guam*. Where do you fit into this crazy business?"

Don glanced around and then looked back to Carol. "We don't have to stand here talking like this," he said. "There must be somewhere around here where we can sit down and grab a sandwich or something. How are you fixed? Are you busy?"

"Not that busy," Carol answered. "Come on. I'll show you the way to the maindeck cafeteria."

"It's bad news all-round," Don said over a half-eaten turkey club twenty minutes later. "Norfield doesn't have any choice. We're having to back down all the way along the line. Without the power relays, the whole lunar construction program, and therefore the colonies program too, will have to be shut down. It could take years to begin to pick up the pieces, never mind to start putting them back together again. In fact they might never get put together again; my feeling is that Garfax will just keep squeezing harder and harder, and take everything we can produce. Our whole space budget will end up being used to expand his economy. And there's no way out. If we don't play ball, he'll start nuking the cities. He's insane enough to do it, too."

"But where will that leave you, Don?" Carol asked, horrified. "Your whole future is tied up in the program . . . everything you've worked for in years. Where's your job if the program gets shut down?"

Don pulled a face and spread his hands. "Gonzo . . . *kaput*." He shrugged and made a wry grin. "Aw, I'll never wind up on the street, I guess. The department will come up with something else."

"Caretaking Garfax's orbiters for him or something like that," Carol said, sounding suddenly bitter. "Or maybe putting up Mickey Mouse satellites with the change that's left over. That's not the same as the colonies and the next jump outward that you always used to talk about. It's not what you want, is it?"

As she looked across the table at Don, a sudden feeling of loathing surged through her at the vision that appeared in her mind's eye of the leering, gnomish face cackling out of a monitor screen. Perhaps, another part of her mind thought, she was projecting some of her inner feelings about herself outward and personifying them as an external object of hatred. For ten obstinate years she had kept Don at a distance, and now she was twisting things such that Garfax's blackmail became the sole cause of a wasted career. She thought about some of the things Doreen had said, and felt doubts inside suddenly for the first time. Maybe it was meeting him here, seventeen thousand miles out from Earth. What had she been trying to prove over all those years anyway, she wondered. Was she setting Amanda up to go through the same thing again in twenty years time?

Don was watching her silently while he chewed another portion of his sandwich. Carol sensed again the uncanny faculty that he had always possessed of being able to read her thoughts from her eyes. "Don't get hung up over Garfax," he advised her. "I know he's a mean bastard—first your father, your mother, Amanda—and now this. But he's sitting pretty thirty years back in the past. Nobody can touch him."

Carol's eyes narrowed and her expression became puzzled. "What do you mean, 'first your father'?" she asked. "What does my father have to do with Garfax? I'm not with you."

A look of surprise flashed across Don's face, then changed slowly to one of realization. He swallowed the last of his sandwich and pushed the plate away in a heavy, solemn movement. "Of course," he said in a dull voice. "You don't know, do you."

"Know what?" Carol became tense and apprehensive. "Don, what about my father?"

"Not Phillip specifically—the whole *Damocles* mission—" Don bit his lip hard as if wishing that he had never broached the subject, but he could see that he had no choice now but to continue. Carol waited without taking her eyes from his face. "I've been involved in some work that's been going on, sifting through the old archives and trying to figure out exactly what happened with that mission," he said. He paused but there was no letup in Carol's gaze. He went on, "Look . . . there's nothing certain about this, but as far as we can tell it's the only explanation that fits all the facts.

"*Nomad* was discovered drifting through the Belt by an unmanned research probe in 1990. The discovery was kept secret, and the government-slash-military sent a scientific team out under Kreissenbaum in a ship called the *Ulysses* to find out what they could about it. That was all hushed up too. In 1993, Garfax was out of the public limelight for over two months, reported as being sick. We don't think he was sick at all. We're beginning to think he went out to *Nomad* to see it for himself. Just before that time, for no reason that made sense, a fast, Air Force, executive lunar shuttle was fitted with long-range drives. Its log for the following two months contains evidence of being falsified. That must have been when they'd finally figured out what *Nomad* was all about."

Don sighed and gave a weary shrug. "You can fill in the rest. A large-scale engineering mission was organized to follow in a hurry, which was the *Damocles* mission of course—too big to cover up. So the meteor story was invented as a blind, and the people who went on the mission left believing that was what they were going out there to fix. But, very strangely, their whole communications system failed when they were over halfway there—not just the primary system, mind you, but all the back-ups too." Don cocked a sardonic eye at Carol and gave her a moment for the implications to sink in. "We can guess that when the mission arrived at *Nomad* it found Garfax and his people waiting, and learned for the first time what the job was really all about.

"And because of another piece of bad luck, they were never able to tell anyone about what they knew because they never came home. According to the files, the *Ulysses* vanished without explanation at around that period too. Obviously that was how Garfax, Kreissenbaum and their people got back, presumably bringing *Nomad*'s receiver with them." Don looked up to meet Carol's eyes for a second. He showed his empty palms, and then slumped back in his seat. There was nothing more to say.

Carol's face had turned white, and she was gripping the edge of the table with fingers that showed knuckles looking as if they were about to burst out of her skin. "*Damocles* was sabotaged!" she whispered, staring at Don in horror. "It was fixed to explode on the way home." She began trembling and unconsciously drove a knuckle between her teeth. "Oh my God . . . ! He had them all killed. Garfax had the whole mission wiped out. That . . . monster . . . *killed* my father!"

Don reached across the table and squeezed her hand. "I'm sorry," he said. "I guess I forgot for a moment that you couldn't have known about any of that. It would have been better if I hadn't brought the matter up." He tried to move his hand away, but Carol entwined her fingers and gripped more tightly.

"You know me better than that, Don," she said, forcing a weak grin. "I'll take it the way it is, whatever it is." Her fingers touched the ring he was wearing. She looked down and noticed it for the first time. Her face jerked upward sharply.

"When?" she asked in a voice that had choked before she could stop it.

"Four months ago." Don's face mirrored the dismay in her eyes. "I waited . . ." he stammered. "I wanted to . . . but all those years . . . ?" He shook his head. "You blew it, Carol. How long did you think we could go on like that?"

They had dinner together later and spent the rest of the evening after Carol came off duty in the officer's bar drinking and talking. Throughout it all she acted normally. The tears came later, when she was alone in her cabin.

Somehow, eventually, she got to sleep. It was a restless, tossing, dream-ridden sleep. In her dream she saw a lonely, sad-faced woman staring out through a window as she played a piano, while behind her on the floor a caricature of Amanda arranged glowing jewels and geometric symbols into patterns. From somewhere out in space, along a line that diminished away into infinity, a thousand *Nomad*s were hurling brightly wrapped gifts from a thousand years of time at the little girl playing on the floor. A thousand packages were coming together to form a flood that began falling toward the tiny figure, menacing . . . looming . . . crushing. Amanda, looking down, was oblivious of the danger. The woman at the piano played on, heedless. Carol tried to cry out a warning but found that she had no voice. In the background, the face of Garfax was cackling insanely. The mountain of packages was falling. . . .

Carol came awake in her bunk, sweating and shaking. She lay in the darkness breathing heavily as the last shreds of the dream fell away and the familiar confines of the cabin reasserted themselves. The reality of the dream had gone, but the memory of the images persisted. She could see it again—a thousand *Nomad*s all beaming back from different places at the same point in the past. Or maybe the same *Nomad* captured at a thousand points along the line that traced its existence . . . concentrating the energy of a thousand futures on a single instant.

Suddenly Carol was wide awake. She stared into the darkness and conjured up the picture again in her mind. A thousand Nomads *concentrating* . . . *focus-*

ing . . . multiplying their power. The same *Nomad* duplicated a thousand times at a thousand points along its future.

The thought in her mind was insane, surely. "Why not?" she asked herself aloud. Everything else about *Nomad* was insane. Why not . . . ?

She thought about it for a half hour without moving, and then said, "Computers, background lighting." A low-level illumination came on around the cabin. Carol hauled herself up into a sitting position and pulled a wrap around her shoulders. "Intercom," she instructed.

"Intercom," a synthetic voice acknowledged.

"Put me through to Dr. Donald Yaiger, visiting the *Guam* from Washington."

After a few seconds the flatscreen vipanel beside her pivoted round to face in her direction, and a moment later came to life to show Don, blinking and rubbing sleep from his eyes. "What is it . . . ? Hey, Carol! What's the matter? Is something up?"

"Don, I've got to talk to you." Carol's voice was low and crisp with urgency. "No it can't wait until morning. I'm in G-37. Can you get here right away?"

Don's mind returned fully to consciousness before the protest that was forming instinctively on his mouth turned into words. "Okay," he said simply. "Give me a minute to rinse my face and get into some things. I'll be there right away."

"The whole operation will be controlled by computers installed in *Nomad* and connected into *Nomad*'s direction system." Carol, now dressed in fatigues, was talking rapidly as she paced from one side of the cabin to the other while Don listened from the chair by the worktable below the bookshelves. "The computers will be programmed to translate the receiver's spacetime coordinates into optical data-forms compatible with *Nomad*'s equipment. In other words, the programs in those computers will determine where in time the energy is sent from, and the point in the past that it's sent to. Okay?"

"Okay," Don confirmed, nodding. "And you're in charge of the group writing those programs. So?"

"Well, you're the physicist. Tell me if there's any reason why this couldn't work." Carol paused for a moment to collect her thoughts. "From what I can make out of the things Kreissenbaum has said, the whole timeline that lies ahead of *now* into the future is all equally *real* . . . as real as the instant we're at right now. Is that correct?"

"It seems that way," Don agreed.

"So every instant along that timeline—every nanosecond of it—contains a *Nomad,* right? And every one of those Nomads could beam its energy back to the same, precisely defined, instant in the past." She wheeled round to face Don suddenly. Don's jaw dropped as the first hint of what Carol was getting at dawned on him. She nodded, then went on. "Suppose we wrote a program in which the instructions to commence transmitting were repeated to execute a billion times at microsecond increments, say, into the future. Then even if the timeline is plastic, at the same instant in, oh, I don't know, some kind of 'hypertime' —while that timeline still existed—all those copies of *Nomad* would commence beaming at slightly different intervals spaced sequentially along it. Now suppose that they *all* were aiming at the same point in the past that Garfax specified. What would happen to the receiver?"

Don gaped at her for a few seconds. "You'd have to build some kind of updating mechanism into it," he said. "Every discrete point would need its own measure of elapsed time to hit the target."

"A standard program offset would do that," Carol said. "That'd be no problem. We could handle it."

Don thought for a moment longer. *"Jesus!"* he whispered hoarsely. "The receiver would get zapped with a billion times more energy than it was supposed to handle . . . unless I'm missing something. You'd be sending a zigaton bomb back up the timeline!"

Carol stopped pacing and nodded her head in satisfaction. A strange light was gleaming in her eyes. "That's the way it seemed to me," she said. She stared Don directly in the face. "So that bastard wants our energy, huh? Okay, why don't we let him have some? Why don't we let him have a billion times more than he ever dreamed of?"

Don raised the issue at a meeting of D.S.R.P. scientists and government advisors held on the *Guam* first thing the following morning. By lunchtime Norfield and his staff in Washington had become involed, and by late afternoon the plan was being examined in detail. The consensus was that nobody could say for sure whether or not it would work, or offer any precise explanation of why it would have worked if it did. On the other hand, nobody could come up with any conclusive argument as to why it shouldn't work either. It was no more or no less crazy than everything else connected with *Nomad*. And it was, after all, the only alternative to total and ignominious surrender that anybody had thus far been able to suggest.

Norfield gave his approval. For two hectic weeks, while formal discussions continued with Garfax and his aides ostensibly to finalize details of the imminent operations, another team, composed of Don's physicists and Carol's programmers, worked secretly to develop the real programs that would be running when the day came for the blackmailers to collect.

In the process of working with and concentrating on the project for days at a time, Carol found new thoughts slowly taking shape in her mind, which she kept to herself. She built some additional modules into the programs and told nobody about them, not even Don.

The face of Garfax looked out of one of the screens on Carol's console and beamed its crooked smile.

Seventy miles away from the *Guam, Nomad* was hanging in space surrounded by its entourage of ten-mile-diameter solar relay orbiters, each fifty miles out. Inside *Nomad,* the control computers were installed and running, awaiting further commands from the *Guam*'s supervisory system. The relays and *Nomad*'s time-beam transmitter were synchronized to begin operating simultaneously on receipt of a master signal.

Carol was alone in a small communications direction center that opened off from one side of the main control deck, handling the link to the computers inside *Nomad.* She had planned it that way.

"Five minutes to zero," Garfax declared cheerfully. "Why such serious faces there? This is a big day. We should all be celebrating. Just think, in five minutes time we'll have changed thirty years of history for the better. Who knows what great things may emerge from this moment? You should be proud and confident . . . with visions of things to come."

Norfield was watching from another screen without saying anything. He was troubled, Carol knew from what Don had told her of the discussions with Washington, by what had been accepted as the unavoidable price of the gamble: if everything worked as hoped, a large piece of Nebraska would disappear from the map, and with it a lot of people who weren't mixed up in Garfax's blackmail and who knew nothing about it. True, they existed nearly thirty years in the past, and maybe the blame could be rationalized as falling squarely on a long-gone Administration, but that didn't alter the fact that they were people—innocent people.

But Carol had other plans which didn't call for the damaging of so much as a blade of grass in Nebraska. She turned her head toward a microphone beside her and said quietly, "Computers, activate program TIMESCAN and unlock communicator coordinates on this channel."

"TIMESCAN running," the machine's voice confirmed. "Channel coordinates unlocked. Awaiting instructions."

Carol took a deep breath and steeled herself. Garfax was talking into the auxiliary communications channel of *Nomad*'s receiver from where it was installed below the Columbus complex in 1996. Carol was about to disconnect the channel through to her console from that point in time and scan backward through earlier periods of *Nomad*'s history—to a time before the receiver had ever been brought to Earth at all.

"Go back ten months," she instructed. Garfax vanished from the screen. The faces on the other screens continued to act normally; their channels were still locked on the Garfax of 1996 and were carrying a normal dialogue. Only the channel switched through to Carol's console had been unlocked to scan back along the timeline.

A picture appeared on the screen after a few seconds. It was of a man, who looked as if he could have been a technician of some kind, working with his back to the viewing point. Suddenly he raised his head, glanced back over his shoulder, and then whirled around in sudden astonishment.

"What's going on?" he demanded. "Who turned that thing on? Where did you come from? You're an Air Force major . . . What—"

"It would take far too long to explain, and I haven't got much time," Carol said. "Just answer a couple of questions, please. Are you down a shaft underneath the Columbus complex?" The technician just nodded. "'You're working on the installation of the receiver?" Again a mute nod. "How long ago did the receiver arrive there?"

"Two months," the technician mumbled. "It was shipped here from Edwards Space Base—at night—all secret. That's all I know."

"Thank you," Carol said. "Computers, resume scanning. Back another three months."

This time she found herself talking to a bewildered

government scientist aboard the spacecraft *Ulysses*. "Let me see if I can guess," she said. "You're taking the receiver from the Belt back to Earth. The *Servochron* transmitter has been sent on a thirty-year round-trip, and the *Damocles* ship recently had a nasty accident. What do I get, ten out of ten?"

"Goddammit, who are you?" the scientist choked, turning purple. "That's highly classified information. I've never seen you before. On whose authority—"

"It doesn't matter," Carol told him. "Computers, resume scanning. Take it back another month."

She tracked the receiver back to the time at which it had formed part of *Nomad*. There were lots of different people around it at various, closely spaced times. Evidently a lot of work was going on in and around *Nomad*. As she had already guessed, she ascertained that they were members of the *Damocles* mission. However, she didn't ask to speak to Colonel Phillip Waverley.

She went back further and was greeted by an astounded general and a white-haired civilian, both wearing overjackets that carried the Damocles emblem on the right breast pocket.

"You're with the *Damocles* mission that arrived from Earth not long ago," she stated without preliminaries. "How long ago did the mission arrive at the *Servochron?*"

The general returned a puzzled look. "At the *what*, Major? Who the hell are you? What is this thing you're talking out of? Where are you talking from?"

"Oh, I see," Carol said. "It's still early days there. They haven't told you what it is yet. How long ago did the mission arrive, sir? It's extremely important."

"A week ago," the general told her. "Do you know what this alien thing is? We were told we were being sent out to steer off a rogue meteor. What's that insignia on your jacket? I don't recognize the unit. Which command of the Air Force are you from?"

Carol ignored the question. "When the mission arrived, who was already there waiting? Was Garfax there, and a scientist called Kreissenbaum . . . and maybe a few others?"

"Major, this kind of cross-examination of a senior officer is most irregular," the general protested. "I must insist that I talk to—"

"Yes, they were all here," the white-haired civilian came in, seeing that she seemed to know more than he or the general. "I don't know why or how. The vessel *Ulysses* was here too, and it was supposed to have disappeared over a year ago. There's something very odd about this whole affair. I don't know who you are or how you know what you seem to know, but it would assist us greatly if—"

"Computers, resume scanning." Carol thought for a second. The *Damocles* ship had arrived at *Nomad* a week before that last point. Three days cruising would put it well out of the danger zone. "Go back another ten days," she instructed. Surely this would be the last stop, she thought.

The screen cleared again, and Carol felt a sudden surge of jubilation. This was going to be better than she had dared hope. She was looking at the familiar gnomish face, only this time it wasn't cackling. It was open-mouthed with surprise and shock, and its beady eyes were popping from their sockets beneath the tuft of unruly hair.

"Good day, Mr. President," Carol grated. "I've been waiting a long time."

Garfax blinked uncertainly. "Who are you? You're not from the *Ulysses*. What are you doing here . . . ? Are you here?" Two more figures joined him on the screen, evidently attracted from somewhere nearby by his agitation.

"Ah, Mr. Josephson and Professor Kreissenbaum," Carol said. "I'm *so* delighted." It was going to be even better.

"Who is she?" Kreissenbaum demanded, turning sharply toward Garfax. "How does she have access to the device? Where is she speaking from?"

"Major Carol Waverley, United States Air Force,"

she informed them. "Speaking from 2023." Three dumbfounded stares confronted her. "Why so surprised?" she asked. "You've had more than two years to figure out what the *Servochron* is, haven't you? You must have all the answers by now. Why else would the President have gone out there?"

"How much do you know about this?" Josephson growled, beginning to sound alarmed.

"Oh, I know everything," Carol answered. "It didn't occur to you that after thirty years we might have put a lot more of the pieces together than you allowed for, did it? I know about your plans to send the *Servochron* off on a thirty-year orbit while you take the receiver back to Nebraska. I also know about your little plan to bomb the *Damocles* mission ship after all the dirty work has been done for you." She paused for a moment and smiled sweetly. "But of course, that hasn't happened yet, has it? In fact, if my figures are correct, the *Damocles* ship should be approaching you right now, about three days out. What do I get, ten out of ten?"

"Somebody's leaked the whole thing," Josephson groaned, turning a shade paler.

"Impossible!" Garfax insisted. "We've got it all tied up. No chance."

"It's not a leak," Kreissenbaum said. "Didn't you hear what she said? She's talking from 2023. Something must have gone wrong further down the timeline."

As the argument on the screen degenerated into a babble, Carol turned her face toward the microphone and recited calmly, "Computers, activate program BLITZKREIG, prime orbiters, initialize main power beam, release target vector director, and lock to coordinates registered on this channel."

"BLITZKRIEG running, orbiters primed and checking positive," the computer confirmed. "Main power beam initialized and checking positive, vector director released and checking positive, coordinates from communicator channel copied and verified. Awaiting instructions."

"Set all beams to maximum power, set incremental repetition factor to one billion, unlock trigger and focus on coordinates as set," she commanded.

"Beams one through six set at two trillion watts, repetition factored at one billion, trigger unlocked, focus set on coordinates as read, status checks at condition *green,*" came the response.

"Who's she talking to?" Kreissenbaum demanded. "What kind of gibberish is that?"

"Explain yourself, Major," Garfax ordered. "What are you doing?"

"You wanted energy," Carol told him simply. "You're about to get it."

"No . . . you've got it all wrong!" Josephson yelled, his voice rising in sudden alarm. "Not *here* . . . not *now*! That's over two years away yet. You can't—"

"Oh yes I can. And it's coming down the line at a billion times the strength you expected. Never mind how. It'd take too long to explain. So long, guys."

"You're mad!" Kreissenbaum screamed. "You don't know what you're—"

"Stop!" Garfax shouted. "As your President I order you to—"

Carol turned her head away. "Computers, disengage safety interlocks and stand by to fire."

"Confirm order to disengage safety interlocks?"

"Confirmed."

"Interlocks disengaged. Standing by."

"Fire!"

A blaze of whiteness erupted in space a million miles ahead of the ship that was moving outward from the orbit of Mars. For a brief instant its light rivalled that of the sun and lit up the surface and structure of the ship from directly ahead. Painted near the ship's nose was a large emblem showing a red sword against a black background.

General Phillip Waverley, U.S.A.F. (Retired), was sitting in a recliner on the patio by the pool at the back of the house, enjoying the last of the fine summer. Beside him his son-in-law was lounging in a deck chair, sipping from a can of cool beer and chewing peanuts. The sounds of excited voices came intermittently through the open French windows from inside the house.

"Executive job with the lunar program, eh?" Phillip said, nodding approvingly. "Just what you needed. They'll be sending you out on some trips after a while, I'd guess." He grinned. "I always said we'd make a spaceman out of you one day."

"I reckon you're right," Don agreed, not sounding too displeased at the thought. "I'll have to move some to catch up with your side of the family though. What with Carol on the *Guam* and the number of miles you've logged across the solar system . . ." He left the sentence unfinished.

"You haven't exactly been wasting your time," Phillip reminded him. "I wouldn't be surprised if you end up seeing more of what it's all about than I ever did, never mind how many years I did or how many miles I covered. You'll be right in there where it matters . . . making it all happen." He shrugged and rubbed his chin. "All I ever did was follow orders, when all's said and done."

A short silence descended while Phillip watched a squirrel scrambling in one of the trees that stood behind the house, and Don finished his beer.

"How old were you when you made your first deep-space trip?" Don asked at last.

Phillip thought for a moment. "Oh . . . somewhere around my early thirties, I guess . . ." A distant look came into his eyes. "It was the *Damocles* mission of 1993, the one I told you about before. The mission that never happened, remember?"

"The meteor that you said wasn't a meteor. It blew up or something, didn't it?"

"They told us it was a meteor," Phillip said, nodding slowly. "But when we were about a million miles out from it, it went up like a piece of the sun. I never heard of any meteor doing anything like that." He turned his head toward the spot where Don was sitting. "And I'll tell you something else . . . I saw the pictures that were reconstructed from the optical scans just before it blew. No meteor ever that looked like that, either. There was something very funny about that whole mission."

"What did it look like?" Don asked, intrigued.

"Aw, it wasn't too clear . . . just some patches of light that made a shape against the starfield . . . . But it didn't look *natural* . . . not to me anyhow. It was too symmetrical, and it had circles round it. Looked sort of like a square strawberry. And then all our communications with Earth failed when we were on the way out, so we couldn't tell anybody about it until after we got back. That just couldn't have happened, but it did." Phillip nodded decisively. "There sure was something peculiar about that whole mission all right."

At that moment Amanda came running out of the house through the French windows. "Daddy, Grandpa, you've got to come inside now. Grandma's opening her presents."

Phillip looked around at her. "You're right," he said. "We're not doing very much to make this a party, are we? Come on then. Let's go inside and see what she's got." He rose to his feet; Amanda clasped his hand and led him back into the house. Don crushed the empty can in his hand, tossed it into the trash bin by the pool, got up, and followed.

Doreen was sitting on the sofa in the living room unwrapping a large package resting on her knees while David, Amanda's six-year-old brother, watched goggle-eyed from beside her. Carol looked up from the arm chair by the grand piano.

"You're just in time," she said, looking at Don. "We're just opening the parcel your parents sent from Florida."

"I didn't know people still got birthday presents when they're *fifty-four,*" Amanda said, perching on the arm of Carol's chair. "I think it's wrong to have to wait until you're that *old* before you can have all your presents. Why can't people have all of them when they're still little? Then they wouldn't have to wait years and then only be able to play with them for a short time."

"Fifty-four isn't old,'" Carol reproached. "And if you got all your presents at once, you'd have nothing to look forward to. Oh look, a pair of Ming vases. Don, they're beautiful!"

"Oh, I must call them today and thank them," Doreen said delightedly. "Phil, aren't they exactly what we needed for the dining room?"

"Very pretty," the general conceded gruffly.

"When I'm older I'm going to be a scientist," Amanda said. "I'll invent a time-machine that will send all the presents I'm going to get between now and when I'm fifty-four back to today. Then I'll be able to play with all of them today."

"You'd have to be a pretty clever scientist to invent something like that," Don told her, laughing.

"Why?" Amanda objected. "They have time-machines in the movies."

"They're just stories," Don said. "They don't really exist. They can't. Such things are impossible."

"Why are they impossible? I don't think they are. I'm going to invent one anyway."

"Your father is a scientist already, don't forget," Carol said. "You'll have a hard time if you start arguing with him about things like that. If he says they're impossible, I'd believe it. He ought to know."

"But why?" Amanda insisted, staring up at Don. "Why aren't they just like any other machine? Other machines aren't impossible."

"Oh hell," Don muttered, scratching the back of his neck. "It'd take a lot of explaining, and I think you'd need to get a little further on at school before we could really talk about it. Why don't we leave it for some other time?" He looked around for a way out. "Let's open another present. That green one looks interesting. I wonder what's in there."

Doreen placed the vases on a side table well out of David's reach, and leaned across to pick up the green-wrapped package. Amanda jumped down from the arm of Carol's chair and moved closer to watch. Don and Phil grinned at each other.

"Kids!" Don snorted. "Time-machines to send back birthday presents."

Philip pulled a cigar from the pocket of his shirt. "They get some crazy ideas all right," he agreed. He shrugged and jammed the cigar between his lips. "Who knows? Maybe nothing's impossible."

"Maybe." Don didn't sound convinced.

Phillip flicked his lighter and brought the flame up to the tip of his cigar. "Well, I heard what my daughter said," he grunted. "I'm not going to argue. After all, you're the scientist." ☆

Chains of Air, Web of Aether

Philip K. Dick

The planet on which he was living underwent each day two mornings. First CY30 appeared and then its minor twin put in a feeble appearance, as if God had not been able to make up his mind as to which sun he preferred and had finally settled on both. The domers liked to compare it to sequential settings of an old-fashioned multi-filament incandescent bulb. CY30 gave the impression of getting up to about one-hundred-fifty watts and then came little CY30B which added fifty more watts of light. The aggregate lumina made the methane crystals of the planet's surface sparkle pleasantly, assuming you were indoors.

At the table of his dome Leo McVane drank fake coffee and read the newspaper. He felt anxiety-free and warm because he had long ago illegally redesigned his dome's thermostat. He felt safe as well because he had added an extra metal brace to the dome's hatch. And he felt expectant because today the food man would be by, so there would be someone to talk to. It was a good day.

All his communications gear fumbled along on autostasis, at the moment, monitoring whatever the hell they monitored. Originally, upon being stationed at CY30 II, McVane had thoroughly studied the function and purpose of the complexes of electronic marvels for which he was the caretaker—or rather, as his job-coding put it, the "master homonoid overseer." Now he had allowed himself to forget most of the transactions which his charges engaged in. Communications equipment led a monotonous life until an emergency popped up, at which point he ceased suddenly to be the "master homonoid overseer" and became the living brain of his station.

There had not been an emergency yet.

The newspaper contained a funny item from the United States Federal Income Tax booklet for 1978, the year McVane had been born. These entries appeared in the index in this order:

Who Should File
Widows and Widowers, Qualifying
Winnings—Prizes, Gambling and Lotteries
Withholding—Federal Tax

And then the final entry in the index, which McVane found amusing and even interesting as a commentary on an archaic way of life:

Zero Bracket Amount

To himself, McVane grinned. That was how the United States Federal Income Tax booklet's 1978 index had ended, very appropriately, and that was how the United States, a few years later, had ended. It had fiscally fucked itself over and died of the trauma.

"Food ration comtrix," the audio transducer of his radio announced. "Start unbolting procedure."

"Unbolting under way," McVane said, laying aside his newspaper.

The speaker said, "Put helmet on."

"Helmet on." McVane made no move to pick up his helmet; his atmosphere flow rate would compensate for the loss; he had redesigned it, too.

The hatch unscrewed, and there stood the food man, headbubble and all. An alarm bell in the dome's ceiling shrilled that atmospheric pressure had sharply declined.

"Put your helmet on!" the food man ordered angrily.

The alarm bell ceased complaining; the pressure had restabilized. At that, the food man grimaced. He popped his helmet and then began to unload cartons from his comtrix.

"We are a hardy race," McVane said, helping him.

"You have amped up everything," the food man observed; like all the rovers who serviced the domes he was sturdily built and he moved rapidly. It was not a safe job operating a comtrix shuttle between mother ships and the domes of CY30 II. He knew it, and McVane knew it. Anybody could sit in a dome; few people could function outside.

"Stick around for a while," McVane said after he and the food man had unloaded and the food man was marking the invoice.

"If you have coffee."

They sat facing each other across the table drinking coffee. Outside the dome the methane messed around but here neither man felt it. The food man perspired; he apparently found McVane's temperature level too high.

"You know the woman in the next dome?" the food man asked.

"Somewhat," McVane said. "My rig transfers data to her input circuitry every three or four weeks. She stores it, boosts it and transmits it. I suppose. Or for all I know"

"She's sick," the food man said.

McVane said, "She looked all right the last time I talked to her. We used video. She did say something about having trouble reading her terminal's displays."

"She's dying," the food man said, and sipped his coffee.

In his mind, McVane tried to picture the woman. Small and dark, and what was her name? He punched a couple of keys on the board beside him, her name came up on its display, retrieved by the code they used. Rybus Rommey. "Dying of what?" he said.

"Multiple sclerosis."

"How far advanced is it?"

"Not far at all," the food man said. "A couple of months ago she told me that when she was in her late teens she suffered an what—is it called? Aneurysm. In her left eye, which wiped out her central vision in that eye. They suspected at the time that it might be the onset of multiple sclerosis. And then today when I talked to her she said she's been experiencing optic neuritis, which—"

McVane said, "Both symptoms were fed to M.E.D.?"

"A corrolation of an aneurysm and then a period of remission and then double vision, blurring . . . you ought to call her up and talk to her. When I was delivering to her she was crying."

Turning to his keyboard, McVane punched out and punched out and then read the display. "There's a thirty to forty percent cure rate for multiple sclerosis."

"Not out here. M.E.D. can't get to her out here."

"Shit," McVane said.

"I told her to demand a transfer back home. That's what I'd do. She won't do it."

"She's crazy," McVane said.

"You're right. She's crazy. Everybody out here is crazy. You want proof of it? She's proof of it. Would you go back home if you knew you were very sick?"

"We're never supposed to surrender our domes."

"What you monitor is so important." The food man set down his cup. "I have to go." As he got to his feet he said, "Call her and talk to her. She needs someone to talk to and you're the closest dome. I'm surprised she didn't tell you."

McVane thought, I didn't ask.

After the food man had departed, McVane got the code for Rybus Rommey's dome, started to run it into his transmitter, and then hesitated. His wall clock showed 18:30 hours. At this point in his forty-two-hour cycle he was supposed to accept a sequence of high-speed entertainment audio and video taped signals emanating from a slave satellite at CY30 III; upon storing them he was to run them back at normal and select the material suitable for the overall dome system on his own planet.

He took a look at the log. Fox was doing a concert that ran two hours. Linda Fox, he thought. You and your synthesis of old-time rock and modern-day streng. Jesus, he thought; if I don't transcribe the relay of your live concert every domer on the planet will come storming in here and kill me. Outside of emergencies—which don't occur—this is what I'm paid to handle: information traffic between planets, information that connects us with home and keeps us human. The tape drums have got to turn.

He started the tape transport at its high speed mode, set the module's controls for receive, locked it in at the satellite's operating frequency, checked the waveform on the visual scope to be sure that the carrier was coming in undistorted, and then patched into an audio transduction of what he was getting.

The voice of Linda Fox emerged from the strip of drivers mounted above him. As the scope showed, there was no distortion. No noise. No clipping. All channels, in fact, were balanced; his meters indicated that.

Sometimes I could cry myself when I hear her, he thought. Speaking of crying.

Wandering all across this land,
My band.
In the worlds that pass above,
I love.
Play for me you spirits who are weightless.
I believe in drinking to your greatness.
My band.

And, behind Linda Fox's vocal, the syntholutes which were her trademark. Until Fox, no one had ever thought of bringing back that sixteenth-century instrument for which Dowland had written so beautifully and so effectively.

Shall I sue? shall I seek for grace?
Shall I pray? shall I prove?
Shall I strive to a heavenly joy
With an earthly love?
Are there worlds? are there moons
Where the lost shall endure?
Shall I find for a heart that is pure?

What Linda Fox had done was take the lute books of John Dowland, written at the end of the sixteenth century, and remastered both the melodies and the lyrics into something of today. Some new thing, he thought, for scattered people as flung as if they had been dropped in haste: here and there, disarranged, in domes, on the backs of miserable worlds and in satellites—victimized by the power of migration, and with no end in sight.

Silly wretch, let me rail
At a trip that is blind.
Holy hopes do require

He could not remember the rest. Well, he had it taped, of course.

. . . no human may find.

Or something like that. The beauty of the universe lay not in the stars figured into it but in the music generated by human minds, human voices, human hands. Syntholutes mixed on an intricate board by experts, and the voice of Fox. He thought, I know what I must have to keep on going. My job is my delight: I transcribe this and I broadcast it and they pay me.

"This is the Fox," Linda Fox said.

McVane switched the video to holo, and a cube

formed in which Linda Fox smiled at him. Meanwhile, the drums spun at furious speed, getting hour upon hour into his permanent possession.

"You are with the Fox," she said, "and the Fox is with *you.*" She pinned him with her gaze, the hard, bright eyes. The diamond face, feral and wise, feral and true; this is the Fox/Speaking to you. He smiled back.

"Hi, Fox," he said.

Sometime later he called the sick girl in the next dome. It took her an amazingly long time to respond to his signal, and as he sat noting the signal-register on his own board he thought, Is she finished? Or did they come and forcibly evacuate her?

His microscreen showed vague colors. Visual static, nothing more. And then there she was.

"Did I wake you up?" he asked. She seemed so slowed down, so torpid. Perhaps, he thought, she's sedated.

"No. I was shooting myself in the ass."

"What?" he said, startled.

"Chemotherapy," Rybus said. "I'm not doing too well."

"I just now taped a terrific Linda Fox concert; I'll be broadcasting it in the next few days. It'll cheer you up."

"It's too bad we're stuck in these domes. I wish we could visit one another. The food man was just here. In fact he brought me my medication. It's effective but it makes me throw up."

McVane thought, I wish I hadn't called.

"Is there any way you could visit me?" Rybus asked.

"I have no portable air, none at all."

"I have," Rybus said.

In panic he said, "But if you're sick—"

"I can make it over to your dome."

"What about your station? What if data come in that—"

"I've got a beeper I can bring with me."

Presently he said, "Okay."

"It would mean a lot to me, someone to sit with for a little while. The food man stays like half an hour, but that's as long as he can. You know what he told me? There's been an outbreak of a form of amyotrophic lateral sclerosis on CY30 VI. It must be a virus. This whole condition is a virus. Christ, I'd hate to have amyotrophic lateral sclerosis. This is like the Mariana form."

"Is it contagious?"

She did not directly answer. Instead she said, "What I have can be cured." Obviously she wanted to reassure him. "If the virus is around . . . I won't come over; it's okay." She nodded and reached to shut off her transmitter. "I'm going to lie down," she said, "and get more sleep. With this you're supposed to sleep as much as you can. I'll talk to you tomorrow. Goodbye."

"Come over," he said.

Brightening, she said, "Thank you."

"But be sure you bring your beeper. I have a hunch a lot of telemetric confirms are going to—"

"Oh, fuck the telemetric confirms!" Rybus said, with venom. "I'm so sick of being stuck in this goddam dome! Aren't you going buggy sitting around watching tape drums turn and little meters and gauges and shit?"

"I think you should go back home," he said.

"No," she said, more calmly. "I'm going to follow exactly the M.E.D. instructions for my chemotherapy and beat this fucking M.S. I'm not going home. I'll come over and fix your dinner. I'm a good cook. My mother was Italian and my father is Chicano so I spice everything I fix, except you can't get spices out here. But I figured out how to beat that with different synthetics. I've been experimenting."

"In this concert I'm going to be broadcasting," McVane said, "the Fox does a version of Dowland's *Shall I Sue*."

"A song about litigation?"

"No. 'Sue' in the sense of to pay court to or woo. In matters of love." And then he realized that she was putting him on.

"Do you want to know what I think of the Fox?" Rybus asked. "Recycled sentimentality, which is the worst kind of sentimentality; it isn't even original. And she looks like her face is on upside down. She has a mean mouth."

"I like her," he said, stiffly; he felt himself becoming mad, really mad. I'm supposed to help you? he asked himself. Run the risk of catching what you have so you can insult the Fox?

"I'll fix you beef stroganoff with parsley noodles," Rybus said.

"I'm doing fine," he said.

Hesitating, she said in a low, faltering voice, "Then you don't want me to come over?"

"I—" he said.

"I'm very frightened, Mr. McVane," Rybus said. "Fifteen minutes from now I'm going to be throwing up from the IV Neurotoxite. But I don't want to be alone. I don't want to give up my dome and I don't want to be by myself. I'm sorry if I offended you. It's just that to me the Fox is a joke. I won't say anything more; I promise."

"Do you have the—" He amended what he intended to say. "Are you sure it won't be too much for you, fixing dinner?"

"I'm stronger now than I will be," she said. "I'll be getting weaker for a long time."

"How long?"

"There's no way to tell."

He thought, you are going to die. He knew it and she knew it. They did not have to talk about it. The complicity of silence was there, the agreement. A dying girl wants to cook me a dinner, he thought. A dinner I don't want to eat. *I've got to say no to her. I've got to keep her out of my dome.* The insistence of the weak, he thought; their dreadful power. It is so much easier to throw a body-block against the strong!

"Thank you," he said. "I'd like it very much if we had dinner together. But make sure you keep in radio contact with me on your way over here—so I'll know you're okay. Promise?"

"Well sure," she said. "Otherwise—" She smiled. "They'd find me a century from now, frozen with pots, pans and food, as well as synthetic spices. You do have portable air, don't you?"

"No, I really don't," he said.

And knew that his lie was palpable to her.

The meal smelled good and tasted good but halfway through, Rybus excused herself and made her way unsteadily from the matrix of the dome—his dome—into the bathroom. He tried not to listen; he arranged it with his percept system not to hear and with his cognition not to know. In the bathroom the girl, violently sick, cried out and he gritted his teeth and pushed his plate away and then all at once he got up and set in motion his in-dome audio system; he played an early album of the Fox.

Come again!
Sweet love doth now invite
Thy graces, that refrain
To do me due delight . . .

"Do you by any chance have some milk?" Rybus asked, standing at the bathroom door, her face pale.

Silently, he got her a glass of milk, or what passed for milk on their planet.

"I have anti-emetics," Rybus said as she held the glass of milk, "but I didn't remember to bring any with me. They're back at my dome."

"I could get them for you," he said.

"You know what M.E.D. told me?" Her voice was heavy with indignation. "They said that this chemotherapy won't make my hair fall out but already it's coming out in—"

"Okay," he interrupted.

"Okay?"

"I'm sorry," he said.

"This is upsetting you," Rybus said. "The meal is spoiled and you're—I don't know what. If I'd remembered to bring my anti-emetics I'd be able to keep from—" She became silent. "Next time I'll bring them. I promise. This is one of the few albums of Fox that I like. She was really good then, don't you think?"

"Yes," he said tightly.

"Linda Box," Rybus said.

"What?" he said.

"Linda the box. That's what my sister and I used to call her." She tried to smile.

"Please go back to your dome."

"Oh," she said. "Well—" She smoothed her hair, her hand shaking. "Will you come with me? I don't think I can make it by myself right now. I'm really weak. I really am sick."

He thought, You are taking me with you. That's what this is. That is what is happening. You will not go alone; you will take my spirit with you. And you know. You know it as well as you know the name of the medication you are taking, and you hate me as you hate the medication, as you hate M.E.D. and your illness; it is all hate, for each and every thing under these two suns. I know you. I understand you. I see what is coming. In fact it has begun.

And, he thought, I don't blame you. But I will hang onto the Fox; the Fox will outlast you. And so will I. You are not going to shoot down the luminiferous aether which animates our souls.

I will hang onto the Fox and the Fox will hold me in her arms and hang onto me. The two or us—we can't be pried apart. I have dozens of hours of the Fox on audio and video tape, and the tapes are not just for me but for everybody. You think you can kill that? he said to himself. It's been tried before. The power of the weak, he thought, is an imperfect power; it loses in the end. Hence its name. We call it weak for a reason.

"Sentimentality," Rybus said.

"Right," he said sardonically.

"Recycled at that."

"And mixed metaphors."

"Her lyrics?"

"What I'm thinking. When I get really angry I mix—"

"Let me tell you something. One thing. If I am going to survive I can't be sentimental. I have to be very harsh. If I've made you angry I'm sorry but that is how it is. It is my life. Someday you may be in the spot I am in and then you'll know. Wait for that and then judge me. If it ever happens. Meanwhile this stuff you're playing on your in-dome audio system is crap. It has to be crap, for me. Do you see? You can forget about me; you can send me back to my dome, where I probably really belong, but if you have anything to do with me—"

"Okay," he said, "I understand."

"Thank you. May I have some more milk? Turn down the audio and we'll finish eating. Okay?"

Amazed, he said, "You're going to keep on trying to—"

"All those creatures—and species—who gave up trying to eat aren't with us any more." She seated herself unsteadily, holding onto the table.

"I admire you."

"No," she said, "I admire *you*. It's harder on you. I know."

"Death—" he began.

"This isn't death. You know what this is? In contrast to what's coming out of your audio system? This is life. The milk, please; I really need it."

As he got her more milk he said, "I guess you can't shoot down aether. Luminiferous or otherwise."

"No," she agreed, "since it doesn't exist."

Commodity Central provided Rybus with two wigs, since, due to the chemo, her hair had been systematically killed. He preferred the light colored one.

When she wore her wig she did not look too bad, but she had become weakened and a certain querulousness had crept into her discourse. Because she was not physically strong any longer—due more, he suspected, to the chemotherapy than to her illness—she could no longer manage to maintain her dome adequately. Making his way over there one day he was shocked at what he found. Dishes, pots and pans and even glasses of spoiled food, dirty clothes strewn everywhere, litter and debris . . . troubled, he cleaned up for her and, to his vast dismay, realized that there was an odor pervading her dome, a sweet mixture of the smell of illness, of complex medications, the soiled clothing, and, worst of all, the rotting food itself.

Until he cleared an area there was not even a place for him to sit. Rybus lay in bed, wearing a plastic robe open at the back. Apparently, however, she still managed to operate her electronic equipment; he noted that the meters indicated full activity. But she used the remote programmer normally reserved for emergency conditions; she lay propped up in bed with the programmer beside her, along with a magazine and a bowl of cereal and several bottles of medication.

As before, he discussed the possibility of getting her transferred. She refused to be taken off her job; she had not budged.

"I'm not going into a hospital," she told him, and that, for her, ended the conversation.

Later, back at his own dome, gratefully back, he put a plan into operation. The large AI System—Artificial Intelligence Plasma—which handled the major problem-solving for star systems in their area of the galaxy had some available time which could be bought for private use. Accordingly, he punched in an application and posted the total sum of financial credits he had saved up during the last few months.

From Fomalhaut, where the Plasma drifted, he received back a positive response. The team which handled traffic for the Plasma were agreeing to sell him fifteen minutes of the Plasma's time.

At the rate at which he was being metered he was motivated to feed the Plasma his data very skillfully and very rapidly. He told the Plasma who Rybus was—which gave the AI System access to her complete files, including her psychological profile—and he told it that his dome was the closest dome to hers, and he told it of her fierce determination to live and her refusal to accept a medical discharge or even transfer from her station. He cupped his head into the shell for psychotronic output so that the Plasma at Fomalhaut could draw directly from his thoughts, thus making available to it all his unconscious, marginal impressions, realizations, doubts, ideas, anxieties, needs.

"There will be a five-day delay in response," the team signalled him. "Because of the distance involved. Your payment has been received and recorded. Over."

"Over," he said, feeling glum. He had spent everything he had. A vacuum had consumed his worth. But the Plasma was the court of last appeal in matters of problem-solving. WHAT SHOULD I DO? he had asked the Plasma. In five days he would have the answer.

During the next five days Rybus became considerably weaker. She still fixed her own meals, however, although she seemed to eat the same thing over and over again: a dish of high-protein macaroni with grated cheese sprinkled over it. One day he found her wearing dark glasses. She did not want him to see her eyes.

"My bad eye has gone berserk," she said dispassionately. "Rolled up in my head like a window shade." Spilled capsules and tablets lay everywhere around her on her bed. He picked up one of the half-empty bottles and saw that she was taking one of the most powerful analgesics available.

"M.E.D. is prescribing this for you?" he said, wondering, Is she in that much pain?

"I know somebody," Rybus said. "At a dome on IV. The food man brought it over to me."

"This stuff is addictive."

"I'm lucky to get it. I shouldn't really have it."

"I know you shouldn't."

"That goddam M.E.D." The vindictiveness of her tone was surprising. "It's like dealing with a lower life form. By the time they get around to prescribing, and then getting the medication to you, Christ, you're an urn of ashes." I see no point in them prescribing for an urn of ashes." She put her hand up to her skull. "I'm sorry; I should keep my wig on when you're here."

"It doesn't matter," he said.

"Could you bring me some Coke? Coke settles my stomach."

From her refrigerator he took a quart bottle of cola and poured her a glass. He had to wash the glass first; there wasn't a clean one in the dome.

Propped up before her at the foot of her bed she had her standard-issue TV set going. It gabbled away mindlessly, but no one was listening or watching. He realized that every time he came over she had it on, even in the middle of the night.

When he returned to his own dome he felt a tremendous sense of relief, of an odious burden being lifted from him. Just to put physical distance between himself and her—that was a joy which raised his spirits. It's as if, he thought, that when I'm with her I have what she has. We share the illness.

He did not feel like playing any Fox recordings so instead he put on the Mahler Second Symphony, *The Resurrection.* The only symphony scored for many pieces of rattan, he mused. A Ruthe, which looks like a small broom; they use it to play the bass drum. Too bad Mahler never saw a Morley wah-wah pedal, he thought, or he would have scored it into one of his longer symphonies.

Just as the chorus came in, his in-dome audio system shut down; an extrinsic override had silenced it.

"Transmission from Fomalhaut."
"Standing by."
"Use video, please. Ten seconds till start."
"Thank you," he said.
A read-out appeared on his larger screen. It was the AI System, the Plasma, replying, a day early.

SUBJECT: RYBUS ROMMEY
ANALYSIS; THANATOUS
PROGRAM ADVICE: TOTAL AVOIDANCE ON YOUR PART
ETHICAL FACTOR: OBVIATED
THANK YOU

Blinking, McVane said reflexively, "Thank you." He had dealt with the Plasma only once before and he had forgotten how terse its responses were. The screen cleared; the transmission had ended.

He was not sure what "thanatous" meant, but he felt certain that it had something to do with death. It means she is dying, he pondered as he punched into the planet's reference bank and asked for a definition. It means that she is dying or may die or is close to death, all of which I know.

However, he was wrong. It meant *producing death.*

Producing, he thought. There is a great difference between *death* and *producing death.* No wonder the AI System had notified him that the ethical factor was obviated on his part.

She is a killer thing, he realized. Well, this is why it costs so much to consult the Plasma. You get—not a phony answer based on speculation—but an absolute response.

While he was thinking about it and trying to calm himself down, his telephone rang. Before he picked it up he knew who it was.

"Hi," Rybus said in a trembling voice.

"Hi," he said.

"Do you by any chance have any Celestial Seasonings Morning Thunder tea-bags?"

"What?" he said.

"When I was over at your dome that time I fixed beef stroganoff for us I thought I saw a cannister of Celestial Seasonings—"

"No," he said, "I don't. I used them up."

"Are you all right?"

"I'm just tired," he said, and he thought, She said "us." She and I are an "us." When did that happen? he asked himself. I guess that's what the Plasma meant; it understood.

"Do you have any kind of tea?"

"No," he said. His in-dome audio system suddenly came back on, released from its pause mode now that the Fomalhaut transmission had ended. The choir was singing.

On the phone Rybus giggled. "Fox is doing sound on sound? A whole chorus of a thousand—"

"This is Mahler," he said roughly.

"Do you think you could come over and keep me company, Rybus asked. "I'm sort of at loose ends."

After a moment he said, "Okay. There's something I want to talk to you about."

"I was reading this article in—"

"When I get there," he broke in, "we can talk. I'll see you in half an hour." He hung up the phone.

When he reached her dome he found her propped up in bed, wearing her dark glasses and watching a soap opera on her TV. Nothing had changed since he last had visited her, except that the decaying food in the dishes and the fluids in the cups and glasses had become more dismaying.

"You should watch this," Rybus said, not looking up. "Okay; I'll fill you in. Becky is pregnant but her boyfriend doesn't—"

"I brought you some tea." He set down four tea-bags.

"Could you get me some crackers? There's a box on the shelf over the stove. I need to take a pill. It's easier for me to take medication with food than with water because when I was about three years old . . . you're not going to believe this. My father was teaching me to swim. We had a lot of money in those days; my father was a—well, he still is, although I don't hear from him very often. He hurt his back opening one of those sliding security gates at a condo cluster where . . ." Her voice trailed off; she had again become engrossed in her TV.

McVane cleared off a chair and seated himself.

"I was very depressed last night," Rybus said. "I almost called you. I was thinking about this friend of mine who's now—well, she's my age, but she's got a class 4-C rating in time-motion studies involving prism fluctuation rate or some damn thing. I hate her. At my age! Can you feature that?" She laughed.

"Have you weighed yourself recently?" he asked.

"What? Oh, no. But my weight's okay. I can tell. You take a pinch of skin between your fingers, up near your shoulder, and I did that. I still have a fat layer."

"You look thin," he said. He put his hand on her forehead.

"Am I running a fever?"

"No," he said. He continued to hold his hand there, against her smooth damp skin, above her dark glasses. Above, he thought, the myelin sheath of nerve fibers which had developed the sclerotic patches which were killing her.

You will be better off, he said to himself, when she is dead.

Sympathetically, Rybus said, "Don't feel bad. I'll be okay. M.E.D. has cut my dosage of Vasculine. I only take it t.i.d. now—three times a day instead of four."

"You know all the medical terms," he said.

"I have to. They issued me a P.D.R. Want to look at it? It's around here somewhere. Look under those papers over there. I was writing letters to several old friends because while I was looking for something else I came across their addresses. I've been throwing things away. See?" She pointed and he saw sacks, paper sacks, of crumpled papers. "I wrote for five hours yesterday and then I started in today. That's why I wanted the tea; maybe you could fix me a cup. Put a whole lot of sugar in it and just a little milk."

As he fixed her the tea, fragments of a Linda Fox adaptation of a Dowland song moved through his mind.

Thou mighty God, that rightest every wrong . . .
Listen to Patience in a dying song.

"This program is really good," Rybus said, when a series of commercials interrupted her TV soap opera. "Can I tell you about it?"

Rather than answering, he asked, "Does the reduced dosage of Vasculine indicate that you're improving?"

"I'm probably going into another period of remission."

"How long can you expect it to last?"

"Probably quite a while."

"I admire your courage," he said. "I'm bailing out. This is the last time I'm coming over here."

"My courage?" she said. "Thank you."

"I'm not coming back."

"Not coming back when? You mean today?"

"You are a death-dealing organism," he said. "A pathogen."

"If we're going to talk seriously," she said, "I want to put my wig on. Could you bring me my blond wig? It's around somewhere, maybe under those clothes in the corner there. Where that red top is, the one with the white buttons. I have to sew a button back on it, *if* I can find the button."

He found her her wig.

"Hold the hand mirror for me," she said as she placed the wig on her skull. "Do you think I'm contagious? Because M.E.D. says that at this stage the virus is inactive. I talked to M.E.D. for over an hour yesterday; they gave me a special line."

"Who's maintaining your gear?" he asked.

"Gear?" She gazed at him from behind dark glasses.

"Your job. Monitoring incoming traffic. Storing it and then transferring it. The reason you're here."

"It's on auto."

"You have seven warning lights on right now, all red and all blinking," he said. "You should have an audio analog so you can hear it and not ignore it. You're receiving but not recording and they're trying to tell you."

"Well, they're out of luck," she responded in a low voice.

"They have to take into account the fact that you're sick," he said.

"Yes, they do. Of course they do. They can bypass me; don't you receive roughly what I receive? Aren't I essentially a backup station to your own?"

"No," he said, "I'm a backup station to yours."

"It's all the same." She sipped the mug of tea which he had fixed for her. "It's too hot. I'll let it cool." Tremblingly, she reached to set down the mug on a table beside her bed; the mug fell, and hot tea poured out over the plastic floor. "Christ," she said with fury. "Well, that does it; that really does it. *Nothing* has gone right today. Son of a bitch."

McVane turned on the dome's vacuum circuit and it sucked up the spilled tea. He said nothing. He felt amorphous anger all through him, directed at nothing, fury without object, and he sensed that this was the quality of her own hate: it was a passion which went both nowhere and everywhere. Hate, he thought, like a flock of flies. God, he thought, how I want out of here. How I hate to hate like this, hating spilled tea with the same venom as I hate terminal illness. A one-dimensional universe. It has dwindled to that.

In the weeks that followed he made fewer and fewer trips from his dome to hers. He did not listen to what she said; he did not watch what she did; he averted his gaze from the chaos around her, the ruins of her dome. I am seeing a projection of her brain, he thought once as he momentarily surveyed the garbage which had piled up everywhere; she was even putting sacks outside the dome, to freeze for eternity. She is senile.

Back in his own dome he tried to listen to Linda Fox but the magic had departed. He saw and heard a synthetic image. It was not real. Rybus Rommey had sucked the life out of the Fox the way her dome's vacuum circuit had sucked up the spilled tea.

And when his sorrows came as fast as floods,
Hope kept his heart till comfort came again.

McVane heard the words but they didn't matter. What had Rybus called it? Recycled sentimentality and crap. He put on a Vivaldi concerto for bassoon. There is only one Vivaldi concerto, he thought. A computer could do better. And be more diverse.

"You're picking up Fox waves," Linda Fox said, and on his video transducer her face appeared, star-lit and wild. "And when those Fox waves hit you," she said, "you have been *hit!*"

In a momentary spasm of fury he deliberately erased four hours of Fox, both video and audio. And then regretted it. He put in a call to one of the relay satellites for replacement tapes and was told that they were back-ordered.

Fine, he said to himself. What the hell does it matter?

That night, while he was sound asleep, his telephone rang. He let it ring; he did not answer it, and when it rang again ten minutes later he again ignored it.

The third time it rang he picked it up and said hello.

"Hi," Rybus said.

"What is it?" he said.

"I'm cured."

"You're in remission?"

"No, I'm cured. M.E.D. just contacted me; their computer analyzed all my charts and tests and everything and there's no sign of hard patches. Except of course I'll never get central vision back in my bad eye.

But other than that I'm okay." She paused. "How have you been? I haven't heard from you for so long—it seems like forever. I've been wondering about you."

He said, "I'm okay."

"We should celebrate."

"Yes," he said.

"I'll fix dinner for us, like I used to. What would you like? I feel like Mexican food. I make a really good taco; I have the ground meat in my freezer, unless it's gone bad. I'll thaw it out and see. Do you want me to come over there or do you—"

"Let me talk to you tomorrow," he said.

"I'm sorry to wake you up but I just now heard from M.E.D." She was silent a moment. "You're the only friend I have," she said. And then, incredibly, she began to cry.

"It's okay," he said. "You're well."

"I was so fucked up," she said brokenly. "I'll ring off and talk to you tomorrow. But you're right; I can't believe it but I made it."

"It is due to your courage," he said.

"It's due to you," Rybus said. "I would have given up without you. I never told you this but—well, I squirreled away enough sleeping pills to kill myself, and—"

"I'll talk to you tomorrow," he said, "about getting together." He hung up and lay back down.

He thought, When Job had lost his children, lands and goods, Patience assuaged his excessive pain. And when his sorrows came as fast as floods, Hope kept his heart till comfort came again. As the Fox would put it.

Recycled sentimentality, he thought. I got her through her ordeal and she paid me back by deriding into rubbish that which I cherished the most. But she is alive, he realized; she did make it. It's like when someone tries to kill a rat. You can kill it six ways and still it survives. You can't fault that.

He thought, That is the name of what we are doing here in this star system on these frozen planets in these little domes. Rybus Rommey understood the game and played it right and won. To hell with Linda Fox.

And then he thought, But also to hell with what I love.

It is a good trade-off, he thought: a human life won and a synthetic media image wrecked. The law of the universe.

Shivering, he pulled his covers over him and tried to get back to sleep.

The food man showed up before Rybus did; he awoke McVane early in the morning with a full shipment.

"Still got your temp and air illegally boosted," the food man said as he unscrewed his helmet.

"I just use the equipment," McVane said. "I don't build it."

"Well, I won't report you. Got any coffee?"

They sat facing each other across the table drinking fake coffee.

"I just came from the Rommey girl's dome," the food man said. "She says she's cured."

"Yeah, she phoned me late last night," McVane said.

"She says you did it."

To that, McVane said nothing.

"You saved a human life."

"Okay," McVane said.

"What's wrong?"

"I'm just tired."

"I guess it took a lot out of you. Christ, it's a mess over there. Can't you clean it up for her? Destroy the garbage, at least, and sterilize the place; the whole goddam dome is septic. She let her garbage disposal get plugged and it backed up raw sewage all over her cupboards and shelves, where her food is stored. I've never seen anything like it. Of course, she's been so weak—"

McVane interrupted, "I'll look into it."

Awkwardly, the food man said, "The main thing is, she's cured. She was giving herself the shots, you know."

"I know," McVane said. "I watched her." Many times, he said to himself.

"And her hair's growing back. Boy, she looks awful without her wig. Don't you agree?"

Rising, McVane said, "I have to broadcast some weather reports. Sorry I can't talk to you any longer."

Toward dinner time Rybus Rommey appeared at the hatch of his dome, loaded down with pots and dishes and carefully wrapped packages. He let her in, and she made her way silently to the kitchen area where she dumped everything down at once; two packages slid off onto the floor and she stooped to retrieve them.

After she had taken off her helmet she said, "It's good to see you again."

"Likewise," he said.

"It'll take about an hour to fix the tacos. Do you think you can wait until then?"

"Sure," he said.

"I've been thinking," Rybus said as she started a pan of grease heating on the stove. "We ought to take a vacation. Do you have any leave coming? I have two weeks owed me, although my situation is complicated by my illness. I mean, I used up a lot of my leave in the form of sick leave. Christ's sake, they docked me one-half day for a month, just because I couldn't operate my transmitter. Can you believe it?"

He said, "It's nice to see you stronger."

"I'm fine," she said. "Shit, I forgot the hamburger. Goddam it!" She stared at him.

"I'll go to your dome and get it," he said presently.

She seated herself. "It's not thawed. I forgot to thaw it out. I just remembered now. I was going to take it out of the freezer this morning, but I had to finish some letters . . . maybe we could have something else and have the tacos tomorrow night."

"Okay," he said.

"And I meant to bring your tea back."

"I only gave you four bags," he said.

Eying him uncertainly, she said, "I thought you

brought me that whole box of Celestial Seasonings Morning Thunder Tea. Then where did I get it? Maybe the food man brought it. I'm just going to sit here for a while. Could you turn on the TV?"

He turned on the TV.

"There's a show I watch," Rybus said. "I never miss it. I like shows about—well, I'll have to fill you in on what's happened so far if we're going to watch."

"Could we not watch?" he said.

"Her husband—"

He thought, She's completely crazy. She is dead. Her body has been healed but it killed her mind.

"I have to tell you something," he said.

"What is it?"

"You're—" He ceased.

"I'm very lucky," she said. "I beat the odds. You didn't see me when I was at my worst. I didn't want you to. From the chemo I was blind and paralyzed and deaf and then I started having seizures; I'll be on a maintenance dose for years. But it's okay? Don't you think? To be on just a maintenance dose? I mean, it could be so much worse. Anyhow, her husband lost his job because he—"

"Whose husband?" McVane said.

"On the TV." Reaching up she took hold of his hand. "Where do you want to go on our vacation? We so goddam well deserve some sort of reward. Both of us."

"Our reward," he said, "is that you're well."

She did not seem to be listening; her gaze was fastened on the TV. He saw, then, that she still wore her dark glasses. It made him think, then, of the song the Fox had sung on Christmas Day, for all the planets, the most tender, the most haunting song which she had adapted from John Dowland's lute books.

When the poor cripple by the pool did lie
Full many years in misery and pain,
No sooner he on Christ had set his eye,
But he was well, and comfort came again.

Rybus Rommey was saying, "—it was a high-paying job but everyone was conspiring against him; you know how it is in an office. I worked in an office once where—" Pausing, she said, "Could you heat some water? I'd like to try a little coffee."

"Okay," he said, and turned on the burner. ☆

Grimm's Law

L. Neil Smith

Smoke from Bernie Gruenblum's cigar drifted through the Langrenus-Tsiolkovsky shuttle, earning him the malevolent glances of his fellow passengers. Smoking in a pressurized conveyance was poor etiquette, but Bernie was determined to enjoy whatever luxuries time permitted.

The fact that this might conflict with the comfort of others did not occur to him. Despite years of training to the contrary, it was difficult to regard those around him now as real. He had less reason than most to regard the past as prologue, but the old saw about the dead past burying its own dead was constantly in the back of his mind.

Bernie shrugged, then slumped in his seat to avoid the icy stares, and watched as the five-thousand-meter crater walls sped by the rising shuttle. Puffing his cigar, he reflected on the incivilities of even so advanced an age as this. Still, at home, decent tobacco was hard to get—"Kansas Grass" being a contemptuous term (borrowed from an earlier time and a different variety of Prohibition) to describe what was illegally available there. Bernie, time permitting, never missed an opportunity to obtain a better quality product.

The sun sank with every kilometer the shuttle penetrated into the terminator; Bernie grinned as he thought about that other opportunity which had come his way back in Langrenus. Feminine companionship was one thing they couldn't outlaw back home, but the pleasure-bent can do phenomenal things at one-sixth G.

Arriving in Grissom, a quiet little suburb of the Tsiolkovsky Research Complex, Bernie descended via drop-tube to the sixteenth level. There was still time for a beer or three in a tavern he recalled. A couple of left turns put him in front of Youssef's Arabian Nights, pleased he'd remembered its location.

He entered and sat down near the end of the bar next to a lanky stranger staring woefully into the amber depths of a beer. Bernie found the man's martyred expression mildly ludicrous, but for conversation's sake was about to offer some condolence, when a woman of mastodonian proportions charged through the door, incongruously brandishing an umbrella. The rage in her bloodshot eyes would have done credit to the Great White Whale attacking the *Pequod.*

"So there you are, George Mittlemoss, you slimy little shrimp!" She emphasized each word with a sharp jab of her umbrella at a wispy little man in shabby civilian clothes sitting at the opposite end of the bar. "So this is where you go when you tell me you're at the library! I might have known! Mother always said you were a philandering worm!"

The little man clawed frantically at the bar beside him. Sensing impending calamity, Youssef the proprietor tried vainly to insert himself between the antagonists, only to have to duck the erratic swings of the woman's umbrella himself. Finally he sprang lightly over the bar, snatched a fragile-looking stool, and advanced slowly behind its minimal protection, an expression on his Semitic face like that of a lion-tamer suddenly realizing he has chosen the wrong profession.

Achieving a strategic position, Youssef lashed out and seized the umbrella's haft just above the Leviathan's fat fingers. This was a mistake, as she probably outmassed him by a hundred kilos. Struggling against his grip, she swung not only the umbrella, but the astonished bartender as well, over and around her head. The man hung on grimly, having gained sufficient velocity to do himself and his establishment no small damage if he were to let go.

Finally, hauling himself closer to the center of rotation, he sank his teeth into the woman's hand—a second mistake. She let out a trumpet of rage and released the umbrella. It and the unfortunate bartender sailed down the length of the bar, cleaving a gracefully arching wake of liquid, bottles, glasses, napkins, and pickled eggs. Bernie and his neighbor, the latter's face bearing a weary look of yet another imposition, ducked back just in time to let Youssef toboggan past and thud into the large front window.

The pane groaned, absorbing the energy of the flying man, and gave it back, flinging the bartender against Bernie's companion, carrying them both into a group of patrons seated at a table near the bar. A shimmering curtain of alcohol and other debris, the result of Youssef's original trip down the bar, drenched them all amidst a heap of legs, arms, bodies, and chairs.

With surprising adroitness, Youssef gathered his wits and feet about him and charged back into the fray, umbrella raised above his head like a scimitar. Mrs. Mittlemoss stood sulkily clutching her wounded digit, her cetacean bulk overshadowing the original object of her attentions, who was cowering between two barstools. She cursed him vehemently.

"SHADDUP!" The bartender blasted over the flood of epithets, "Goddamit, lady, I don't care if your old man's an *axe-murderer,* I want you the hell out of here, right now!"

The woman's little raisin eyes slowly widened as she turned to focus them on Youssef. In the ensuing silence, the little man timidly emerged from his shelter under the bar, his small, thin voice cutting through the room.

"Es tut mir leid," he said, a tear trembling on his lower eyelashes, *"aber Herr Schankwirt, g-gnädige Frau, ich hab' keine Englisch . . ."*

The woman fainted.

"Well fry me in salad oil!" Beads of beer glistened on

Bernie's coverall. He turned to his companion in misfortune who was daubing miserably at the spreading stains on his suit. "Mistaken identity'd be bad enough, but mistaken *nationality?*"

"Damn it all," said the man, "now I'll go home smelling like a brewery! Sidney, may he rot in Cleveland, will have quite a laugh—but Martha will kill me. . . . Excuse me, did you say something?"

"Just wondered if it's like this around here all the time." Bernie picked up a fresh beer supplied gratis by the establishment.

"I should hope not! Grissom is a respectable little warren." He surveyed the barroom. "I wonder how she ever got past the Eugenics Board!" Stains now covered half the area of his jacket, abetted, no doubt, by his mopping at them with the bar rag. He thrust out a damp hand. "My name's Horace Homer—but for godsake, call me Hap."

Bernie placed a fresh rag in Hap's outthrust hand and introduced himself. "Too bad about the suit. Take it topside and hang it out the lock for a couple seconds. Then you can *shake* the stains out." He glanced at his empty glass and Youssef brought another round. "Last time I was through here they'd just dug this level, and it was quiet, even then. Haven't seen a fracas like this since my last trip to Europe."

"We don't see an awful lot of excitement here," agreed Hap, "Like I said, Grisssom is a nice, quite little—"

"Didn't mean that flying trapeze act," Bernie shook his head, "I meant that little *deutscher* getting mistook for Mr. Mittlemoss. She must need contacts."

The lady in question had been revived and commenced a subdued argument with the proprietor over damages. That she lacked her former ardor may have been due to the fact that Youssef still possessed the confiscated umbrella. The little German was working his way through a series of free drinks.

"Have you been to the Moon often?" Hap asked conversationally.

"More times'n I can remember," Bernie replied, "I'll remember this trip, though. Never like this in Oklahoma City, worse luck."

The serving robots had cleared up the mess and were now shuffling around like chrome-plated Charlie Chaplins, offering alcoholic amends to the bruised and shaken clientele. One little machine cleared off the end of the bar and brought Bernie and Hap yet another unordered round. Bernie gravely shook hands with the automaton, and it scuttled away delightedly to fetch Hap another dry towel.

Hap had discovered to his annoyance that his pants needed "vacuuming", too, and was trying to hide the embarrassing stain from public view. He watched Bernie salt his beer to a monumental head. "When did you say you were in Europe? We were there, once, on our honeymoon. Paris—dirty, hot, and smelly. And the bloody *weight*. I thought I was going to die of a coronary at the tender age of—

"—and I'll tell you something else." He leaned forward secretively. "Some of those places, the ones in the country, didn't even have—well, maybe a little shack out there, naked on the surface of the planet, but . . ." He whispered, "I'm afraid I wasn't quite myself for almost a month. Never did trust patent medicines."

Bernie grinned. "Yeah, it can be pretty bad if you're used to cultural refinements. Be thankful you didn't go with me—outhouses were an unheard-of luxury, way back then."

"Back *when?*"

Bernie colored suddenly, glanced at his watch and shrugged mentally. Well, why not? Taking a breath, he said quietly, "Third century—A.D."

Hap laughed. "Well, I've heard some wild stories in bars. This one should be a winner." Swivelling on his stool, he pushed his face down at Bernie's, nose-to-nose. "You're a Time Traveler."

Bernie cleared his throat, grinned sheepishly, and had to clear his throat again. "Well, I suppose you could put it that way." He glanced at his watch, then shoved his sleeve back and held a thin hairy wrist under Hap's nose. The location of the instrument was novelty enough in an era of finger timepieces. The large, square-faced machine was divided vertically into twin displays:

+20.0751	+22.7875
JUL 06	OCT 09
1703:56.9	0603:53.4

"Centuries and decimal fraction," explained Bernie, "this being A.D. 2007, and the year about half gone. The one on the right is my home time." Taking the watch off, he turned it over and handed it to Hap:

CONGRATULATIONS! CADET GRADUATE (TEMPORAL) BERNARD M. GRUENBLUM ODF(T) 5327796 87659921-A OCHSKAHRT MEMORIAL ACADEMY, CLASS OF 2221

"Elaborate," Hap replied, "a good barroom story with a good prop to back it up. Get it Earthside, or have it specially made?" The story sounded lame, even to himself. He glanced at his own fingerwatch, tiny, sophisticated, operating on body heat, then at Bernie's again as he handed it back.

"Got it the day I graduated," Bernie said with pride, "sixteenth in a class of nearly six thousand."

"And they gave away six thousand of these at your commencement?"

"Every year. 'Course below the top hundred graduates, the pile-dampers are only cadmium, and the case is platinum *plated,* instead of the real—"

"You know," Hap shook his head, "I ought to get up right now and leave before I start believing this nonsense. But Sidney and Martha are back there, waiting, so I probably won't."

Bernie said nothing, but simply raised his eyebrows at his empty glass. Youssef brought over more beer and picked up the bill Bernie tossed on the bar. They watched the fat woman, who was now conversing earnestly with an armed gentleman in uniform. The bartender shook his head, a resigned smile on his lips, and returned to the cash register. Bernie grinned; he preferred sittting at the bar, since bartenders are usually more interesting than Charlie Chaplin robots.

Hap did leave, but it was a short trip to acknowledge the physiological effects of beer. As he returned, he was looking at his watch again. "Seventeen-fifteen," he stated. "Another forty-five minutes and I can go home—my brother-in-law, Sidney, will be at his Save Our Lunar Environment meeting. That crumb never even *saw* Our Lunar Environment—can't trust him with anything more complicated than a fork, let alone a pressure suit. I wish he'd give up. He *knows* the Immigration Authority'll never let him settle permanently, the miserable, parasitic, worthless, lousy, stupid . . ."

"Schmuck?" suggested Bernie.

"Schmuck. I do love my wife, but Sidney makes me wonder if there's anything to heredity. Say—maybe he's not really . . ." He was lost momentarily in some pleasant fantasy concerning Sidney's possible origins. "At least he hasn't found this bar yet. He prefers staying at home, sitting in *my* chair, drinking *my* liquor, while gleefully denouncing the effort and technology that produced them. Why he should be the only relative of ours who drops in for five months at a stretch is—"

"I like *my* brother-in-law, he hardly ever comes to visit. He's a frog-fur rancher out on Milhous—Beetle Juice IX. Before he took up the simple life, he was a philologist—you know, one of those academics who figures out where words come from? Cared more about morphemes and phonemes than—but he was a decent sort, and not one of those eggheads who look down their noses at Academy grads. Hell, I got more education in my left big toe than those professors have in their whole dissertations—just don't let it stick out around the edges. Didn't spend ten years learning to jockey an Ochskahrt around for nothing. You can't be ignorant and do that—probably helps to be a little nuts, though."

"Oxcart?"

"Ochskahrt—like on the watch engraving. He was—uh, *is* a twenty-first-century physicist looking for an anti-Einsteinian spaceship drive. Found it, too, only he blew himself and half a million other folks into little bits doing it. Dug himself a hole a hundred klicks wide an more'n two deep—big monument right in the middle, up in my time. Government boys finally figured out how to make things work without embarrassing side-effects. In fact, they're *still* not sure how old Ochskahrt managed to make an ash of himself."

The Ochskahrt Memorial Academy was originally set up to train FTL pilots. Then somebody equated an equation a little differently, and a ship got home before it left—time travel. It was easy to see how the original calculations implied it, once it had been accomplished but did you ever figure out what part of your anatomy houses your hindsight?

Anyway, that's when they started the Temporal Division. Right away, it was a big flop. Why? Well, first off, only about ten percent of Academy grads go Temporal—there's a real pioneering spirit up home these days, and all the bright young folks want the Romance of the Spaceways.

And those damned spacers get all the publicity. Hero types. They get the glory, while all we do is ferry a lot of graybeards around—historians, anthropologists, dinosaur-diggers. And do we get any thanks for that? You go and figure it—nobody likes to see his own private preserve, where he's used to letting his opinions run wild, turned into an exact science. One reason, maybe, they're always so tough on old Ochskahrt.

There's another reason we're poor relations. No appropriations from the government or private foundations. Lotta ideological fourflushers had to pack their carpetbags and crawl back into the woodwork, once Temporal started running. Religions, too. You'd be surprised what a crud your favorite saint or guru might turn out to be in everyday life.

So while the spacers pop in and out of the universe, blazing paths of glory, we just go on keeping our mouths shut and doing our job. Academy likes it better that way, anyhow—they keep a pretty tight rein on this time travel jazz. Hafta. We don't know how much it'd take to mess things up—our present, yours, too—beyond repair. Nobody's anxious to find out, either. Bend anything back and forth enough and it'll fatigue.

But hell, *anybody* can con a starship—I could do it with the computer down. Let one of those thumbfingered spacers loose, and he'd run my baby right into a paradox, sure as shootin'.

"And, they call us *Little Green Men!"* Bernie brushed his hand down the green jumpsuit he wore and took another swallow of beer. "Of course a few things have happened to give us an idea the past is fairly elastic. That's how we got the *Little Green Men* tag hung on us. Whenever one of the boys slips up and lets the yokels catch a glimpse—easy to do, as you can't let your passengers off without dropping shields—we're either a Heavenly Omen or an Invasion from Outer Space.

"Hell, our ships manipulate enough energy to shove a medium-sized planet out of orbit anyway, and some of it's bound to leak, especially when you're overworked and overdue for a 5000-year overhaul." Bernie's spare frame shifted inside his coverall as he relaxed and wet his voice again. Hap had given up all pretense of disbelief and merely sat there, waiting for Bernie to continue.

"Well, after I'd graduated and done my six as an observer, I got my own ship and my brother-in-law comes to see me. Bernie, he says, could you swing a little weight and get a shuttle for me? He'd been working on something special for years and never got a chance at field confirmation. Everybody had priorities ahead of him.

I say to him it seems other fields have their glory-grabbers, too, and on accounta that, and because he was my favorite (only) brother-in-law, I'd see what I could do. But I warned him a newly commissioned officer swings about as much weight as a Styrofoam plumb-bob.

I asked him what he had in mind. So he commences to lay something on me called "The Progression of Mutes"—otherwise known as Grimm's Law.

Never did get it all straight. Somewhere back in the third or fourth century, the languages that were scheduled to turn into English and German suddenly changed the pronunciation of a lot of their consonants—as if everyone who spoke them got a toothache or a headcold all at the same time.

Well, look—in Latin you got *pater, mater, frater,* right? So how come we end up with father, mother, brother? They're really the same words, but the consonants are shifted ahead, kinda like musical chairs.

There's a definite pattern to this mulberry bush. A guy named Jacob Grimm—yeah, one of the fairy-tale brothers—figured out how it happened. But not why. As usual, there were other guys involved—Rask, and Verner—but Grimm got all the glory.

Anyway, they figured it happened sort of like a plague, spreading out from central Europe, but missing the Slavs and Scandinavia. Max—my brother-in-law—thought he had it nailed down where it all started. All he wanted was to get back there and find out why.

It took three years for Max to get all approved and cleared, pretty speedy considering the calculations necessary to predict what changes might occur if, say, you moved a pebble that some historical person was supposed to have stepped on. Or not stepped on.

And he spent months in training—you don't want the natives seeing through your cover, after all. You train while the bureaucratic wheels grind, and if, after all that effort, they turn you down, tough luck. You wind up speaking three or four languages nobody else knows, or using table manners that'd get you kicked out of the Kremlin.

Last thing they do is run a guesstimate on whether your project's worth all the calculated risks. Usually, after billions of computer-hours are invested, some desk-jockey vetoes everything. All the same, plenty of trips get made. I wouldn't be surprised if you've already run into some of our folks and never knew it.

Their cover's usually good, because we can't afford to take chances. We won't prevent wars or epidemics, or even save somebody's grandma from a trainwreck. Hell, we can't even save old Ochskahrt and half a million other folks with him. Nobody wants to have the past jerked out from under him. The future has to look out for its own interests.

So Max was lucky to get clearance at all. He and an ethnologist and a couple of linguistics guys were to spend a couple of weeks in Iberia recording Basques arguing over wine, women, and sheep, then spend the same two weeks in Germany listening to Teutonic views on the same subjects. The Basques were a kind of experimental control, as their language isn't related to *anything* this side of Alpha Centauri, and wasn't subject to the Progression of Mutes.

Since there were only four in Max's gang, the Academy dispatched me another group who were going to study Rome just before Alaric the Visigoth opened up the real estate market in 410.

You don't just drop the customers off and go home. It eats energy that way and costs money. S.O.P. calls for hanging around in orbit, nice and inconspicuous, but there's no regulation against going along with a group if you're trained for it and in an interesting neighborhood. The Academy doesn't care for it, but they have to use *some* inducements to get Temporal cadets, and that's about *numero uno*.

I never cared much for being spitted on some sheepherder's pike, so I left Max off in the Spanish Pyrenees and headed for Rome with the other bunch.

Republican Rome was about as prudish as twentieth-century Boston or Moscow, but by the fifth century, they'd loosened up considerably.

So there I was, in a certain establishment just off the Via Vendorii, sipping a bowl of Chianti in the company of a professional daughter of joy, when my watch here gives out with a distress alarm.

Third century. Max.

Well, you try explaining a noisy wristwatch to a fifth-century Roman. I jumped the ignition of someone's noble steed and went roaring off down the street with the horse's owner, the lady of easy virtue, and about half the loafers in Rome running after me shouting Vulgate curses and making Italian gestures.

I dodged into a sidestreet and lost them, then lit out for the vineyards with the old nag floorboarded. Finally called my ship down in a secluded spot—though I'll bet half the prospective saints in Italy had mystic revelations that evening—and was gone in a hurry, with no Air Force, for once, to scramble after *that* U.F.O.

I kept trying to raise Max's party, but all I got was that automated signal. By then I figured they were guests of some local witch doctor—in those days they tied half the rocks in the county to you and threw you in the river. If you floated, you were innocent, a verdict that seldom got reversed by a higher court. Max was asthmatic and wouldn't hold his breath for thirty seconds.

I was sweating by the time I got a fix on them. I went aft and dug out a forcefield generator and a big strobe, figuring to convince the barbarians of a miracle —and my Gold Cup .45 in case they didn't go for it. The automatic's obsolete and illegal as hell for reasons the Academy regards as obvious, but it'll knock down a man and make a horse pretty sick—and regulations don't count when you're dead and gone.

I usually slip out of the Null with so much finesse you can't feel the displaced air, but this time the ship materialized with a Jovian thunderclap I figured would impress the locals. It sure knocked Max and his cohorts flat on their Ph.D.'s. A quick once-over gave me no indication of unfriendlies, but I was out of the hatch with the Colt drawn and the hammer back just the same. All I saw was a tiny clearing full of disconsolate, fur-clad professors looking sheepishly at me as I snaked down the boarding ladder.

I began to feel foolish and holstered the autopistol, making sure the safety was flipped up—damn thing's unsafe to carry any way but at battle-stations. There'd better be a good reason for this fiasco, I figured.

There was.

Max looked at me with tears in his eyes and said *"Pernie! You kotha ghelf us! Somedhinh wenth wronh! We ghoth haughth in dhe shibhth!"*

Hap was nearly cyanotic before he stopped laughing and choking on beer.

"You guessed it," Bernie resumed, "they hadn't caught a cold or a toothache. They never figured out what caused the consonant shift, but they experienced it first hand. A phone call topside for a textual reference had put them wise. They hadn't noticed it among themselves—relativity or something. While every Teuton on the Continent was shoved one notch closer to English, the only four English speakers got shoved one notch ahead!"

There was a moment of silence. "Philology never was quite the same to Max after that. Very embarrassing, considering his profession, to have to learn his native language all over again—and at his age. Took to raising fur-frogs out on Milhous, like I said. They don't care how you talk, long as you feed 'em regular and aerate their roots."

"That," said Hap at last, "is one of the dumber stories I've heard in this place." A sudden change came over his face, a flash of triumph. He swirled the remainder of his drink around the bottom of the stein, tilted it high above his head, and watched it drain slowly into his mouth. "Just one point, if you don't mind. It might help next time you tell it. If your Academy's so damned careful about not monkeying around with the past, how come you're telling me all this?"

Bernie glanced at his watch, determined there wasn't time for another beer. He took out a cigar and lit it, standing up slowly, speaking carefully. "You're right, of course. Normally it'd call for a court-martial. We don't take chances on changing the past." He zipped his green coverall up to his throat, shoved a hand in a pocket and turned to go, then turned back momentarily.

"I gotta take off, now, to pick up my passengers over in Tsiolkovsky. They're physicists, trying to figure out what old Ochskahrt's gonna do wrong twenty minutes from now." ☆

Corpus Cryptic

Lee Killough

Death was a hell of a thing to start Monday.

Dr. Dallas March paused in the doorway of the office where the campus security officer had brought her. The man they wanted her to see was slumped face down across his desk, his scalp shining pale through the thinning strands of his hair. Dallas felt the skeletal figure of her old enemy grinning at her from above him.

Cold rage rushed through her as it always did in the presence of death, as it had ever since the years of her adolescence she spent watching her mother's life leaching away. Her mouth tightened. *Made a successful week-end raid, I see. How did you do it this time?*

Death's mocking smile dared her to find out.

She stepped inside, closing the door behind her, shutting out the curious eyes of the students and faculty who had been gathering in the hall. The eyes of the campus security officers in the room with her were equally curious, but, she knew, for a different reason. She had seen similar expressions all during her residency. *This is a coroner? Hello there, Red.*

One, a plainclothesman slightly taller than herself, said, "I'm David Oaks, Investigations. Where's Dr. Terry?"

"He's out of town this week. I'm Dr. March, his partner." She almost said new partner, but decided that information was irrelevant. "He's made me acting coroner until his return." She rolled the head of the dead man to one side so she could see his face. After seeing so many bodies, there was a temptation to think of them as just cadavers, but she tried to think of them as individuals entitled to the same respect and dignity they had had in life. "Who is he?"

"Dr. Lawrence Morgan. He's—was—a professor of physics. His graduate assistant found him like this when she unlocked the office this morning."

Dallas pulled back the chair. It rolled easily on oiled casters. With the help of an officer, she slid Dr. Morgan onto his back on the floor. He moved limply, without any of the stiffness of rigor mortis. His skin felt cold.

"Do you think it was a heart attack?" the officer asked.

"I really can't say yet."

But his face was peaceful, not distorted as it would have been after an agonal struggle. However he had died, death had come unexpectedly and unfought. *Took him like a sneak thief, didn't you?* The subject appeared to be in his mid-fifties and had once been a very muscular man. He still probably weighed around 85 kilos, but some of it had gone to fat.

"Let's have a look at you, Doctor."

She unbuckled his belt and unzipped his trousers. Rolling him onto his stomach, she pulled his trousers and shorts down.

Someone cleared his throat.

"If you're embarrassed, don't look," Dallas said.

The buttocks carried the bruise-like darkening of hypostasis where gravity had drawn the blood when circulation stopped, indicating he had been sitting in that chair since he died. She pulled up his trousers again, tucking in his shirt tail, and rolled him back over.

"Is the room always this temperature?" she asked. It felt about twenty degrees.

"Yes."

She was calculating what time rigor should have disappeared considering the temperature and Dr. Morgan's physical condition and pre-mortem activity when she became aware of voices carrying from the hall outside.

"Dr. *Morgan!* But I saw him just Friday." A woman's voice.

Dallas grimaced. People would say that, time and time again, as if having seen someone alive made it impossible for him to die. They never seemed to realize that it was such a fragile spark, just a breath and a heartbeat, that made the difference between a vital being and dead meat.

Another voice said, "I can't say I'll miss him."

The voice grew clearer as the door opened to admit another security officer. Dallas, glancing up, caught a glimpse of the speaker, a small, square woman with short graying hair, before the door closed on her again.

"Esther!" The first woman was shocked.

"Don't expect me to be a hypocrite. I've never approved of the man or of his ptolemaic flat-earth attitudes. Men like him drive our best students to other universities."

Their voices faded down the hall.

Dallas sat back on her heels. Rigor had probably disappeared twenty-five or thirty hours after death. However, his skin had the washed pallor of someone newly dead. Ingesta should be fermenting by this time, too, causing bloating. Palpation of Dr. Morgan's stomach revealed none. Judging the time of death would be difficult. The security officers were looking expectant, however. She had to say something. She decided to go by the rigor.

"He died Saturday night at the latest, and possibly as early as Friday. I'll have a better idea after the autopsy."

"When will you do it? We'd like to know how he died as soon as possible," Oaks said. "Deaths are a terrible hassle, especially the pressure from relatives and the insurance companies."

She was just as anxious to know what happened, but not for the sake of relatives or insurance. "I'll post him tomorrow, but it may be Wednesday or

Thursday before the tests are complete." *I'm coming after you, Old One.*

She stood up. "See you in the morning, Doctor." She headed for the door.

Two ambulance attendants were waiting in the hall with a stretcher. She nodded as she left, giving them permission to take the body to the hospital, and walked out to where her car was illegally parked at the curb in front of the ambulance. The new '85 MG Electric was her Done-With-School present to herself.

She sat behind the wheel frowning for a few minutes before she switched on the motor. Dr. Morgan's death bothered her more than most. Rigor gone but decomposition still minimal? That was most peculiar, and disturbing. Right now it was uncomfortable being fresh out of residency and the only pathologist in town. She hoped the autopsy would give her some clear answers.

It did not. If anything, the postmortem only raised more questions. Before touching the body with a knife, she examined the skin closely, looking for any significant signs of trauma: burns, abrasions, lacerations, even needle punctures. All she found was a large contusion on the right temporal bone, above and behind the ear. She parted the hair to study the skin, but could see no bruise. From the size of the swelling, the blow had been a hard one, so the lack of bruising could mean he died before one could form.

"Let's check for leukocytic infiltration," Dallas told the OR nurse who was helping her.

She ran a tissue study using the autopsy room's microscope. There were white blood cells in the field. He had gotten the wound before he died then. The cells would not have been present if the injury had happened after death.

That was the last fact she was able to feel sure about. From the start of the three intersecting incisions that opened the abdomen, the case went from puzzling to bizarre. Not only was there no postmortem tympanites of the digestive tract—examination of the stomach and small bowel contents found the ingesta without even the beginnings of fermentation—but there was no detectable decomposition of any kind.

Dallas scraped the wall of the jejunum and spread the scrapings on a slide. She placed it on the stage of the microscope and bent over the eyepieces—and blinked in disbelief. She shifted the stage, scanning the entire slide. After a long time she straightened up, frowning.

The nurse raised her brows. "What is it? What do you see?"

Dallas shook her head. "Like the famous dog in the night, it's what I *don't* see. He has no intestinal flora."

The nurse's eyes widened. "What?"

"They're all gone."

"I don't remember observing anything like that before."

"Nor I." Dallas eyed the eviscerated corpse on the table. "Let's get cultures of saliva, liver, stomach, jejunum, ileum, and colon. Culture the ingesta, too."

While the nurse took swabbings of the indicated areas and sealed each in a separate sterile tube, Dallas went on with the autopsy. Standing at the sink at the head of the table, she examined the viscera immersed in the water. Slices of the liver, spleen, lungs, and bowel went into formalin. She snipped open the heart to check for valve failure and for chamber enlargement indicative of decompensation. She looked for the scarring of old infarcts, and for plaque and emboli in the major vessels. None. The heart could have gone on beating for another quarter of a century. The lungs looked good, too, minimally tarred by cigarette smoke.

"Let's have a look at the brain, then," Dallas said.

But when the scalp and calvarium were off and the brain out and sectioned, there was nothing there, either. She found no hemorrhage or ischemia to suggest that by some fluke a cardiovascular accident killed Dr. Morgan in such a short time.

Dallas sighed, stretching her aching neck and shoulder muscles, and stood brooding over the gaping gray flesh that hardly looked like a man any longer. She gave one cold shoulder a reassuring pat. "I don't know how he did it to you, but I'll find out yet."

The nurse smiled. "Do you often talk to your patients, Doctor?"

Dallas smiled back. "Why not? They listen in silence and never argue." She grimaced, then became serious again. "However, they usually tell me more about themselves than Dr. Morgan has. Let's be thorough and run a complete set of toxicology tests."

"Sister Mary Luke will throw her rosary at you."

Dallas shrugged. "Life would be dull without a few enemies."

She wished they had a gas chromatograph. It could have identified the molecules of poisons other tests would not pick up. There were disadvantages to practicing in a small town.

When they were finished, they closed Dr. Morgan up with the suture gun and returned him to his refrigerated locker. Dallas was on her way upstairs to the lab with the tray of specimens when she remembered that there was a veterinary school at the university, whose diagnostic laboratory serviced five states. It would be worth giving them a call to see what she might be able to use down there.

She walked into the lab. "Brought a lot of work for you, Sister."

Sister Mary Luke was alone. The empty counter where the lab trays usually sat indicated the other four technicians were out on the floor taking blood. The nun looked from Dallas to the still half-full spindle of requests by the door and sighed. She wore the old-fashioned long habit and wimple, leaving only small hands and a round, freckled face visible of the woman herself. It was enough to express disapproval, however, as Dallas explained what needed to be done with each specimen.

"Yes, Doctor," she said with tight-lipped politeness to each instruction.

"And these are for a complete toxicology series," Dallas finished. She indicated a group including gastric and urinary samples and hair and nail cuttings.

Unexpectedly the nun's eyes brightened. "Do you think he was poisoned?"

Dallas was startled by the relish in her voice. "I hope not."

The nun took the tray. "I like to read murder mysteries. I always enjoy the chance to play detective. I'll start these right away."

"Start the cultures first."

Dallas left the nun regarding the specimens with anticipation and walked over to the phone extension by the blood refrigerator. She looked up the number of the diagnostic lab and punched it.

She was given to a Dr. Miles, who proved very cooperative. "Yes, we have a gas chromatograph. Our toxicologist uses it in his research. We'll be glad to run whatever you want."

"I'll be right down. How do I get there?"

He gave her directions. Before she left, she separated a little of each toxicology specimen into another container. After a moment of thought, she included a section of jejunum, too.

"I'll be back to read those breast sections later," she called to Sister Mary Luke on her way out.

Driving down to the veterinary complex. Dallas took out the roof panel over the seat, letting the vivid Kansas autumn into the car. The air had a smoky tang.

She pulled into the parking lot behind the medical science building. Climbing out, she glanced toward the other two buildings in the complex—the one marked *Teaching* and the huge, sprawling clinic, both handsome structures of buff-colored limestone. She recalled Pete Terry telling her they had equipment the human hospital would never be able to afford, like a

Dupont ACA that would perform forty blood chemistry analyses. That for dogs and cats! Their office SMAC ran twenty-two exams and was considered fine equipment by the local MD's.

She carried her specimens into the building. Three wrong turns and two direction-askings later, she found the diagnostic lab.

Dr. Miles, a small, dark man, greeted her with a smile. "I'm glad you managed to find us, Dr. March. Let me take those."

He looked over what she had brought and she looked past him at the equipment lining the walls and counters. It was impressive. She did not see the ACA, however, and asked about it.

"It's over in clin path at the hospital," Dr. Miles said. "Do you have something you'd like to run through it?"

"No, not today. When do you think the chromatography will be done on my specimens?"

With a rueful grimace, Dr. Miles waved at a counter covered with specimen containers and request slips. "After those. It may not be until tomorrow morning."

"That's okay. Will you call me when they're done, then?"

She drove back to the hospital to evaluate the breast sections and stayed for a frozen section on a tissue sample from a biopsy in progress, then moved down the road a bit to her office at the medical center. A large stack of SMAC profiles sat awaiting her in the middle of her desk. She groaned.

Jenny Gover, the office nurse, grinned. "That's why Dr. Terry took on a partner, Dr. March."

"And then skipped town as soon as I knew my way around." She glanced at her watch, thinking of the blood chemistries and all she had yet to do here and at the hospital. No lunch today. "Bring me some coffee, will you, please?"

She settled into her chair and picked up the first profile.

Late in the afternoon, after finishing microscopic evaluation of uterine tissue from hysterectomies done Friday and Monday, she had a chance to sit down with Sister Mary Luke and go over the results of the toxicology tests on Dr. Morgan. They were all negative. Sister Mary Luke looked not only apologetic but disappointed.

Dallas lifted a brow. "You didn't *want* him to be poisoned, did you?"

The nun's face went the color of her freckles. "Well . . . it would have been interesting."

"Sister, you have the soul of a pathologist."

"Dr. March." A technician at the other end of the lab waved a phone receiver. "Call for you."

Dallas went up to take it. A male voice came over the wire. "This is David Oaks at campus security, Dr. March. I wondered if you are able to tell yet how Dr. Morgan died."

Dallas rubbed her eyes. "No. I know a few things that *didn't* kill him, though."

There was a pause before Oaks said, with great politeness, "That doesn't help me much, I'm afraid. His wife—widow was here a few minutes ago. She wants to know how soon she can have the mortuary pick up the body. She had her insurance agent with her, too. Morgan has a double indemnity clause in his policy. The agent is rooting for suicide, of course. Can it have been?"

"Not the way it looks now." Not unless he had access to some undetectable poison that would also kill all the bacteria in his gut before enough was absorbed to kill him. "Was there a reason in his personal life for suicide, do you know?"

There was certainly no organic reason, no incurable neoplasms or the like. Those were much rarer these days, thanks to the anticarcinogenic vaccines coming on the market.

"Quite the contrary," Oaks said. "Mrs. Morgan was telling me he was one of the two people in contention for appointment as new department head when Dr. Teal retires in December."

Dallas tugged thoughtfully at her lower lip. "How bitter are rivalries for positions like that?"

"What?" Oaks laughed. "Not bitter enough for murder. Though I'm told Dr. Esther Kastens, the other contender, is very vociferous in her criticism of Dr. Morgan." He paused. "When can Mrs. Morgan have her husband's body?"

"I don't know. I have to be satisfied I have all the specimens I need. The cultures and micro exam will take a while yet. I'll let you know."

After she hung up she walked up to the medical library to see what the literature had to say about flora-killing substances. Neomycin would do the job, but it was poorly absorbed from the G.I. tract, so flora was all it killed. There were few recorded instances of allergic reaction or systemic toxic effects from the drug, either. High doses of tetracycline given over long periods of time would also kill flora. She knew from reading Dr. Morgan's medical record the previous afternoon, though, that he had not been taking the antibiotic recently. She decided she was just going to have to wait and see what the gas chromatography showed.

She switched off her light at the emergency entrance and went home.

She spent a restless night wearing a skin diver's suit and swimming after Death in an interminable game of tag through mazes of water-filled tunnels. She finally recognized the tunnels as blood vessels when Death skimmed by her in a surfing position on an erythrocyte. She climbed on another of the concave red disks and gave chase and was just getting good at steering with her weight when she wiped out. The serum waves receded, leaving her on a stretch of fleshy beach.

Death was there ahead of her, stretched out on a beach towel. He spoke in a voice like rattling bones. "Welcome to the Island of Langerhans, my dear. Come sit with me. The time has come to speak of many things, of ships and sails and sealing wax, of—"

Dallas woke up swearing. It was early but she rolled out of bed and went to work anyway.

There was only one other car in the doctors' row of the parking lot at the hospital and inside, down at the far end of the hall beyond the lab, she could see a flurry of activity on the surgical ward that marked the shift change. In the lab the technicians were just picking up their kits and separating the stack of requests by floors. They greeted Dallas with nods and a polite, "Good morning, Dr. March."

Sister Mary Luke was standing at the door of the incubator. She turned with her hands clasped and her face distressed. "Dr. March, I took a look at the Morgan cultures just now."

"What do they look like?"

Her hands dropped to the rosary tucked into her belt. "I think I did something wrong."

Dallas opened the door and slid out the shelf of petri dishes. In each one, an unblemished agar surface gleamed dully back at her, even the dish marked *Colon. E. coli* could usually be found in profusion in any bowel. It was a normal finding, an expected one, but the dish where Sister Mary Luke had streaked the swabbing from Dr. Morgan's colon showed not even a pin-prick of growth.

Dallas stared. Through the mad clashing of thoughts came one lucid one: Dr. Morgan's death and the disappearance of his flora were not due to something he ingested. It would not have had time to reach the colon, too.

"I've reviewed my technique, Doctor, and I can't find an error anywhere. I don't understand this. Shall I do them all again?"

Dallas slid the tray back into the incubator. "No. We'll let these go on a few more days." Not that she expected to see anything more. "It begins to look as if every bacteria in Dr. Morgan is as dead as the man himself." *Made a clean sweep, didn't you? How?* No wonder there was no decomposition or tympanites.

"I've never heard of such a thing before."

"Dr. Morgan is the deadest man in medical history." Dallas felt less flippant than she sounded, though. She picked up the colon culture, frowning. A sterile corpse? It was unbelievable. How in god's heaven could it have happened? The situation gave her goose-pimples.

The door of the lab opened. Dr. Charles Nealey came in wearing surgical greens. "Sister, sweetie, I'd like to see the surgical evaluation on Mrs. Mostert in 215. You ran a cross-match, too, I hope?"

"As the request ordered, Doctor," the nun said. "There are five units of blood ready to go."

"Good. Red, this is another breast biopsy, remember. I'll be wanting a frozen section."

"I remember," Dallas said absently. She still stared into the petri dish.

He came back to look over her shoulder. "Trouble?"

"A problem." She put the dish back in the incubator and closed the door. "I have a dead man."

He chuckled. "That's the way they come in pathology, sweetie."

She arched a brow. "Not usually *this* dead, Doctor. Excuse me." She went to call Dr. Miles.

He was out and the technician who answered knew nothing about her chromatograph readout. "I'll have him call you when he comes back," she promised.

Dr. Miles' call did not come until mid-afternoon at the medical center.

"There are no poisons," he reported, "but we do get a very unusual graph."

Dallas sat straighter. "Unusual how?"

"I think you ought to see it for yourself. Do you have time to come down?"

"I'll make time."

She arrived in ten minutes.

Handing her the readouts, Dr. Miles said, "I presume you're familiar with this procedure."

Dallas nodded. The lighter molecules of the gas made from her specimens reached the detector first, the heavier ones later, and were plotted on an X-Y graph according to time of arrival at the detector and amount present. The value of the gas chromatograph was its speed and the delicacy of its detection of trace elements.

"So." He spread the readouts across his desk. "Each is a bit different, of course, but notice that on every sample, the latter part of the graph is the same. That's where your DNA molecules should be showing up. Reducing the specimen to gas breaks them up to some extent, but normally they show up on the graph as a few fair-sized peaks. This is a sample from some animal tissue I ran as a control. Notice how the heavier molecules usually plot. But look what we have in all *your* readouts, a whole group of very small peaks grouped together at the end."

"Could a poison do this?"

"I asked our toxicologist. He said no."

Dallas drew a long breath. Curiouser and curiouser. Her finger traced the graph line. *What the hell did you do to him, Old One?* "Do you have any idea what caused this?"

"As a matter of fact," he said, "I do."

"What?"

"The small peaks, anyway. I had the girls make up some slides and I ran them through the electron microscope in the physics department."

Dallas blinked. "Already?"

"Well, actually we ran the chromatography late yesterday afternoon and as soon as I saw this I started the girls on the slides. I've been busy for you today, Doctor. I photographed what the E.M. found and sweet-talked Teaching Resources into rushing through developing and printing. Look at these." With the flourish of a magician producing a pigeon from his hat, Dr. Miles laid a stack of photographic prints on top of the readouts. "The top three are liver cells."

Each print showed only one or two cells but it was enough to give Dallas the feeling she had stuck her finger in an electric outlet. In almost half the cells some of the long chromosomes had been broken into pieces. Why only some, she wondered. She looked at them more closely. A number of other cellular structures had odd shapes, too.

"The next pictures are of muscle from the jejunum." Dr. Miles' voice was tight with excitement.

Dallas glanced up at him and shuffled over to the next group of photographs. She stared. "What the hell happened to the actin and myosin?"

Where she should have seen parallel rows of muscle protein, there were lines that swayed and angled and zigged drunkenly. It looked like a TV picture with a failing horizontal hold.

"Unusual, isn't it?"

"Bizarre," Dallas said. Her head felt as if it were filled with fog. "Bizarre like this entire case. Lord. No wonder the man had died, with all that insanity in his cells." *Did you have to be so violent, you miserable bastard?* She rubbed her temples. "And would you believe that in addition to all this, the body was somehow sterilized inside and out?"

Dr. Miles gave a rebel yell that picked everyone in the lab an inch off their stools. "That's like Dr. Kastens' rats, too. I knew it!"

"Kastens!" Dallas stared at him. "From the physics department?" How often that woman's name came up, again and again.

"Right. She brought three rats in here last month. Wanted to know why they died. We took them apart and looked at them with every test and instrument we have, including the E.M. We never were able to determine exactly why they died . . . but they exhibited the same findings your patient does: broken DNA, wavy actin and myosin, and no living internal bacteria."

Dallas felt excitement boiling up from her toes. "Where did she get the rats?" These similarities had to be more than chance.

He shrugged. "She wouldn't tell us. They were laboratory rats is all I can tell you." He picked up the photographs and stood shuffling through the stack. "Damndest thing I've ever seen, and now here's a human with the same anomalies." He looked at her. "May I ask who it is?"

She wanted to tell him. She knew his curiosity must be itching furiously, but . . . "I'd probably better not say. I'm sorry. I promise I'll tell you all about it eventually, though."

He could not hide his disappointment. He handed the pictures back to her along with the chromatograph readouts. "I guess I'll have to settle for that. I hope I was helpful."

"You certainly were. You have records of the findings on the rats, I hope."

"Of course."

"Don't lose them." She stood up. "Thank you very much."

Dallas locked the graphs and pictures in the trunk of the MG and drove over to park close behind the physics building. She looked up Dr. Kastens' office number on the building directory and took the elevator to the third floor. She was acting, she knew, like the foolish amateurs she was so often annoyed by in TV shows and mystery novels. She could be asking for trouble, or a lawsuit. On the other hand, she could hardly take a dead man and three dead rats with molecular disturbances to the campus police and call it evidence of something sinister. She certainly could not go to them with this gut feeling she had about Dr. Kastens.

She knocked on Dr. Kastens' door.

"Come in."

She opened the door. The small, square woman behind the desk looked familiar. After a moment Dallas remembered her. It was the woman she had glimpsed in the hall on Monday, the one who said she would not miss Dr. Morgan.

"You're Esther Kastens?"

"*Dr.* Esther Kastens," the woman corrected. "What can I do for you?"

Dallas lied by inference. "I'm Dr. March. I've just come over from the diagnostic lab at the vet school. I'm very interested in knowing what was being done with the rats you brought in last month."

"Why?" Dr. Kastens' eyes narrowed. "Isn't one dead rat like another?"

Dallas stared at her for a moment before it occurred to her that Dr. Miles might not have told the physics professor what he actually found. She decided it might be wisest to leave the good professor in ignorance for the time being.

"Yes," she said, "except when they die without apparent cause." She waited for Dr. Kastens to answer.

Dr. Kastens frowned at her. Finally she said, "I don't know what was being done with them. My students were running an independent experiment. I didn't ask them what it was. I simply stopped the experiment and had it dismantled. I didn't want to lose a student, too."

Dallas almost snorted aloud at the transparency of the lie. She knew the experiment could not be dismantled, nor was the rest of her story very believable. She could imagine students experimenting on their own, but a professor stopping them and taking apart a dangerous experiment without finding out what it was and why it was dangerous? Nonsense!

While they talked, her eyes were exploring the room. It was cluttered as only a busy person with her mind on many things can clutter a room. One feature was unusual, though: two circular raised platforms a bit less than a meter in diameter, one on each side of the room, with a panel of wires, switches, and dials beside the one to the rear of the desk.

"That looks interesting. What is it?"

Dr. Kastens' voice sharpened. "It has nothing to do with the rats. Is there anything else I can do for you?"

"I guess not. Thank you."

Dallas retreated. In the corridor she considered what to do next. The visit had heightened her suspicion of

Dr. Kastens, but not produced any material evidence.

She went down one floor to a Dr. Morgan's office where she found a girl who proved to be the graduate assistant who first discovered Dr. Morgan's body.

"Is this a regular part of a coronér's job?" the girl asked.

Dallas fudged. "It could help me establish the cause of death. When did you last see Dr. Morgan?"

"About nine-thirty Friday evening. I was on my way home from the library and saw his light on. He has—had a habit of working until all hours when his wife was out of town. I stuck my head in to remind him to go home."

"Did he seem all right then?"

"Perfectly. That's why it was such a shock to find him there like that when I turned the light on."

Turned the light on! Who had turned it off? *That* was something she could ask David Oaks about.

"What do you think of Dr. Kastens?"

The student shrugged. "I didn't know her. Dr. Morgan didn't care for her, but on the other hand, I know students who worship her. She's supposed to be brilliant. She did some of the early work for NASA on the Halley Sail and has connections with the L-5 project. She's always building machines up in her office.

"What kind of machines?"

"God only knows. This is a rather conservative school, not the kind to appreciate its professors playing with wild blue yonder ideas on State time, so she never tells anyone what she's doing."

It was time to become official, Dallas decided. She asked directions to the security office. After stopping off at the library to look up some references and photocopy selected pages, she parked in front of the administration building, took the photographs out of the trunk, and walked around to the security office in back. She asked for David Oaks.

Oaks appeared around a frosted divider that separated the counter area from the rest of the large office. He toasted her with a cup of coffee. "Dr. March, how nice to see you. Come on in." He let her in through a door at the end of the room. "Do you know what happened to Morgan yet?"

"Not exactly. May I have some coffee, too? But I'm beginning to build up a suspicious picture."

Oaks turned his head to look at her and almost poured coffee over his hand. "Oh?" He finished filling the cup and gave it to her, then sat down in another chair, regarding her with a policeman's eyes. "Tell me about it."

She started by telling him about the autopsy. He listened attentively, if uncomfortably. At the end, however, he shook his head.

"I'm afraid I don't see what you find suspicious. If he wasn't poisoned, what is the significance of dead bacteria? I don't understand your excitement over the actin and—myelin, is it? What are they?"

"Myosin," Dallas corrected. "They're the main structural proteins of muscle. Look." She laid the photocopied sheets and photographs in front of him. "These book illustrations are photographs taken through an electron microscope of normal muscle cells. These parallel lines are the actin and myosin. The photographs are also taken through an electron microscope, but of visceral muscle from Dr. Morgan. Look at the lines now. You can see the difference. These photographs"—she shuffled through them—"show chromosomes in cells of liver and intestinal mucosa. See how there are breaks in them?"

He studied the photographs. "So what does it' mean?"

"Something happened to Dr. Morgan that was so traumatic it wrenched his very molecular structure. It killed everything in him."

Oaks frowned. "How can you be sure this isn't a congenital condition?"

"Because," she said, "last month three dead rats with the very same characteristics were brought into the diagnostic lab at the vet school by Dr. Esther Kastens."

He thought about that. He did not look pleased.

Dallas pushed on. "I talked to Dr. Kastens and asked how her rats died."

"Talked to her? You were playing detective, I suppose." He looked even less pleased. "Look, life isn't like a television program."

"Dr. Kastens said the rats died in some student experiment."

"Good. So that explains it."

"She also said the experiment was dismantled, which is an obvious lie. Furthermore, there is a strange machine in her office she wouldn't talk about."

"No," Oaks shouted.

People around the office turned to look at them.

He lowered his voice and leaned toward her, hissing. "There's nothing more complicated than someone dying. It's bad enough if the death is suicide, but I'm not about to let you talk me into a murder investigation. It was probably just some weird accident. Sign the death certificate *'Cause of death unknown'* and let it go at that."

Dallas set her jaw. "I think I'll call an inquest."

He went pale. "But you have no *evidence,* nothing but speculation."

"Someone turned the lights out."

He blinked. "Lights?"

"His graduate assistant saw him late Friday night. The lights were on in his office. They were out when she found him Monday."

He scowled. "That proves nothing. Morgan may have been leaving when he felt ill. He simply sat down without turning them back on."

"He wasn't wearing his overcoat when I saw him. It was still hanging up. There were also two chairs closer to the door than the one at his desk."

Oaks ran his hands through his hair. "For someone so good looking, you're a real pain in the ass." He sighed. "All right, Madam Medical Examiner, what do you want from me?"

"Well, to start with, I'd like a close, uninterrupted look at the machine in Dr. Kastens' office."

She met him at the physics building at six o'clock. Oaks muttered under his breath about amateur detectives all during the ride to the third floor, but he took a key ring out of his pocket when they reached Dr. Kastens' office and unlocked the door. Once they were inside, he locked the door after them.

"Look away."

Dallas laid her coat and purse on a chair and began studying the machine. Everything was just as she remembered it, the two platforms, each with raised metal arms. The one behind the desk had what looked like a control panel. The other—she now noticed—sat over a clear plexiglass base filled with chunks of rock.

"So that's the machine," Oaks said. "How do you think it killed Morgan?"

"I haven't the slightest idea."

Oaks frowned. "Playing with it could be dangerous, then."

She gave him a cheerful grin. "Possibly."

She peered at the panel. On one side was a rocker switch. She pushed it.

The machine made no sound but needles swung over on two indicators. An amber light came on.

Oaks retreated to the door. "I think I'll let you do this by yourself. Someone has to stay able to pick up the pieces."

She wrinkled her nose at him. There was little other instrumentation. Two dials had numbers noted around them in marking-pen ink. Having no idea what the numbers meant, Dallas decided not to touch them. But in the middle of everything a red push button stood out.

She went back to her purse and removed two bottles. The smaller one contained water. The other, with holes punched in the top, held a live mouse. She set the mouse's bottle on the desk and put the bottle of water on the platform with the control panel. Then she pushed the button.

There was a brief play of light between the metal arms. That was all. When it stopped, the platform was empty.

Her exclamation brought Oaks to her side. "Where's the bottle?" he asked.

"I certainly didn't expect anything like that to happen."

"No. If this machine killed him, it doesn't look like we would have found much left of him."

He started to turn away but stopped short, staring at the other platform. Dallas followed his line of sight to the missing bottle of water.

She took a breath. "I think I'd like to see that again."

She carried the bottle back to the first platform and once more pushed the button. Again there was the brief flicker of light, and when it stopped, the bottle was gone. She was watching both platforms this time, though, and saw a similar light between the rods rising over the second one. A quick breath after the bottle had vanished from the first platform, it reappeared on the second.

"I don't believe it," Oaks said, but together with Dallas he looked at the mouse on the desk.

Dallas picked up the bottle. "Sorry, wee one."

While Oaks retrieved the water bottle from the far platform, she put the mouse, still in his container, on the near one. The mouse stood on its hind legs, peering out at them with nose twitching. Dallas pushed the button.

Mouse and bottle reappeared on the far platform with the mouse still stretched up the side, but almost immediately the mouse's legs started folding. It sagged into a still lump of white in the bottom of the bottle.

Dallas dashed over to it. Unscrewing the lid, she tipped the mouse out into her hand. She felt its chest with a gentle forefinger. "Dead."

Oaks ran a hand through his hair. "Oh, God."

"I'll have to necropsy it to be sure, but I'm predicting he'll look just like the rats and Dr. Morgan microscopically."

"My superiors are never going to believe this. It's . . . straight out of Buck Rogers."

He froze as the lock on the door clicked. The door swung open and Dr. Kastens stood in the opening.

Her voice was frigid. "Don't move, either of you. I'm going to call campus security."

Oak fished his identification out of his pocket and dangled it in front of her.

"Oh." Her face remained frozen. "Then may I ask what the campus police and a horse doctor are doing in my office at this hour?" She looked past him to Dallas. "Don't they keep you busy enough over there, dear?" She saw the dead mouse in Dallas' hand. Her eyes jumped to the machine's control panel. Her nostrils flared. "Or *are* you a horse doctor?"

"No. I'm a pathologist, the acting coroner. You *didn't* dismantle the machine that killed the rats."

Dr. Kastens' eyes met Dallas' unwaveringly. She tossed her coat onto her desk. "So?"

"It looks as if it might have been used to kill Dr. Morgan, too," Oaks said.

She snorted. "Ridiculous. Whatever gives you that idea?"

Dallas told her.

Of all the reactions Dallas might have anticipated from the physicist, delight was the last, but Dr. Kastens ignited with the emotion. "Complete sterility? Really? I wish that stupid horse doctor had told me that when I asked about the rats. Here I've been thinking I had failed. This is wonderful." She beamed at the machine. "It can cut the cost of sending parts up to L-5 by millions and revolutionize the canning and meat packing industries."

Oaks was grim. "Don't forget that your matter transmitter was also a murder weapon."

Dr. Kastens turned on him. "It isn't a matter transmitter. It replicates. It scans the molecular structure of the object on the transmission stage, transmits the information, and rebuilds the object on the receiving stage, drawing molecules from the raw material bin." She pointed to the rocks under the receiving platform. "I thought with it we could solve the transportation problem, but apparently even the microseconds required to complete the transmission and replication are too long for all living processes to cease totally and then be able to resume."

Dallas felt a shock of realization clang through her nervous system. "That's why the actin and myosin look as they do. The machine replicates exactly what it scans. Living, moving material won't be in exactly the same position each time the scanning beam passes." *That's a new one for you, Old One, tearing a man's cells apart*. She looked at Dr. Kastens. "Even as a transportation failure, you managed to make good use of it, though."

Dr. Kastens stood up straighter. "I beg your pardon. My machine may have killed Dr. Morgan, but there's no proof *I* used it."

Oaks looked as if he had been stabbed. Dallas could see him visualizing a defense attorney making fools of the prosecution.

"You were the only person who knew what it would do," Dallas said.

The other woman smiled. "You broke in here and learned about it, didn't you?"

Even Dallas winced.

"And how could I do it anyway? Dr. Morgan was at least sixteen centimeters taller than I am and a good deal heavier. Do you propose that I was able to overpower him and throw him into the machine?"

Dallas was prepared for that. "You knocked him out first. I found the contusion on his head. You probably asked him up here Friday night on the pretext of showing him something or talking about your differences. Once he was unconscious, you doubled him up on the transmission stage and turned on the machine."

The physicist's cool smile never wavered. "And just how did I move his dead body down to his office?"

Dallas crossed to the desk chair and slid it back on its casters. "Small aides have been moving large men in wheel chairs for years. There is also an elevator in this building."

Dr. Kastens looked over at Oaks. "You realize, of course, that this evidence is only circumstantial. I think the county attorney will laugh in your face if you try taking this to him." She picked up her coat. "However, you're free to try. Should you want me, I'll be home. Turn out the lights and lock up when you leave." She headed for the door.

Oaks stood watching her go.

"Are you going to let her leave?" Dallas exclaimed.

"Yes." When the door had closed behind the physicist, he went on, "She's right. Someone killed him, and that's all the evidence says."

"But I'm convinced she's guilty!"

"So am I."

"Then what can we do?"

"You stick to being a doctor. Take apart that mouse and document every cell of it. Let me play cop. There must be physical evidence of some kind: hair, fingerprints, cloth fibers. I'll find it. *Then* I can go to the county attorney and ask for her arrest."

Dallas started to protest, but looking down at the mouse in her hand, changed her mind. He was right. Detecting was his job. She had already done hers. *I keep mapping out your methods, Old One. Some day I'll know enough to step in and stop you.*

She put the mouse back in the jar. She remembered she must test the water in the other jar for sterility, too.

"You can tell Mrs. Morgan I'm releasing her husband's body."

"I will. Thank you." He helped her on with her coat. "See you in court."

She nodded. "Good night."

His "Good night" followed her down the hall, but so did Death's dry bones whisper. *Auf Wiedersehen.* ☆

Elbow Room

Marion Zimmer Bradley

Sometimes I feel the need to go to confession on my way to work.

It's quiet at firstdawn, with Aleph Prime not above the horizon yet; there's always some cognitive dissonance because, with the antigravs turned up high enough for comfort, you feel that the "days" ought to reflect a planet of human mass, not a mini-planetoid space station. So at firstdawn you're set for an ordinary-sized day: twenty hours, or twenty-three, or something your circadian rhythms could compromise with. Thus when Prime sets again for firstdark you aren't prepared for it. With your mind, maybe, but not down where you need it, in your guts. By thirddawn you're gearing up for a whole day on Checkout Station again, and you can cope with thirddark and fifthdark and by twelfthdark you're ready to put on your sleep mask and draw the curtains and shut it all out again till firstdawn next day.

But at firstdawn you get that illusion, and I always enjoy it for a little while. It's like being really alone on a silent world, a real world. And even before I came here to Checkout I was always a loner, preferring my own company to anyone else's.

That's the kind they always pick for the Vortex stations, like Checkout. There isn't much company there. And we learn to give each other elbow room.

You'd think, with only five of us here—or is it only four; I've never been quite sure, for reasons I'll go into later—we'd do a lot of socializing. You'd think we would huddle together against the enormous agoraphobia of space. I really don't know why we don't. I guess, though, the kind of person who could really enjoy living on Checkout—and I do—would have to be a loner. And I go squirrelly when there are too many other people around.

Of course, I know I couldn't really live here alone, as much as I'd like to. They tried that, early in the days of the Vortex stations, sending one man or woman out alone. One after another, with monotonous regularity, they suicided. Then they tried sending well-adjusted couples, small groups, sociable types who would huddle together and socialize, and they all went nuts and did one another in. I know why, of course; they saw too much of each other, and began to rely on one another for their sanity and self-validation. And of course that solution didn't work. You have to be the kind of person who can be wholly self-reliant.

So now they do it this way. I always know I'm not alone. But I never have to *see* too much of the other people here; I never have to see them unless I *want* to. I don't know how much socializing the others do, but I suspect they're as much loners as I am. I don't really care, as long as they don't intrude on *my* privacy, and as long as they take orders the way they're supposed to. I love them all, of course, all four or maybe five of them. They told me, back at Psych Conditioning, that this would happen. But I don't remember how it happened, whether it just happened or whether they *made* it happen. I don't ask too many questions. I'm glad that I love them; I'd hate to think that some Psych-tech *made* me love them! Because they're sweet, dear, wonderful, lovable people. All of them.

As long as I don't have to see them very often.

Because I'm the boss. I'm in control. It's *my* Station! Slight tendencies toward megalomania, they called it in Psych. It's good for a Station Programmer to have these mild megalomanic tendencies, they explained it all to me. If they put humble self-effacing types out here, they'd start thinking of themselves as wee little fleabites upon the vast face of the Universe, and sooner or later they'd be found with their throats cut, because they couldn't believe they were big enough to be in control of anything on the cosmic scale of the Vortex.

Lonely, yes. But I like it that way. I like being boss out here. And I like the way they've provided for my needs. I think I have the best chef in the galaxy. She cooks all my favorite foods—I suppose Psych gave her my profile. I wonder sometimes if the other people at the station have to eat what I like, or if they get to order their own favorites. I don't really care, as long as I get to order what I like. And then I have my own personal librarian, with all the music of the galaxy at her fingertips, the best sound-equipment known, state-of-the-art stuff I'd never be able to afford in any comparable job back Earthside. And my own gardener, and a technician to do the work I can't handle. And even my own personal priest. Can you imagine that? Sending a priest all the way out here, just to minister to my spiritual needs! Well, at least to a congregation of four. Or five.

Or is it six? I keep thinking I've forgotten somebody.

Firstdawn is rapidly giving way to firstnoon when I leave the garden and kneel in the little confessional booth. I whisper "Bless me, Father, for I have sinned."

"Bless you, my child." Father Nicholas is there, although his Mass must be long over. I sometimes wonder if this doesn't violate the sanctity of the confessional, that he cannot help knowing which of his congregation is kneeling there; I am the only one who ever gets up before seconddawn. And I don't really know whether I have sinned or not. How could I sin against God or my fellow man, when I am thousands of millions of miles away from all but five or six of them? And I so seldom see the others, I have no chance to sin with them or against them. Maybe I only need to hear his voice; a human voice, a light, not particularly masculine voice. Deeper than mine, though, *different* from mine. That's the important thing; to hear a voice which *isn't* mine.

"Father, I have entertained doubts about the nature of God."

"Continue, my child."

"When I was out in the Wheel the other day, watching the Vortex, I found myself wondering if the Vortex was God. After all, God is unknowable, and the Vortex is so totally alien from human experience. Isn't this the closest thing that the human race has ever found, to the traditional view of God? Something totally beyond matter, energy, space or time?"

There is a moment of silence. Have I shocked the priest? But after a long time his soft voice comes quietly into the little confessional. Outside the light is already dimming toward firstdark.

"There is no harm in regarding the Vortex as a symbol of God's relationship to man, my child. After all, the Vortexes are perhaps the most glorious of God's works. It is written in scripture that the Heavens declare the glory of God, and the firmament proclaims the wonder of His work."

"But does this mean, then, that God is distant, incapable of loving mankind? I can't imagine the Vortex loving anyone or being conscious of anyone. Not even me."

"Is that a defect in God, or a defect in your own imagination, my child, in ascribing limits to God's power?"

I persist. "But does it matter if I say my prayers to the Vortex and worship it?"

Behind the screen I hear a soft laugh. "God will hear your prayers wherever you say them, dear child, and whenever you find anything worthy of worship and admiration you are worshipping God, by whatever name you choose to call it. Is there anything else, my child?"

"I have been guilty of uncharitable thoughts about my cook, Father. Last night she didn't fix my dinner till late, and I wanted to tear her eyes out!"

"Did you harm her, child?"

"No. I just yelled through the screen that she was a lazy, selfish, stupid bitch. I wanted to go out and hit her, but I didn't."

"Then you exercised commendable self-restraint, did you not? What did she answer?"

"She didn't answer at all. And that made me madder than ever."

"You should love your neighbor—and I mean your chef, too—as yourself, child," he reproves, and I say, hanging my head, "I'm not loving myself very much these days, maybe that's the trouble."

Mind, now, I'm not sure there really is a Father Nicholas behind that screen. Maybe it's a relay system which puts me into touch with a priest Earthside. Or maybe Father Nicholas is only a special voice program on the main computer, which is why I sometimes ask the craziest questions, and play a game with myself to see how long it takes "Father Nicholas" to find the right program for an answer. As I said, it seems crazy to send a priest out here for five people. Or is it six?

But then, why not? We people at the Vortex stations keep the whole galaxy running. Nothing is too good for us, so why not my personal priest?

"Tell me what is troubling you, my child."

Always *my child*. Never by name. Does he even know it? He must. After all, I am in charge here, Checkout Programmer. The boss. Or is this just the manners of the confessional, a subtle way of reemphasizing that all of us are the same to him, equal in his sight and in the sight of God? I don't know if I like that. It's disquieting. Perhaps my chef runs to him and tells tales of me, how I shrieked foul names at her, and abused her through the kitchen hatch! I cover my face with my hands and sob, hearing him make soothing sounds.

I envy that priest, secure behind his curtain. Listening to the human faults of others, having none of his own. I almost became a priest myself. I tell him so.

"I know that, child, you told me. But I'm not clear in my mind why you chose not to be ordained."

I'm not clear either, and I tell him so, trying to remember. If I had been a man I would surely have gone through with it, but it is still not entirely easy to be ordained, for a woman, and the thought of seminary, with ninety or a hundred other priestlings and priestlets herded all together, even then the thought made me uneasy. I couldn't have endured the fight for a woman to be ordained. "I'm not a fighter, Father."

But I am disquieted when he agrees with me. "No. If you were, you wouldn't be out here, would you?" Again I feel uneasy; am I just running away? I choose to live here on the ragged rim of the Universe, tending the Vortex, literally at the back end of Beyond. I pour all this uncertainty out to him, knowing he will reassure me, understand me as always.

But his reassuring noises are too soothing, too calming, humoring me. Damn it, is there anyone *there* behind that curtain? I want to tear it down, to see the priest's face, his human face, or else to be sure that it is only a bland computer console programmed to reassure and thus to mock me. My hand already extended, I draw it back. I don't really want to know. Let them laugh at me, if there is really a *they*, a priest Earthside listening over this unthinkable extension of the kilometers and the megakilometers, let them laugh. They deserve it, if they are really such clever programmers, making it possible for me to draw endless sympathy and reassurance from the sound of an alien voice.

Whatever we do, we do to make it possible for you to live and keep your sanity . . . "I think, Father, that I am—am a little lonely. The dreams are building up again."

"Perfectly natural," he says, soothingly, and I know that he will arrange one of Julian's rare visits. Even now I hang my head, blush, cannot face him, but it is less embarrassing this way than if I had to take the initiative alone, unaided. It's part of being the kind of loner I am, that I could never endure it, to call Julian direct, have to take—perhaps—a rebuff or a downright rejection. Well, I never claimed to be a well-adjusted personality. A well-adjusted personality could not survive out here, at the rim of nowhere. Back on Earthside I probably wouldn't even *have* a love life, I avoid people too much. But here they provide for all my needs. All. Even this one, which, left to myself, I would probably neglect.

Ego te absolvo.

I kneel briefly to say my penance, knowing that the ritual is foolish. Comforting; but foolish. He reminds me to turn on the monitor in my room and he will say Mass for me tomorrow. And again I am certain that there is nobody there, that it is a program in the computer; is there any other reason we do not all assemble for Christian fellowship? Or do we all share this inability to tolerate one another's company?

But I feel soothed and comforted as I go down between the automatic sprinklers through the little patch of garden tended so carefully by my own gardener. I catch a glimpse, a shimmer in the air, of someone in the garden, turned away like a distant reflection, but no one is supposed to be here at this hour and I quickly look away.

Still it is comforting not to be alone and I call out a cheery good-morning to the invisible image, wondering, with a strange little cramp of excitement low in my body; *is it Julian?* I see him so briefly, so seldom, except in the halfdarkness of my room on those rare occasions he comes to me. I'm not even sure what he does here. We don't talk about his work. We have better things to do. Thinking of that makes me tremble, squeeze my legs tight, thinking that it may not be long till I see him again. But I have a day's work to do, and with seconddawn brightening the sky, glinting on reflections from which I glance away . . . *you never look in mirrors* . . . I climb up into the seat that will take me up to the Wheel, out by the Vortex.

There is an exhilaration to that, shooting up toward the strange seething no-color of it. There is a ship already waiting. Waiting for *me,* for the Vortex to open. All that power and burning and fusion and raw energy, all waiting for *me,* and I enjoy my daily dose of megalomania as I push the speech button.

"Checkout speaking. Register your name and business."

It is always a shock to hear a voice from outside, a really strange voice. But I register the captain's voice, the name and registry number so that later they can match programs with Checkin, my opposite number on the far side of the Vortex—in a manner of speaking. Where the Vortex is concerned, of course, Near and Far, or Here and There, or Before and After, have no more meaning than—oh, than I and Thou. In one of the mirrors on the wheel I catch a glimpse of my technician, waiting, and I sit back and listen as she rattles off the co-ordinates in a sharp staccato. She and I have nothing to say to each other. I don't really think that girl is interested in anything except mathematics. I drift, watching myself in the mirror, listening to the ship's captain arguing with the technician, and I am irritated. How dare he argue, her conduct reflects on me and I am enraged by any hint of rudeness to my staff. So I speak the code which starts the Vortex into its strange nonspace whorl, the colors and swirls.

This could all be done by computers, of course.

I am here, almost literally, to push a button by hand if one gets stuck. From the earliest days of telemetered equipment, machinery has tended to go flukey and sometimes jam; and during the two hundred years that the Vortex stations have been in operation, they've found out that it's easier and cheaper to maintain the stations with their little crews of agoraphobic and solitary loners. They even provide us with chefs and gardeners and all our mental and spiritual comforts. We humans are just software which doesn't—all things considered—get out of order quite as often as the elaborate self-maintaining machineries do. Furthermore, we can be serviced more cheaply when we *do* get out of order. So we're there to make sure that if any of the buttons stick, we can unstick them before they cost the galaxy more than the whole operating costs of Checkout for the next fifty years.

I watch the Vortex swirl, and my knowledge and judgment tell me the same thing as do my instruments. "Whenever you're ready," I say, receive their acknowledgment, and then the strange metal shape of the ship swirls with the Vortex, becomes nonshape, I almost see it vanish into amorphous nothingness, to come out—or so the theory is—at Checkin Station, several hundred light-years away. Do these ships go anywhere at all, I wonder? Do they ever return? They vanish when I push those buttons, and they never come back. Am I sending them into oblivion, or to their proper prearranged destination? I don't know. And, if the truth be told, I don't really care. For all the difference it makes to me they could be going into another dimension, or to the theological Hell.

But I like it out here on the Wheel. There is *real* solitude up here. Down there on Checkout there is solitude with other people around, though I seldom see them. I realize I am still twitching from a brief encounter with the gardener this morning. Don't they know, these people, that they aren't supposed to be around when I am walking in the gardens? But even that brief surge of adrenaline has been good for me, I suppose. Do they arrange for me to get a glimpse of one of my fellow humans only when I *need* that kind of stirring up?

Back at Checkout—there will not be another ship today—I walk again through the garden, putter a little, cherish with my eyes the choice melon I am growing under glass, warn the gardener through the intercom not to touch it until I myself order it served up for my supper. I remember the satisfaction of the cargo ship waiting, metal tentacles silent against the black of space, waiting. Waiting for me, waiting for my good pleasure, gatekeeper to the Void, Cerberus at a new kind of hell.

Rank has its privileges. While I am in the garden none of the others come near; but I am a little fatigued, I leave the garden to the others and go to my room for deep meditation. I can sense them all around me, the gardener working with the plants like an extension of my own consciousness, I sit like a small spider at the center of a web and watch the others working as I sit back to meditate. My mind floats free, my alpha rhythms take over, I disappear . . .

Later, waiting for my supper, I wonder what kind of woman would become chef on a Checkout station. I *can* cook, I *have* done my own cooking, I am a damn good cook, but I wouldn't have taken a job like that. Is she completely without ambition? I don't see her very often. We wouldn't have much in common; what could I possibly have to say to a woman like that? Waiting, floating, spider in my web, I find I can imagine her going carefully through the motions, and little soothing rituals, chopping the fresh vegetables I fingered in the garden this morning, heating the trays, all the little soothing mindless things. But to spend her life like that? The woman must be a fool.

I come out of the meditative state to find my supper waiting for me. I call my thanks to her, eat. The food is good, it is always good, but the dishes are too hot, somehow I have burned my hand on them. But it doesn't matter, I have something more to look forward to, tonight. I delay, savoring the knowledge, listening to one of my operatic tapes, lost in a vague romantic reverie. Tonight, Julian is coming.

I wonder sometimes why we are not allowed to see one another more often. Surely, if he cares for me as much as he says, it would be proper to see each other casually now and then, to talk about our work. But I am sure Psych is right, that it is better for us not to see each other too often. On Earth, if we grew tired of one another, we could each find someone else. But here there *is* no one else—for either of us. A phrase floats through my mind from nowhere, *chains of mnemonic suggestion,* as I set the controls which will allow him to come, silent and alone, into my room after I have gone to bed.

He has come and gone.

I do not know why the rules are as they are. Perhaps to keep us from quarreling, to avoid the tragedies of the early days of the Vortex stations. Perhaps, simply, to avoid our growing bored with each other. As if I could ever be bored with Julian! To me, he is perfect, even his name. Julian, has always seemed to me the most perfect name for a man, and Julian, *my* Julian, my lover, the perfect man to match the perfect name. So why is it we are not allowed to meet more often? Why can we meet like this, only in the silent dark?

Languorous, satisfied, exhausted, I muse drowsily, wondering if it is some obscure mystery of my inner Psych-profile, that one of us subconsciously desires the old myth of Psyche, who could retain her lover Eros only as long as she never saw his face? I see him only for a moment in the mirror, misty, never clearly perceived, over my shoulder; but I know he is handsome.

I am so sensitive to Julian's moods that I think sometimes I am developing special senses for my love; becoming a telepath, but only for him. When our bodies join it seems often as if I were one in mind with him, touching him, how else could I be so aware of his emotions, so completely secure of his tenderness and his concern? How else could he know so perfectly all my body's obscurer desires, when I myself can hardly bring myself to speak them, when I would be afraid or ashamed to voice them aloud? But he knows, he always knows, leaving me satisfied, worn, spent. I wish, with a longing so intense it is pain, that the regulations by which we live would let him lie here in my arms for the rest of the night, that I could feel myself held close and cherished, comforted against this vast, eternal loneliness; that he could cuddle me in his arms, that we could meet sometimes for a drink or share our dinner. Why not?

A terrible thought comes to me. They give me everything else. My own cook. My own gardener. My technician. My personal priest.

My very own male whore.

I cannot believe it. No, no. No. I do not believe it. Julian loves me, and I love him. Anyhow, it would not suit the Puritan consciences of our legislators. No, I can't see it; how would they justify it on the requisition forms? *Whore, male, one, Checkout Programmer, for the use of*. No, such a thing couldn't happen. Surely they just hired some male technician, determined by Psych-profile to have the maximum sexual compatibility with myself. That's bad enough, heaven knows.

Now an even more frightening thought surges up into my conscious mind. Can it be possible—oh, God, no!—that Julian, *my* Julian, is an android?

They have designed some of them, I know, with extremely sophisticated sex programs. I have seen them advertised in those catalogs we used to giggle over when we were little girls. I am sick with fear and dread at the thought that during those conditioning trances which I have been conditioned to forget, I gave up all that data about my secret dreams and desires and sexual fantasies, so that they might program them all into the computer of an android, and what emerged was . . . Julian.

Is he a multipurpose android, perhaps, then? Hardware, no more, both useful and economical; perhaps that gardener I see dimly sometimes, like a hologram, in the distance. He could, of course, be the gardener, though in the brief glimpses of the gardener I had the impression the gardener was a woman. Who can tell, with these coveralls we all wear, uniform, unisex? And it would look better on the congressional requisitions:

Android, one, multiprogrammed, Checkout Station, for the maintenance of. And a special sexual program would only be a memo in the files of Psych. Nothing to embarrass anyone—anyone but me, that is, and I am not supposed to know. Just another piece of Station hardware. For maintenance of the Station. And of the Station Programmer. Hardware. Yes, very. Oh, God!

I have no time now for worrying about Julian, or what he is, or about my own dissatisfactions and fears. I cannot take any of these disquieting thoughts to that computerized priest, if he is indeed only a sophisticated computer, a mechanical priest-psychiatrist! Is he another android, perhaps? Or is he indeed the same android with still another program? Priest and male whore at the flip of a switch? Am I alone here with a multipurpose android serving all my functions? No time for that. A ship is out there, waiting for me; and my instruments tell me, as I ride out to the Wheel, even before I get the message; that ship is in trouble.

Perhaps all the signs, all my fears that I am going mad, are simply signs of developing telepathic potential; I never believed that I was even potentially an esper, yet somehow I am aware of nearly everything my technician said to the ship's captain. I did not understand it all, of course, I have no technical skill at all. My skills are all executive. I can barely manage to make my little pocket calculator figure out the tariffs for the ships I send into the Vortex; I joked with Central that they should allow me a bookkeeper, but they are too stingy. But even though I did not understand all of what the technician said, when I read the report she left for me, I know that if the ship went into the Vortex in this state, it might never emerge; worse, it might create spatial anomalies to disturb the fields for other ships and put the Vortex very badly out of commission. So I know that they dare not pass through that gate; I cannot follow the precise mathematics of the switch, though, and I feel like a fool. When I was in preparatory school I tested highest in all the groups, including mathematical ability. But I ended up with no technical skill. How, I wonder, did that happen?

Later I have leisure to visit the captain by screen. He is a big man, youthful, soft-spoken, his smile strangely stirring. And he asks me a strange question.

"You are the Programmer? Are you people a clone?"

"Why, no, nothing like that," I say to him, and ask why.

"The technician—she's very like you. Oh, of course, you are nothing alike otherwise, she's all business—a shame, in a lovely young woman! I could hardly get her to say a pleasant word to me!"

I tell him that I am an only child. Only children are best for work like this; the necessary isolation from peer groups. A child reared in a puppy-pack, under peer pressure from siblings and agemates, becomes other-directed; dependent upon the opinions and the approval of others, without the inner resources to tolerate the solitude which is the breath of life to me. I am even a little offended. "I can't see the slightest resemblance between us," I tell him, and he shakes his head and says diplomatically that perhaps it is a similarity of height and coloring which misled him.

"Anyway, I didn't like her much, she flayed me with her tongue, kept strictly to business—you'd think it was my *fault* the ship was out of commission! You're much, *much* pleasanter than she is!"

And that is as it should be, I am the one with leisure for reflection and conversation; it wouldn't be right for my technician to waste her time talking! So we talk; we even flirt a little. I am aware of it; I pose and preen a little for him, letting the animal woman surface from all the other faces I wear, and finally I agree to the hazardous step, to visit him on his ship.

So strange, so strange to think of being with one who is not carefully Psych-profiled to be agreeable to me. There is nothing in the regulations against it, of course, perhaps they believe our love of solitude will keep us away as it has always done before, for me. Even a little welcome, alien. But when I am actually through the airlock I am shocked into silence by the strange faces, the alien smells, the different body-chemistry of strange male life. They say that men give off hormones, analogous to pheromones in the lower kingdoms, which they cannot smell on one another; which only a woman is chemically able to smell. I believe it, it is true, the ship reeks of maleness. Ushered into a room where I may strip my suit I avoid the mirror. *Never look into a mirror, unless . . . unless . . .* why would Psych have imprinted that prohibition on me? I need to see that my hair is tidy, my coverall free of grease. Defiantly I look into it anyway, my head swims and I look away in haste.

Fear, fear of what I may see, my face dissolving, identity lost . . . stranger, not myself, unknown . . .

A drink in my hand, flattery and compliments; I find I am hungry for this after long isolation. Of course I am selfish and vain, it is a professional necessity, like my little touch of daily megalomania. I accept this, and revel in seeing others, interacting with strange faces—*really* strange, not programmed to my personal needs and wishes. Yes, I know I need to be alone, I remember all the reasons, but I know also, too well, the terrible face of loneliness. All my carefully chosen companions are so dovetailed to my personality that talking to them is like . . .

. . . . . like talking to myself, like looking in a mirror . . .

Two drinks help me unwind, relax. I know all the dangers of alcohol, but tonight I am defiant; we are off duty, both the captain and myself, we need not guard ourselves. Before too long I find the captain's hands on me, touching me, rousing me in a way Julian has not done since his first visits. I give myself over to his kisses, and when he asks the inevitable question I brace myself for a moment, then shrug and ask myself *Why not?* His touch on me is welcome, I brush aside thoughts of Julian, even Julian has been too carefully adjusted, dovetailed, programmed to my own personality; perhaps even a little abrasiveness helps to alter the far-too-even tenor of the days, to create something of the necessary *otherness* of love-making. That is what I have missed, the otherness; Julian being too carefully selected and Psych-profiled to me.

If a love-partner is too similar to the self there is not the needed, satisfying *merging*. Even the amoeba which splits itself, infinitely reduplicating perfect analogies of its own personality and awareness, feels now and then the need to merge, to exchange its very protoplasm and cell-stuff with the *other*; too much of even the most necessary similarity is deadly, and makes of lovemaking only a more elaborate and ritualized masturbation. It is good to be touched by *another*.

Together, then, into his room. And our bodies merge abruptly into an unlovely struggle at the height of which he blurts out, as if in shock, "But you couldn't *possibly* be that inexperienced . . . " and then, seeing and sensing my shock, he is all gentleness again, apologetic, saying he had forgotten how young I was. I am confused and distressed; *I* inexperienced? Now I am on my mettle, to prove myself equal to passion, sophisticated and knowledgeable, tolerating discomfort and strangenesses, to think longingly of Julian. It serves me right, to be unfaithful to him, Psych was right, Julian is exactly what I need; I know, even while the captain and I are lying close, afterward, all tenderness, that I will not do this again. The regulations are wise. Back to the Station, back to my quarters, blur the experience all away in sleep, all of it . . . *awkwardness, struggle that felt like rape* . . . no, I will not do this again, I know now why it is forbidden. I do not think I will confess it even to the priest, I have done penance enough. Seal it all away in some inaccessible part of my mind, the bruising and humiliation of the memory.

Flotsam in my mind from the vast amnesia of the training program, as I seek to forget, that conditioning they will never let us remember; that I am suitable for this work because I dissociate with abnormal rapidity. . . .

And next morning at firstdawn I go up even before breakfast to the Wheel; their repairs are made and they do not want to lose time. The captain wants to speak with me, but I let him speak with the technician while I watch out of sight. I do not want to look into his face again; I never want to see again in any face that mixture of tenderness, pity—contempt.

I am glad to see their ship dissolve into the vast nonshape of the Vortex. I do not care if their repairs have been made properly or if they lose themselves somewhere inside the Vortex and never return. Watching their shape vanish I see a face dissolving in a mirror and I am agitated and frightened, frightened . . . they are not part of my world, I have seen them go, I have perhaps destroyed them. I think of how easy it would have been, how glad I would have been if my technician had given them the wrong program and they had vanished into the Vortex and come out . . . nowhere. As I have destroyed everything not the self.

Julian has been destroyed for me too . . .

Maybe there is nothing out there, no ship, no Vortex, nothing. Everything comes into the human mind through the filters of self, my priest created to absolve a self which is not there, or is it the priest who is not there at all? Maybe there is nothing out there, maybe I created it all out of my own inner needs, priest, ship, Station, Vortex, perhaps I am still lying in the conditioning trances down there on Earth, fantasizing people who would help me to survive the terrors of loneliness, perhaps these people whom I see, but never clearly, are all androids, or fantasies born of my own madness and my inner needs . . . a random phrase floats again through my mind, *always the danger of solipsism. in the dissociator, the feeling that only the self exists . . . eternal preoccupation with internal states is morbid and we take advantage . . .*

Was there ever a ship out there? Did my mind create it to break the vast monotomy of solitude, the loneliness I find I cannot endure, did I even fantasize the captain's gross body lying on my own?

Or is it Julian that I created, my own hands on my body, fantasy . . . a half-lighted image in a mirror . . .

The terrible solitude, the solitude I need and yet cannot endure, the solitude that is madness. And yet I need the solitude, so that I will not kill them all, I could murder them as all the earlier Vortex stations murdered another, or is it only suicide when there is nothing but myself?

Is the whole cosmos out there—stars, galaxies, Vortex—only an emanation of my own brain? If so, then I can unmake it with a thought as I made it. I can snatch up my cook's kitchen knife and plunge it into my throat and all the stars will go away and all the universes. What am I doing in the kitchen . . . the cook's knife in my hand . . . here where I never go? She will be angry; I am supposed to give her the same privacy I yield to myself, I call out an apology and leave. Or is that pointless, am I crying out apology or abuse to myself? I have had no breakfast, at this hour, near thirddawn, the cook always prepares, I always prepare breakfast, I meditate while breakfast is prepared and served to me on my tray, facing the mirror from which I emerge . . . I am the other, the one with leisure for meditation and reflection—the executive, creative, I am God creating all these universes inside and outside of my mind . . . dizzied, I catch at the mirror, the knife slips, my face dissolves, my hand bleeds and all the universes wobble and spin on their cosmic axes, the face in the mirror commands in the voice of Father Nicholas "Go, my child, and meditate."

"No! No!" I refuse to be tranquilized again, to be deceived . . .

"Command over-ride!" A voice I do not remember. "Go and meditate, meditate . . ." *meditate, meditate . . .*

Like the tolling of a great bell, commanding, rising out of the deeps, the voice of God. I meditate, seeing my face dissolve and change . . .

No wonder I can read the technician's mind, I am the technician. . . .

There is no one here. There has never been anyone here.

Only myself, and I am all, I am the God, the maker and unmaker of all the universes, I am Brahma, I am the Cosmos and the Vortex, I am the slow unravelling . . .

. . . *unravelling of the mind* . . . .

I stumble to the chapel, images dissolving in my mind like the cook's face with the knife, into the confessional, the confessional I have always known is empty, sob out a prayer to the empty shrine, *Oh, God, if there is a God, let there be a God, let there be somebody there. . . . or is God too only an emanation of my mind . . .*

And the slow dissolve into the mirror, the priest's voice saying soothing things which I do not really hear, the mirror as my mind dissolves, the priest's voice soothing and calm, my own voice weeping, pleading, sobbing, begging . . .

But his words mean nothing, a fragment of my own disintegration, I want to die, I want to die, I am dying, gone, nowhere . . .

The phenomenon of selective attention, what used to be called hypnosis, a self-induced dissociation or fugue state, dissociational hysteria sometimes regarded as multiple personality when the fragmented self-organized chains of memory and personality sets organize themselves into different consciousness. There is always the danger of solipsism, but the personality defends itself with enormously complex coping mech-

anisms. For instance, although we knew she had briefly attended a seminary, we had not expected the priest. . . .

"*Ego te absolvo.* Make a good act of contrition, my child."

I murmur the foolish, comforting, ritual words. He says, gently, "Go and meditate, child, you will feel better."

He is right. He is always right. I think sometimes that Father Nicholas is my conscience. That, of course, is the function of a priest. I meditate. All the terrors dissolve while I sit quietly in meditation, spinning the threads of this web where I sit, happy at the center, conscious of all the others moving around me. I must be developing esper powers, there is no other explanation, for while I sit quietly here meditating in the chapel the soothing vibrations of the garden come up through my fingers while my gardener works quietly, detached and calm, in my garden, growing delicious things for my supper. I love them all, all my friends around me here, they are all so kind to me, protecting my precious solitude, my privacy. I cannot cook the lovely things he grows, so I sit in my cherished solitude while my cook creates all manner of delicious things for my supper. How kind she is to me, a sweet woman really, though I know that I would have nothing to say to a woman like that. I waken out of meditation to see supper in my tray. How quickly the day has gone, seventhdawn brightening into seventhnoon, and darkness will be upon all of us again soon. How good it is, how sweet and fresh the food from my own garden; I call my thanks to her, this cook who spends all her time thinking up delightful things for me to eat. She must have esper powers too, my prize melon is on my tray, she knew exactly what I wanted after such a day as this.

"Good-night, dear cook, thank you, God bless you, good-night."

She does not answer, I know she will not answer, she knows her place, but I know she hears and is pleased at my praise.

"Sleep well, my dear, good-night."

As I go to my room through the dimming of eighth-dark, it crosses my mind that sometimes I am a little lonely here. But I am doing important work, and after all, the Psych people knew what they were doing. They knew that I need elbow room. ☆

The Nobel Laureate

Robert H. Curtis

The members of the Council were uncertain. Usually there was harmony but whenever administration of this particular population was on the agenda, uncharacteristic sighs echoed through the chamber.

"Should we give up?" the Director asked patiently. He queried merely to elicit a response, not to indicate preference.

"I don't believe that they are capable of learning, real learning," the Minister of State said bitterly. "I gave Cleon to the Athenians and they chose to allow him to desecrate a portion of their history and for how long did they remember?"

"Ah yes, Cleon," the Minister of Music recalled. "Now I used a different approach. I gave the lyre to Nero along with a generous spirit. The lyre to soothe, the spirit to be distributed." He shook his head, disturbed by the recollection. "For the end result, I accept neither credit nor blame. But the point is that although inadvertent, it paralleled the purposeful exercise of our esteemed Minister of State. Again, they failed to reject tyranny. And I echo his pessimism. For how long did they remember?"

"During what they called the Dark Ages, I gave them what they called the black plague and repeated the dose several times. They profited not." The Minister of Health was inclined toward dogmatism and toward punishment.

"I gave them Torquemada," the Minister of Justice said simply.

Each of the Ministers spoke in turn and the litany of repeated failure was unpleasant to hear and seemed to answer the initial question of the Director.

Finally it was the turn of the Minister of Art. He was the oldest and wisest of them and they deferred to him. He always spoke last. The Director wanted it that way.

"One might argue," the Minister of Art said, "that we are being a bit impatient." He turned to the Minister of Music. "After all, Rome wasn't built in a day."

The Minister of Music smiled politely at the small joke.

"But," the Minister of Art continued, "we are not being impatient. I, for one, insist that we have too often been troubled by them. They have a parable: *burnt child fire dreadeth.* Though given the opportunity to avoid the flame, they consistently have chosen to feed it. Often, their so-called lower forms act with more humanity than they do."

"Furthermore," the Minister of Knowledge added, "so many of them prefer neither to contemplate nor to learn. They seem to eschew their brain's highest cortical operations and opt instead for its thalamic response of blind rage."

"Exactly," the Minister of Art said. "And they never blame themselves for the results; so my plan, provided of course that we agree, is finally to change all that. Now I have in mind this no-talent guy who . . ."

Was the jangling a real sound or did it belong to a world of dreams? And as the unconscious of his subconscious wrestled with the noise, a constant anxiety reasserted itself. What in this world *is* real? And then the core of his discomfort. Was *he* real and had his work in truth culminated in the miracle that his mind, night after night, refused to accept. *Cogito, ergo sum?* Finally he became aware simultaneously, of the telephone ringing and of his heart pounding. He looked over at the alarm clock which glowed in the dark: 3:15 A.M. It had to be very bad—mother or father. He wasn't that kind of doctor, not in practice, not the kind who was frequently summoned from sleep by insistent ringing demanding services. He was a researcher, so the call meant personal news. He turned on the end table light and reached for the phone. Out of the corner of his eye, he saw Ruth, roused from a deep slumber, looking worried and helpless.

"Hello."

"Doctor Goldberg?"

"Yes, this is Avrum Goldberg." Get on with it man.

"You've heard the news? About the prize?"

"No. Who is this?" Avrum was relieved that the call was not about one of his parents.

"Fred Emerson, sir. UPI. Sorry about the hour but I thought you'd be up. The news came in from Stockholm. You've won the 1983 Nobel Prize in Medicine. Congratulations." There was a brief pause. "Can you give me a statement, sir?"

Avrum held his hand over the receiver. He pointed to his chest. "Nobel Prize, Medicine," he whispered to his wife. Suddenly, her arms encircled him. She was sobbing, and he could feel the dampness of her tears.

"Are you still there?"

"Yes. Emerson is it? I'm thrilled and surprised and honored and every damn cliché you can think of to tell your wire service. It's wonderful and you can wake my family and me any time you want with news like this. Thank you."

"Weren't you pretty certain that you would get the prize, Doctor Goldberg? I mean, the nature of your work . . ."

"I knew I was in the running but let me tell you Emerson, I'm surprised. Very surprised. Really surprised. And thrilled and honored." Euphoria was overtaking him.

"How do you plan to spend the prize money?"

"Well, look, Mr. Emerson. It's not even 3:30 yet

and I want to discuss what you've told me with my family. I'll have more answers later. There's usually a press conference for this sort of thing, isn't there?"

"Yes, sir. They're planning to set something up later in the day. At the hospital if that's convenient with you."

"I'll be there. And please come up and introduce yourself, Emerson. I want to meet the man who first told me the news and shake his hand."

"See you at four P.M. then, Doctor. That's the time I heard mentioned."

"Thanks again." Avrum slowly placed the receiver back in its cradle. He moved with the same deliberation and precision he had applied to his research work and that had led him, inexorably, to the pinnacle of recognition of which he had just been apprised. Then he let out several war whoops and he and Ruth danced, hora style, around the bedroom as the bewildered faces of their three children appeared one by one at the door.

"Listen Goldbergs," Ruth announced to her startled brood. "Your father has just won the Nobel Prize."

"But Avrum, are you sure?" Mrs. Sarah Goldberg's voice in Santa Monica, California, retained the accents and emphases of its genesis in Krakow, Poland. And her question reassured her son that living the good life in sunny California had deprived her not at all of her inbuilt pessimism and compulsion.

"Yes, Mother. I'm sure. The phone has been ringing all morning. I finally took it off the hook." This is ridiculous, Avrum thought. Here I am a forty-one-year-old winner of the Nobel Prize and I still have to convince my mother that I'm a good boy. "Listen, let me talk to Dad for a minute."

Now the voice at the other end was hoarse and the accent was German. Hans Goldberg was an emotional man and obviously had begun to cry when his wife relayed the news that their son was transmitting from New York. "Avrum. We're so proud of you, your mother and me. You've made an old man very happy. You've always been a hard worker and a good boy and a smart boy. You deserve the prize. But I was as proud of you yesterday as I am today. Still, you've made an old man very happy."

"What's with the *old* bit, Dad?" Avrum noted that his father's priorities regarding his only child were still intact. California had not corrupted Hans any more than it had Sarah. "You're sixty-six and Mother is sixty-one. You're not fossils."

"You're right, Avrum. Your mother says I have a tendency to make us sound decrepit. But I can tell you one thing, I feel twenty years old right now."

"Wonderful, Dad. Just don't do anything foolish."

After Avrum hung up the phone, he thought about his parents and all they had given him. He wondered about the horrors of their European life of which they never spoke.

The auditorium of New York Hospital was filled with reporters and cameramen. The cameramen were lined up along both side aisles and the ceiling lights reflected off the flash units. Midway down the center aisle, the pool television cameraman was watching the monitor as he received instructions from the director who was sitting in a truck parked on York Avenue. An assistant sat in the center chair of the stage platform, alone in the glare of the TV floodlights. Even though it was past 4 P.M., nobody from the hospital staff had entered the room yet and this added to the tension. Even the most experienced and cynical of the newsmen assembled here for the press conference felt unfamiliar tingles in his spine because in many ways, this was the most important event he had ever covered. The hubbub of conversation paradoxically was more restrained than usual. This was a solemn, albeit joyous occasion. Few in the room—practically no one of the over-forty group—had escaped the ravages of cancer. Not the direct ravages, for this was the working press, healthy and vigorous for the most part. But almost everyone had a mother or a father, or a grandparent, or a brother or sister, or a child, or an aunt or uncle who had either succumbed to cancer or had barely escaped, thereafter carrying the scars of terror the disease inflicted. And now, today, the work of Dr. Avrum Goldberg had received official sanction. Finally, with the endorsement of the Swedish Academy, the long-awaited cure was authenticated. It was all right to breathe easier. This was for real.

Fred Emerson, sitting in the front row, noted the time. At precisely 4:05 P.M. the procession came in from the wings. Though almost everybody wore a white laboratory coat, Emerson recognized Dr. Goldberg at once. The Nobel Laureate, holding the hand of his wife, actually looked like the photographs of him on file. Emerson rushed up to the stage and maneuvered past the entourage toward the center.

"Dr. Goldberg," he shouted above the din, for a great roar of voices and applause had accompanied the entrance of the scientist. "It's me, Fred Emerson." Avrum looked blank. "From last night—the telephone! You remember," Emerson said with some desperation in his voice. Then Avrum Goldberg smiled in recognition and shook hands with Emerson and introduced him to Ruth. After a brief conversation, Emerson yielded to the stares of the doctors and made his way to his seat.

A tall, dignified man with white hair walked up to the microphone and waited for the room to become quiet. "Is this working?" he inquired of the audience about the mike. Assured that all was in order, he began: "Members of the Press. My name is Edgar Carmichael and I am the Director of New York Hospital. Dr. Hanford—"—he pointed to the stocky man behind him—"is the Dean of Cornell University Medical College and the men and women sitting here are Chiefs of Departments. I have been asked to represent them all on this historic occasion. The awarding of any Nobel Prize is momentous enough but I think that nobody in the field of science is unaware that the achievement of our distinguished Professor of Physiology, Dr. Avrum Goldberg, is unique even among recipients of that highest honor. His contribution ranks among the very foremost achievements in the entire history of medicine. I have obviously ignored Avrum's request to omit any accolades but I will say no more, other than to voice the sentiments of our faculty and medical staff. We thank God for Dr. Avrum Goldberg. And now, our Nobel Laureate will take over. Avrum."

There was time-out for picture taking. After introducing his wife to the press, Avrum walked to the wings and induced his three young children to pose with them. As soon as the photographers finished, Ruth returned to her seat and the children returned to their refuge. Finally, Avrum stood alone in front of the microphone. The noise in the crowded auditorium stilled completely, and the silence was almost palpable.

"I think I'll run this like a Presidential press conference," the Nobel Laureate announced. "I mean, how many times in your life are you afforded this kind of power?" The ensuing laughter punctured the tension. Avrum waited for quiet. Standing there, he looked terribly young, more like a college athlete than a scientist.

"I have an opening statement—"laughter again—"and then I'll try to answer any questions you have. To begin with, I am deeply grateful to Dr. Carmichael, to Dean Hanford, and to the entire faculty. This is a wonderful family to be part of. And I am also grateful to the Nobel Prize Committee although I must admit that my life has been complicated by this unfamiliar spotlight. Also, let me make certain that you realize, and this is not perfunctory, that in scientific research, any person receiving credit for his or her work does so really as a symbol for thousands of colleagues in the present and in both the recent past and the distant past. For scientific research is a cooperative venture and progress in the field is made over a very broad and deep foundation. The remarks which follow take into account what I have just said.

The work in which our team has been and is engaged is not based on a new principle. Attempts to fool the cancer cell have been going on since medical research in the cancer field first was started. We are fortunate that the methods we have employed have finally succeeded and that the many forms of cancer are now reversible. I say many forms because I wish to emphasize that we have not discovered the *cause* of cancer. We do assume that there are *multiple* causes which may include metabolic changes of aging, viruses and so forth. What we *have* accomplished is the stymieing of the cancer cell regardless of the factors that caused it to become malignant. We have been able, by gene splicing, to make the cancer cell incorporate, to accept into its structure, a chemical substance which then prevents the cell from multiplying. Cell division, mitosis, of the cancer cell can no longer take place. We have rendered it sterile. Thus we force the malignancy to die out instead of spreading. Of equal importance, normal cells are *not* affected and their division continues as usual. May I have the first slide, please."

The lights in the auditorium were dimmed, and Avrum proceeded to show a series of eleven colored slides and give commentary explaining each of them. After twenty minutes, he had finished and the lights were turned on again. Then he invited questions from the audience. The questions, technical at first, were answered with explanations devoid of confusing jargon. Finally, the queries took a more personal direction.

"Have you decided how you'll spend the prize money, Professor Goldberg?" That from a reporter from *Newsweek*.

"Not yet," Avrum answered, "but I can assure you that part of it will be used completely selfishly." Laughter.

"Will your family accompany you to Sweden for the acceptance?" A *New York Times* reporter.

"We all hope to make the trip."

"Do any of your children plan to follow in your footsteps, Doctor Goldberg?" This one from Fred Emerson.

"I hope, Mr. Emerson, that one of them will choose science some day because I know of no more exciting career. But let me tell you their current plans. David, age ten, tight end for the Giants; Philip, age seven, space-shuttle pilot; Anne, age four, mother of two children and President of the United States."

There were other questions but finally, Dr. Carmichael rescued the Nobel Laureate and signalled an end to the press conference by a simple "Thank you, Avrum." As reporters rushed to file their stories, Avrum shook hands with the assembled faculty. He spoke briefly with each. When her husband was through, Ruth retrieved the children from their off-stage hiding place. Then the Nobel Laureate and his family walked out of the auditorium.

"Therefore," the Minister of Art concluded, "you see the necessity for cooperative action."

"It is your opinion that the one in question is the right clay, so to speak?" the Director asked.

"Yes. He is of the right clay. Unmolded, he would spend his days performing menial duties and drinking beer," the Minister of Art replied. "But with each of our hands applied to this clay, he will serve our purpose. Should they fail to reject him, the aftermath will leave them no doubts that their days of whimsical choices have ended. We will show them, once and for all, that it is by their own hand and by their own hand alone that they will either survive or perish. If, in the face of this aftermath, they elect to carry out business as usual, so be it."

"I shall give him madness," the Minister of Health volunteered.

"I shall transform his voice," the Minister of Rhetoric chimed in and then each spoke in turn once more.

When they had finished, the Director sat back and enunciated the consensus. "We are agreed that there is no other way."

"I shall begin then," the Minister of Art said quietly.

The sallow-faced youth walked into the Academy of Fine Arts and entered a small office on the ground floor. Inside the office, a man, obviously not happy to see him, motioned for him to sit down, and began to talk after the youth had complied.

"The results this year are no better than last year. You have again failed your entrance examinations. I must be blunt because really my young fellow, this is the kindest way. You are wasting your time trying to become an artist. You must face the fact that you have no talent, simply no talent at all. Try another field."

I shall give him early failure.

The youth stared at the older man for several seconds, then stood up and left the room. The place was Vienna. The year was 1908. In 1913, the young man, thinking it was his own idea, travelled to Munich to take up residence. And his madness grew. And his xenophobia grew. And his political power grew in concert with the ability of his voice to stir hatred. And then in 1942, Avrum Goldberg died in an ovum of his mother in Auschwitz and in a spermatozoon of his father in Dachau. ☆

All That Glitters

G. C. Edmondson

Getting on. Frank wasn't sure how old he was because he didn't have a calendar. Spring. But was it March or May? In his private chronology it was shootin-star month. And if the danged snow ever cleared out he was going to have to get to town and see about his teeth which were aching like eternal damnation.

He brought his rifle to his shoulder and tried to draw a bead on the lightning-struck bull pine across the meadow. After a moment he sighed and lowered the gun. It was a 50-70 Springfield Government Breech Loader and had been new about the same time Frank was.

Shep studied him worriedly. He remembered when the dog would have pranced rings around him. Now their tracks were side by side in the mushy snow. There were fresh droppings near the bull pine. Frank squinted and couldn't tell if they were deer or elk. He studied droppings and tracks, trying to decide how many hours old. Shep sniffed and lost interest.

But these were the only tracks this morning. Frank belched sourdough and began following the trail as Shep paced soberly beside him, glancing up from time to time.

Frank was still straight and his hair only beginning to gray. He walked with the careful economy of motion that goes with age, carrying the breech loader at port arms. They followed tracks toward the place up the hillside where game trails crossed, their traffic thickened by the block of salt he had packed in twelve years ago to permeate the soft rock face of the lick. Only very gradually did Frank sense something was wrong.

It was too quiet even for this barren land. Not a single chicken, which is what people up here call the ptarmigan. Nor were there any of the sparrowlike snow birds whose names he had never bothered to learn. By now he surely should have heard the raucous squawk of some ruffnecked scavenging crow.

It was natural for Frank and Shep to walk in their little circle of silence as all the woods creatures acknowledged their passage, but this time the silence was all-pervading. That could only mean some other large animal was loose in the woods.

No moose or elk would provoke this universal watchfulness. And even if it weren't still early for them to be out Frank knew a grizzly wasn't all that terrifying to his neighbors. He glanced down at Shep and realized how old his dog was getting. If Shep sensed anything different, he wasn't saying. Then abruptly the dog's hackles rose and he gave a deep, almost subsonic hint of a growl.

Frank squinted toward where Shep was pointing, and up on the hillside near the lick he saw it. It was impossible to believe his eyes so Frank didn't. Instead, he squinted and tried to look slightly to one side until the formless quivery mass wavered and finally congealed into two separate entities, one vertical and the other not. "Be danged if I don't get me some glasses," Frank muttered.

Shep was still edgy but stuck close to Frank as they walked toward the vertical and horizontal blurs. Another hundred yards and Frank realized he had come upon the one thing he had never expected to find out here. The man wore a ragged mackinaw rather like his own. His dog must be getting on in years too, considering his lack of curiosity.

Man and dog stood silent waiting for Frank to finish climbing the hill. As he approached closer, Frank's eyes cleared momentarily and he saw the stranger had a rifle too. Shep's subsonic warning became more insistent. "Now don't you go startin' no fights with peaceable strangers," Frank growled back. He nodded at the stranger. "Howdy," he said, working the word carefully past his aching jaw.

The stranger raised his right hand high and for an instant Frank thought he was an Indian. Then as they came closer he could see grizzling hair and weathered skin much like his own. The two were about the same height, and the stranger seemed just as at home up here as Frank. Shep and the stranger's dog surveyed each other warily.

"Seen any game?" Frank asked. There were other questions he would rather ask—like "What the hell you doin' in my backyard?" But in the days when Frank's character had still been setting you just didn't say things like that to strangers.

The other man's voice was odd. Once when he had not had a dog to talk to Frank's voice had gotten that way from long disuse. Give him time, he told himself. His voice'll come back to him. There was an instant of awkward silence and then finally the stranger croaked, "Howdy."

At precisely the same moment they shushed their bristling dogs. Frank decided the stranger had been out here quite a while from the woodsy way he was acting. Funny they had never cut each other's sign before. An unwelcome suspicion was building in Frank's mind. He was getting on. Eyes going. Maybe the stranger had been here quite a spell and Frank, getting so careless, had walked right over all the signs. "Nice country," he hinted.

If the stranger knew what Frank was asking he gave no sign. But he didn't have the confused, hostile air that often came from too many months of solitude. Instead he seemed neutral—waiting. After a slightly-too-long interval he finally said, "Yes."

Frank could see him clearly now. There was something vaguely familiar about the stranger. It took a moment before he knew what it was. The stranger looked a little like the older brother he had not seen for thirty years. Not the way Leonard had looked, but the way he might look if he were still alive. "Thought I saw elk sign this morning," Frank said. He was babbling, but the stranger had been out here too long. Somebody had to help him back to civilization. "Name's Frank," he offered.

Another long silence and then a barely perceptible croak. Frank thought the stranger was repeating his name and then he understood. The stranger's name was Fred.

"It'll come back," Frank said. "First year up here I danged near forgot how to talk too." He still wasn't talking too well with that aching jaw but that was nobody else's business.

"Elk," the stranger said. "Saw one." He pointed.

Frank nodded. "C'mon, Shep," he said. Hackles still up, Shep followed him off in the direction the stranger had pointed. No use rushing things, Frank guessed. Give the stranger time to get used to the idea of other humans. Must be as much of a strain for him as it was for Frank to discover that neither of them was alone since the Indians had started to die off. "You come on around some day soon now and we'll have us a feed," he called back.

Another slightly-too-long interval, and then the stranger croaked. "Tomorrow."

A quarter mile ahead Frank saw more fresh droppings and knew the stranger had steered him right. He glanced back and saw the man and dog still standing there by the lick, apparently they hadn't moved since first he had seen them. But by then Frank's eyes had once more melded them into the same amorphous lump. Shep growled, then sniffed at the fresh droppings and showed an interest he had not evinced back down in the meadow. Frank checked the load in his breech loader and began following the tracks where the elk had pawed through the mushy snow for grass and moss.

Shep's ears lay back and he went into a point. Frank

squinted. There was the elk. The bull had not seen them. He was in range. Frank shouldered the rifle and squinted. This time his eyes were clear. He whistled, and the bull elk obligingly raised its head. Frank fired and the animal disappeared behind billows of black powder smoke. For an instant it felt as if the side of his face was coming off. Then his jaw subsided back to its regular ache. The smoke cleared and he saw he had made a clean kill.

Shep lapped blood and made the most of a kidney while Frank dressed out the elk and spent the greater part of the day cutting it into manageable pieces which he hung from branches out of reach of all the forest creatures who liked fresh meat as much as he did. Finally he packed liver and tongue and some of the other more perishable parts into his rubberlined meat sack and started hoofing it back to the cabin.

Suddenly he remembered the stranger. If he was still at the lick Frank reckoned he'd tell him where the kill was hung, invite him to take a piece. But when he and Shep arrived at the lick the stranger was gone. Not a stranger, he reminded himself. Man's name was Fred.

That night Frank and Shep shared a skilletful of sliced liver salted, floured and peppered. He wished for onions but the dried onions were finished along with just about everything else. He wondered how Fred was fixed. Once he had had time to get over his woodsiness maybe they could trade a few odds and ends to make life easier until the snow was gone.

And tomorrow he would have to start slicing all that meat thin; get it at least part dry in the month that was left before fly time. But that could wait till tomorrow. Tonight, full of fresh meat for the first time in over a month and with his jaw aching a little less than usual, Frank suddenly became aware of how his whiskers were itching. He began stropping his cut-throat razor while another kettle of snow warmed on the sheetiron stove.

He tried to shave around the angry red lump on

his jaw and then, halfway through shaving, stopped to squint into the cracked mirror. Suddenly he knew why the stranger had seemed so familiar. Should have guessed it when he saw how much like Shep the stranger's dog had been. Now he knew where he had seen Fred's face before. He was shaving it. Even to the same reddish lump on the right side of his jaw. "And I thought *he* was woodsy," Frank said. Shep looked up at him and wagged his tail.

Man can't get to Frank's age without thinking once in a while about the inevitable. But now that he was faced with new evidence of how quickly everything was closing in on him Frank's first and most painful thought was for a dog grown too old to forage for himself. *I'll have to kill Shep first.* He was tempted to do it right now without any more hesitation or thinking it over. Then he decided he might as well wait a while. Maybe he would get better before the elk was all gone. So instead, he banked the fire and went to bed.

Sleep did not come as easily as it had when a body was new and everything happened for the first time. There had been a girl once. After fifty years he was hard put to remember what she looked like. She had been young, had loved to go to barn dances. He had been young too. In those days he had known with a young man's certainty that all problems could be solved with gold—if he could just find some.

"You don't think about anybody but yourself," Effie had said.

Frank had not answered, had only wished he had followed his first impulse to skin out without saying goodbye to anybody. "I'll come back once I strike it," he had lied. Had he known he was lying?

"No you won't." Effie had been wise beyond her years. "You'll chase off and have a high old time and after a while I'll find me another feller and when you get around to comin' home there won't be nothin' to come back for."

Effie had been right except for one thing: Frank had

never come back. He sighed and from the deerskin at the foot of the bed Shep replied in kind. No use feeling sorry for himself now. Frank had lived the life he wanted. Man lives alone, he might as well expect to die alone. Come to think of it, didn't everybody?

But maybe in the morning his eyes would be better. Maybe the winter-long lump in his jaw would turn out to be only a tooth after all. Anybody could have an off day. Even if he was going woodsy, Frank suspected he wasn't as woodsy as the stranger—as Fred. Finally he slept.

There was a skim of ice on the bucket when he woke up, but it wasn't frozen solid like a month ago. He boiled up oatmeal mush and shared it with Shep, who liked his half with a little more sugar. Breakfast finished, he headed back up to bring the elk home one piece at a time—if a wolverine or a lynx hadn't beaten him to it. They were still a quarter mile below the lick when Shep reminded him about Fred and his dog. Frank squinted. His eyes seemed better this morning. He saw something blurry uphill and then the blur became Fred and his dog.

Man and dog waited as motionless as yesterday. Frank felt a tiny prickle of sweat that was not all due to climbing a hillside in a mackinaw during a thaw. He kept squinting, trying to see what Fred really looked like. Each time the blurry figures at the lick drifted into focus they seemed slightly different. He glanced down at Shep. "We all got to go," he muttered, but the dog's hackles were up as he approached the other dog.

Finally they faced one another again. "Howdy," Fred said in that rusty-gate voice. Frank was relieved to discover that the other man was not really his mirror image, that there was only a superficial resemblance. Back before the Indians had all started dying off from measles he had an elderly friend who had confessed he couldn't tell one white man from another. Maybe Frank had been here so long his own people were starting to blur together.

"Knocked over some meat yesterday," he said. "Could you use a quarter?"

The stranger nodded and they began walking up toward the kill, dogs observing a canine protocol and keeping a careful distance. "Nice country," the stranger finally said. His voice sounded better today. Frank guessed he had been practicing.

"There." Frank pointed where he had hung the quartered elk. There were fox tracks in the snow where blood had dripped but nothing had gotten to the carefully hung meat. "Take your pick," he said. When the stranger pointed at a hind quarter he wondered if the man was ignorant. The tasty parts were all up front and closer to the bone. Hindquarter meat was for dogs or for jerking. But maybe Fred was just being polite. Frank concealed a shrug and moved on to the next tree where he had hung a forequarter. He got packstraps around it while Shep worried away at a piece of gut the foxes hadn't managed to finish. Fred's dog remained aloof.

Frank slipped his arms into the packstraps and got the tumpline over his forehead. He turned to see if Fred was ready. Fred was. He stood waiting. On the mushy snow before him were a thigh and shinbone and the outer hoof shells the old Indians used for rattles. The bones were white and dry as if they had been boiled clean in a glue factory.

Frank blinked. Abruptly he remembered that Fred had brought neither meat sack nor packstraps. To conceal his confusion he looked away. Shep still played with a length of gut, tossing it and growling. The other dog sat and watched. "Got to get me some specs," Frank muttered. But when he turned back the other man had knapsack straps biting heavily into the shoulders of his mackinaw and there was no hint of leached-out bone. They walked back to the lick in silence. "Come on down and have some soup?" Frank asked.

Fred shook his head. "Got to start jerkin' this," he explained.

Frank was relieved. With the way his jaw was pounding he had had all the company he needed for a few days.

Winter hung on longer than he had expected and for the next couple of weeks Frank sawed and split wood until finally one morning the wind reversed and the chinook turned every creek into a river, every low spot into a lake. The spring thaw was always the worst time of year. Frank stuck pretty much to the cabin waiting for the mud to dry, knowing that as soon as the worst of the runoff was over the whole country would be alive with mosquitoes, no-see-ums and the deerflies whose bite felt like the stab of a red hot knitting needle.

But he had no whiskey, and the only way he could stop thinking about the constant throbbing ache of his swollen jaw was to stay busy. He surveyed the gamy interior of his cabin—the natural consequence of a man living alone without running water. Finally he put on his gum boots and trudged down to the creek with a pair of buckets. When he got there the creek was filled with the fine white glacial milk that a later generation would liken to first rinse out of a cement mixer.

Now what? Frank had seen plenty of glacial milk in the larger streams. Usually they didn't run clear until late summer just before the salmon run. But this was the first time the stream below his cabin had ever been filled with the stuff. He brought the buckets of white water back up to the cabin and put them to settle—which would take all day. And while the water was settling he fried a bannock for lunch, stuffed it in the pocket of his mackinaw and started upstream. He hadn't gone more than three miles before he saw what was stirring things up.

It was the dangdest looking sluice box Frank had ever seen. Seemed to be made out of cardboard or waxed paper or something like the celluloid collar he had once worn for an evening of salooning back when he was younger. But it seemed to work all right. He couldn't get it through his head how anything that thin and flimsy could stand up to the full flow of the creek and the pounding abrasion of constant shovelsful of rocks and gravel. Not a seam in it. Now how could anybody pack in a forty-foot-long sluice box all in one piece? Anyhow, somebody had done it and that somebody had to be Fred.

Frank was studying the flimsy-looking sluice box when Shep's ears abruptly lay back. He turned and there was Fred with his dog.

"Howdy," Fred said.

"Finding any?" Frank asked.

The stranger shook his head.

"Never saw one like that before," Frank said. He went to the bottom of the sluice where there was carpetlike material apparently glued to the bottom of the flume to catch whatever fines got past the riffles. "How often do you clean it?" he asked.

"Two or three times a day."

Frank pointed at the matting which was so incrusted with flour gold that it was actually yellow. "Must be six ounces there," he said.

"Oh, that." The stranger dismissed the yellow metal.

For an instant Frank felt cupidity. There had been a time in his life when gold had been very important but that had been before he had learned that a greater quantity of the stuff seemed only to equal a bigger headache and the rest of the year went along pretty much the same whether he took out barely enough for flour and bacon or . . . how many pairs of boots could a man wear in a year? He stared at the gold matted carpet. Enough to do him for years. He sighed. "Hope you ain't gonna take it all down into town at once."

Fred looked at him and for an instant Frank's vision shimmered and he thought he was seeing something else. Then the stranger came back into focus. "Why not?" Fred asked.

"Nice country up here. People down in town get

wind of that and you'll have so danged many shysters, whores, claim jumpers . . ."

"Oh!" From his horrified expression Frank guessed Fred couldn't have experienced many gold rushes. "But—" Fred hesitated. "Do they come for this—for gold?"

It was Frank's turn to stare.

"Want it?" Fred asked.

"Want what?"

"The gold."

Frank sighed. Not just his eyes. . . . Now he was hearing things. He squinted Fred back into focus and tried to hold him there. "You offerin' to give me the gold?"

"I could give you more only I've been throwing it away."

Frank was tempted to pinch himself but he didn't want to seem simple in front of a stranger. "If you ain't lookin' for gold with this outfit, then what in thunder are you lookin' for?"

Fred shifted on his feet and Shep growled. Frank glanced down and for an instant the other man's dog was no dog at all. He glanced at Shep who remained totally canine. Fred was struggling and Frank remembered how woodsy the man had been the first time they had met. "Can't find the word."

There was a silence. "I'm not from around here," Fred finally added.

"Didn't figure you was an Injun."

"I mean your language. I don't speak English good."

"Seems like you talk it near's good as I do."

"Just so, and ary a word better. If you knew the name of what I'm looking for then I'd know it."

Later when he was alone Frank was to decide it was just plain cowardice that made him abruptly turn and head back to the cabin with a hasty, "Goldang it! Just remembered I left somethin' on the stove."

Sitting on a peeled log in front of the cabin he studied Shep. "You think I'm crazy?" he asked. If the dog knew, he wasn't committing himself. That left Frank back where he had started. He wished he knew the stranger better. Then he finally knew what it was he really wished—apart from his jaw to quit aching. "Funny," he told Shep. "Always got along fine by myself. Now why would I go thinkin' I need somebody else?"

He couldn't confide in the stranger. The stranger—Fred, was woodsy. No telling how long he'd been out here alone putting up that funny sluice box and building fires on the creek bed to soften up gravel, shovel it into neat piles and get ready once the spring thaw made water available to wash his pay dirt through the sluice.

But the whole thing was impossible. In the years he had spent alone here Frank had dug that creek from end to end—had dug this whole country from the Caribou Trail to the Klondike. He had gotten placer gold, flour, an occasional nugget. But never had he struck anything like Fred was getting out of old, worked-over ground. And Fred wasn't even hunting gold!

Frank knew there were more valuable things than gold. Diamonds, for instance. And platinum. But there were no diamonds in this country. Platinum? That was scarce, Frank didn't even know how to recover it. Besides, no matter what he was looking for, what kind of fool would go throwing gold away?

"Crazy," he muttered. "There ain't no Fred. I been up here too long."

And yet Frank didn't think he was crazy. Man lives any time in this country, he gets plenty of chances to see men who've worked too hard, put up with too much misery and deprivation. They always turned suspicious—ended up killing their partners, their dogs, everything not a part of themselves. And not uncommonly, once they had killed off everyone else, those unhappy men would try to bite the muzzle off a shotgun. "Don't want to kill nobody," Frank muttered. "Went out of my way to be friendly, didn't I?"

Shep thumped his tail against Frank's shin.

Frank studied the ageing dog. "You're supposed to know things like that," he said. "Is Fred and his dog real—or am I just seein' things?"

Shep stopped thumping his tail and turned to look into Frank's eyes. Frank sat there a long time, then remembered the buckets of mud he had taken in to settle. They were reasonably clear now. He skimmed and poured carefully and then spent the rest of the day swamping out the accumulated grime in his cabin. But all day long he kept returning to the question, no more able to stop picking than he was to quit poking a tongue at his aching jaw. "Wish I had some whiskey.

But he didn't and next morning the creek still ran milky and that, he realized, meant something. If he was seeing things it was a remarkably consistent hallucination that would send mud three miles downstream to foul his water supply—glacial milk that persisted whether or not he thought about Fred. He finished breakfast and tried to make up his mind. There was nothing to be gained by sticking around here chasing his tail and asking himself if he was cracked—broken like so many others by this country.

"But I like it here," he muttered as Shep joined him for the walk upstream.

The sluice was still there, milk pouring from its lower end. At the top something like an endless chain dredge bucket was dumping gravel into the sluice. Then as his eyes cleared Frank saw it was not a machine: just Fred hunched over and tossing his shovel regularly.

Fred straightened up. "Howdy."

This time Frank noted that his dog was not there. Still Shep regarded the stranger with stifflegged wariness.

"Want gold?" Fred asked.

"You still givin' it away?"

"I—" Fred shrugged and for an instant something in Frank's eyes made him shimmer. "I'm lookin' for another metal," he explained as he settled back into reality. "Fact is, I'm havin' such a hard time findin' it, I wondered if maybe you'd like to trade."

Frank studied him for a startled moment. "What can I trade you for gold?"

"Meat."

"You ate up that whole quarter already?"

Fred started to nod, then changed his mind. "Still got plenty. But my dog eats a lot too and I got to tend this sluice while the water's high and—"

It sounded reasonable—reasonable as anything he might expect from a man who threw away gold. "Reckon I could split anything I shoot," Frank agreed.

"Over there."

The tailings carpet had been ripped from the bottom of the sluice. The gold-incrusted fabric lay in jumbled yellow folds amid the bare bones of several kinds of animal. Fred must have a real craving for meat. "I'll bring you whatever I can find," Frank promised, and picked up the carpet, trying not to shake flour gold from its drying nap. Beneath the carpet was a pile of nuggets. The largest, the size of a quail's egg was of such a blatant yellow that he thought it might be copper. He put his tongue on it and there was the dull, nothing taste of gold instead of the slight sharpness of a base metal.

"Appreciate it about the meat," Fred said, and went back to shoveling. Frank got the carpet into his meat sack along with the nuggets and went back down to his cabin. Once there he stirred up the fire in his sheet iron stove.. When it was going good he stuffed the carpet in and opened drafts and damper.

The stove began erupting, spouting thick greasy smoke at every crack. Then suddenly it was roaring and so red hot that Frank rushed down to the creek for buckets of muddy water lest he lose the cabin. When he returned the place was full of acrid smoke, but the stove and pipe were no longer so bright red. But godamighty, what a stink!

He opened the tiny "window" in the opposite wall. It was not the burning-feathers stink of woolen carpeting. Nor was it the burning-grass stink of the coco matting sluice boxes usually had in place of Turkey carpet. Eyes streaming and lungs burning, Frank hastened outside to stand upwind waiting for the smoke to stop. When the carpet had finally burned out he went back into the cabin to make acrid comment on the way soot smuts had obliterated his spring housecleaning. "Next time he gives me a piece of matting, be danged if I don't build a fire outside," he promised.

The firebox of his sheetiron stove was incrusted with melted gobs of something like the glassy mess Frank remembered around the edges of the sugaring-off pans in his mapled boyhood. He resolved to ask Fred what the hell kind of a carpet that was. But meanwhile he shoveled the ashes carefully from the stove, took them down to the creek, and panned out danged near seven ounces.

"Better go shoot a moose," he muttered as he spooned flour gold into a paper funnel and thence into an empty whiskey bottle. He would have felt quite cheerful about all that much gold except the memory of sugaring-off brought another memory of Maw. The last time he had sugared-off Maw's jaw had been swollen and lumpy too. "And they say it don't run in families!" he growled as he went in to bed.

To Frank's mild amazement he found not moose but more elk sign next morning and it turned out to be a fairly good day. His jaw didn't ache quite so constantly; his eyesight had improved, and the elk promised to dress out well over four hundred. He made the kill well up the hillside where there was still a foot of rotten snow that made it easy to horse the whole carcass into a toboggan and drag it downhill to within a mile of Fred's diggings. There, well away from the bloody remnants of butchering, he rigged tackle and hoisted the animal up a skinned pole pending its dismembering.

"No need to bother cutting it up," Fred said when Frank came by with tongue and liver. "I'll lug it down the rest of the way come nightfall. By the way, there's some more gold."

This time the patch of Turkey carpet was neatly wrapped in what Frank first thought was one of those pokes the Eskimos made of walrus gut. Then from the transparent regularity of the poke he knew it had to be something different. "Never had a piece of carpet stink like that stuff you give me t'other day," he said.

"Stink?"

"When I burned it."

"Oh. Should've warned you about that."

"What kind of cloth is it?"

"I don't know the word." Where Fred came from it was something that started with *ack*—Frank couldn't remember the rest of it.

"Ain't seen your dog around."

Fred pointed and Frank realized that Shep's hackles were not rising against Fred. He was reacting to the other dog, which had been nowhere in sight an instant ago. Frank felt a sudden suspicion. "You—" He didn't finish the question. Obviously, if Fred could stand out here all the equinoctial day long shoveling pay dirt he wasn't afraid of sunlight. He thanked Fred for the gold and hastened back to the creek bank in front of his cabin where he built a fire and after the smoke died down he panned out the ashes for another three ounces.

Frank sat for a long time looking at the whiskey bottle half full of gold. If he lived twice as long as a man his age had any right to expect, there was enough here to keep him in tobacco and flour—if he could just get it out.

But doing so posed a new set of problems. If Frank showed up in town with that much gold, all the things he had warned Fred about would come true. The country would fill up with claim jumpers and confidence men—it would turn into another Klondike. Neither of them needed that. He would have to stash the gold somewhere and only take in small amounts. As long as he was scratching away barely making wages nobody was going to come stampeding up this creek to spook all the game and make life miserable. Frank calculated the country was ample for himself and Shep. If Fred and his dog continued eating at their present rate, however, it wouldn't be long before he had to hunt farther away from home. And meanwhile, who else would be hunting?

Fred was handing out gold the way butchers gave away liver. And Frank was beginning to believe all of this was really happening. Now, which of them was the crazier? He studied the bottle of dust a while longer, then studied his immediate surroundings until he saw a suitable spot beneath the splayed roots of a spruce. Fred gives. Someday Fred might want to take. Frank decided to wait until after dark to stash his hoard.

He guessed he was lucky it was still early enough in the spring for day not to last all night long. Shep accompanied him out to bury the bottle. As he finished Frank suddenly knew that in a day or two he was going to be wondering if he hadn't dreamed all this—that it was pointless to hide something if he was going to wear a trail out to this spruce making sure it was still here.

Drive a stake in the ground in the opposite direction from the cabin and if the stake was still there tomorrow—it would mean nothing. If there really was a bottle of gold dust Fred could remove it without touching the stake. He gave a growl of disgust and took the bottle back into the cabin. "I'd give it to you," he told Shep, "if you could find half the bones you bury."

Shep wagged his tail briefly but offered no suggestions.

Frank's next kill was well up the mountain. Directly above Fred's diggings as near's he could figure it. Despite last week's chinook there was still some snow at this altitude and he was having a fairly easy time dragging the buck head first so its close-laying hair glided smooth as an iced runner in winter. He came to a dropoff and saw a mile of creek spread in looping curves below him. Fred's diggings were in the middle and he could see the pasteboard sluice box without even squinting. The creek downstream was milky, the piled pay dirt already half gone. It was not until he had studied the panorama for some time that Frank finally realized what he could not see. There was not the slightest sign of cabin, tent, cave, smoke—no hint of human habitation. Where the hell did Fred hole up?

Despite the easy descent Frank was tired by the time he had dragged the buck down to Fred's diggings. His jaw was serving notice again and the sudden stabs of pain made his vision shimmer. By now he was used to having to squint Fred and his dog into focus every time he approached.

"Howdy!" Fred sounded jovial. "More meat? Just in time."

Frank slipped out of the tumpline harness and sat on the buck until he could catch his breath. "Just in time?" he echoed. "You'n that dog must've put away a ton in the last ten days."

"We do eat a lot," Fred agreed. "But we went pretty hungry during the winter. And we're puttin' up some of it for a trip." Just as Frank was noting that Fred's voice and mannerisms were practically an echo of his own, the stranger's voice changed timbre. "I s'pose it makes you wonder," he conceded.

Frank allowed as how he had been gettin' a mite curious. "Mainly, I don't see no signs of a cabin," he explained.

As he said that, Frank was horrified to see the shimmery outlines of a trapper's cabin directly across the creek from him. Then just as he was turning to go home and kill himself the cabin disappeared.

"Sorry," Fred said. "It just happens. I didn't mean to spook you thataway."

"You?"

Fred shrugged. "Told you I come from quite a ways off. You wouldn't believe how many miles. But it's far enough for folks to have different ways."

"How many miles?"

Fred sighed. "Put down a one and then write a mile of naughts behind it."

Frank knew better. "Ain't no place on Earth farther than twelve and a half thousand miles."

"You're right. No place on Earth."

"Wish you wouldn't do this," Frank protested. "Been feelin' a little peaked lately."

"I know. Been feelin' kind of bad about it."

"You?"

"Nothin' much wrong with your eyes," Fred said. "Thing is, I don't really look like this."

"You ain't human?" As he said it Frank knew he had been skirting around this question ever since he had first made Fred's acquaintance. He remembered Shep's attitude toward the stranger's dog. "Your dog ain't no dog either, is he?"

"My dog is part of me."

Frank struggled to digest this.

"Foxes, snowshoes, caribou all change color with the snow," Fred explained. "Only I do it all year round. Always try to look like something harmless."

"Are you?"

"Are *you?*"

"Don't rightly know," Frank conceded. "S'pose it depends on whether the critter's askin' looks tasty."

"By the way, I saved you some more gold."

"You know what gold's worth?"

"I do now."

Frank considered the implications. "Don't want no trouble," he said. "If you're goin' to start wantin' it back—"

Fred shook his head. "If it'd buy what I need things'd be different. But the metal I need seems t'be pretty scarce in these parts. All the time I been diggin' here I ain't come up with more'n half an ounce."

"And you still don't know what it's called?"

"If you knew I would."

Frank sighed. "What's it look like?"

"A little like silver. Heavier but not as shiny."

Frank knew there were any number of scarce metallic elements. But he didn't know enough to connect up descriptions with names. "How much you need?"

"Couple more ounces."

"Goin' to be a pretty rich feller when you get home?"

"Goin' to take all of it just to get there."

"Use it for money, do you?"

Fred shook his head. "Use it the same way you'd use cordwood in a steamer."

"Got your own steamer?"

"Stashed. My ship looks kind of funny and makes a lot of noise."

That explained the racket Frank had heard one night at the beginning of shootin'-star month. "Y'ain't been here long then?"

" 'Bout the middle of shootin'-star month."

Frank stared. "How'd you know about that?"

"You must've figured it out by now."

Frank guessed he had. "Funny," he muttered. "Never really thought I was crazy."

"You're not."

"Must be if I'm swallowin' all this." Frank looked down at Shep, who seemed to have accepted the stranger and his now-absent dog. Even when Fred shimmered for a moment and looked very different from an old man in a mackinaw, Shep remained calm. Frank rubbed his eyes. "Either Shep ain't seein' it or it ain't happenin'."

"Shep believes his nose instead of his eyes. I stopped trying to smell like a dog."

"Sure you ain't a devil or an angel or somethin'?"

"No such luck. I can't tell your fortune or give you three wishes."

"You're doin' somethin' the way you're alluz a jump ahead of me."

"Can't even see deep into your mind," Fred explained. "Once you bring something up to the surface, about the time you're goin' to say it I can usually make it out. That's how I learned t'talk English."

"You really are from quite a spell down the road,"

Frank said. "And your name ain't Fred. You was going to call yourself Frank and then changed your mind."

"You hit it," Fred agreed. "I kind of cottoned to how you wasn't too happy with a stranger in your backyard. There's two of us gonna be happier when I'm gone."

"You ain't figurin' on stayin' then? By the way, what *is* your name?"

"Man ain't got no language ain't got no name either." Fred shrugged. "Nice country you got here but it's a little hot for me."

"You think it's hot now, just wait till summer when the flies and the sun are both out all night long."

"Exactly. Just as soon's I pan me out another couple of ounces of fuel you'll have the whole country to yourself again—providin' you don't tell everybody about all that gold. By the way, there's another tailings mat over by the bones."

"Been meanin' to ask you about them bones," Frank began."

"Been meanin' to tell you. But I was afraid you might be a little weak in the stomach."

"Oh?"

"Next time you knock over some meat, don't bother to clean it."

"You eat 'em whole?"

Fred nodded.

Frank guessed he wouldn't be too sorry to see the last of Fred. "Uh, that stuff you're lookin' for—could I see some of it?"

Fred produced a tiny vial of some translucent material and handed it to him. The vial was much heavier than Frank had expected. He studied the grayish metallic powder that rolled around inside of it and had a sudden inspiration. "Arsenic?"

Fred was silent a moment. Frank knew the stranger was sifting through his, Frank's, knowledge of heavy-metal poisons. "No. Pretty sure it ain't arsenic," Fred finally said.

Frank wet his finger and shook the uncorked vial against it. He put finger to mouth and tasted the tiniest possible amount. There was a faint metallic taste and nothing else.

Fred didn't even look like Fred for a moment. "No!" he yelled. "Dangerous!" We are not alike but it can burn any life. Quick! Wash out your mouth and whatever you do, don't swallow!"

Frank shrugged and handed back the vial. "Man'd get pretty tired of living if he didn't take a few chances." But Fred was so insistent that he gave up and went down to the creek to wash his mouth out with clear water from above the sluice.

But Fred was still het up over his tasting it. "Poison," the stranger insisted. "I should never have let you touch it."

Frank shrugged. Then the full realization hit him. "My dog," he began.

Fred was holding something that looked like a piece of pipe with the ends stopped up. He passed it over Frank's face and there was a whining like some lovesick mosquito.

"I must touch you," Fred said, "put things in your mouth." He seemed to be expecting Frank to refuse.

"Like a dentist? While you're at it maybe you could jerk out that tooth."

There was a flicker of hesitation, then Fred said, "But there is nothing wrong with your teeth."

Frank sighed. "Kind of figgered that." Shep studied him soberly. Frank began aiming his rifle. Then his vision blurred and he couldn't trust himself to make a clean shot.

For an instant he was so dizzy he had to sit down. When he could see again he sensed the stranger's fingers probing his jaw from the inside. "Yes," Fred sighed. "Here life has gone wild."

There was a sudden sharp pain that exploded upward from his jaw clear through his head until Frank knew even the roots of his graying hair were quivering. Slowly the pain subsided. Fred kept slipping in and out of focus as he struggled to make Frank comfortable.

"Sorry I don't know what that metal of yours is," Frank finally managed. "Though I could help look for it."

"Two or three more weeks and I'll have enough, if you can just keep me in meat."

"Right," Frank said. He was beginning to feel a little better now. "Go see'f I can wake up a bear tomorrow. They be skinny this time of year but I guess you won't mind?"

Fred would not.

Frank accepted the piece of gold-incrusted carpet and went home to pan out the ashes. By now the quart whiskey bottle was nearly full of dust. But now his whole mouth was starting to feel as tender as a cheechako's feet. By bedtime he was sincerely regretting his haste to taste Fred's tiny vial of powdered metal. "Wush I had some whiskey," he growled.

Shep glanced up and thumped his tail but the dog had no whiskey either.

Toward midnight Frank decided that tiny taste of metal might have been the nicest thing the creature from so far away could ever have done for him. His whole mouth seemed on fire and he was sweating buckets. Man his age couldn't last through much more of this kind of agony.

But he did and next morning, pale and weak as if he had run out of potatoes and gotten scurvy again, he staggered to the cabin door and studied the sky. Looked like another thaw. Didn't make no difference. Too sick to go hunting today anyhow. He thought about making soup but knew he would never get it past the flaming hell of his jaws. Shep looked at him and whined. Frank realized the old dog's teeth were probably not much better than his own. He got a fire going and boiled up a mess of oatmeal and liver for the dog. Then he went outside and held mushy snow against the side of his face. It dulled the ache a little but when he took his hand away he saw that all the whiskers on that side of his face were coming out by the roots.

Mostly, Frank dozed for the next three—or was it four days? But finally the intense agony was over and he staggered from the cabin feeling slightly better. Didn't feel up to chewing anything but after a cup of oatmeal thinned out with enough water so he could drink it he felt strength returning. Next day he went hunting and got a yearling caribou.

"Feelin' a mite peaked," he told Fred. "Don't suppose you could go a mile or so on t'other side of the creek and get it yourself?"

"Hungry as I am, I reckon I could," Fred said. "Not feelin' well?"

"Sore jaw."

"Oh. Thought I got it all out." Fred didn't have to say any more but he did. The dull flatness of his "Sorry" said it all.

Still, Frank thought he was at least entitled to know the color of the snake that bit him.

"Like any fuel," Fred explained. "It burns. But this fuel burns without air."

"Gunpowder?"

"Gunpowder carries its own air. This metal's got to be kept in small lots or it blows up. It's only safe to clump it together inside my ship's engine."

"Am I going to blow up?"

"No such luck. It's a cold fire."

" 'Tain't phosphorus. I seen that in rat poison."

"No," Fred agreed. "This has a long half-life."

"Half alive? You said you wasn't no spook."

"Didn't mean it that way. I should never have let you handle the stuff. But how could I know you'd put it in your mouth?" He struggled to say something comforting. "We ain't the same kind of animal. Maybe you're stronger."

Frank decided Fred's kind of animal didn't know much about the art of telling lies. " 'Tain't your fault," he said. "You tried to warn me."

There didn't seem to be much more to say. Frank

took another gold-incrusted scrap of carpet back to the cabin and dropped it. He sat looking at Shep, wishing there were some way an old dog could go on living by himself. He wished fleetingly for some way an old man could go on living. Then he sighed and stopped wishing.

But at Frank's age one gets into the habit, no matter how unappetizing the prospect of living. He went into the cabin and began cutting elk steak into tiny bits he could boil and swallow without chewing. Next morning he went out hunting again.

Wasn't Fred's fault. Fred was a funny codger but he'd played square with Frank. Best Frank could do was keep him from going hungry until he had enough gray metal to hit the trail home.

The next time he approached the diggings with news of more meat Fred did not bother about his appearance. Frank stood for some time studying an amorphous something that flowed, loose as a badger in a borrowed skin and twice as ugly. But even without any shovel, Fred's claws made the dirt fly like a monitor nozzle. The sluice was working at full capacity and the creek downstream would never be the same again.

Not that it made any difference to Frank. By the time the creek cleared he would. . . . He was not quite prepared for Fred's hearty "Howdy!"

"Doin' any better?" Frank tried to be polite.

"Hit a pocket. Think I got more'n enough to make it home."

"Two ounces of that poison must go a long way."

"Oh, that's not critical mass. Just enough to top up the breeder."

While Frank struggled to make head from tail, Fred abruptly reacted to his earlier remark. "Yes," he agreed. "It is poison. Is there anything I can do? Would more gold help?"

Frank shrugged. "If it would I reckon we'd have a lot of millionaires named Methusaleh."

"You feel pain?"

"No worse'n usual. Jaw's been sore all winter. Think it's the same thing took my Maw."

"Cancer?" Fred had lifted the forbidden word from Frank's mind and brought it out into the open. There was a long silence and Frank sensed that Fred was skimming him, searching for a full description of that forbidden word. "Yes," the alien finally said. "I knew it was. We used to have a similar ailment."

Frank was mystified by Fred's improved vocabulary. Then he knew the alien was lifting words from his mind that Frank had not thought of for a lifetime—not since a country doctor had talked to Maw about similar ailments.

"I've got to leave soon," Fred continued. "Probably tonight. Thanks for the meat. Best stand upwind when you burn the sluice."

Frank nodded and called Shep. That night he was awakened by what sounded like a rock slide. Then as the sky lit up he guessed it was still shootin'-star month. It wasn't till he was thoroughly awake that he knew what it really was.

Next day he went back up to the diggings. No sign of Fred but the celluloid sluice box was still there, every riffle clogged with gold. Close to a hundred ounces, Frank guessed. He cleaned it out and considered dismantling it but there were still a few piles of pay dirt to be washed. Might as well bring his shovel tomorrow.

Funny thing was, his jaw didn't ache any more. Swelling was down to where he hardly remembered it. He wondered if he was imagining a little hollow where the swelling had been. Would anybody in town believe him if he told them about Fred?

Better not say anything. He had more gold than he'd ever need. Valley was quiet again. Soon the creek would clear up and with Fred gone the game would be back.

Have to sell that gold in danged small lots, or else he'd have so many neighbors there'd be nothin' left to do but take it all and go try living Outside for a spell.

He didn't really want to do that. Neither would Shep. He watched the old dog worrying at a bone and suddenly knew what had happened: all those clean-polished bones when the stranger had finished feeding. "Be goldanged," he muttered as he ran his hand over a faint fuzzy growth of new beard. "I'll just bet you that Fred critter went and bit it all clean out!"

☆

The Subtle Serpent

Charles Sheffield

If the Mattin Drive fails, the Manual provides an explicit and detailed description of the measures to be followed. The ship is to proceed at maximum sub-light speed to the nearest G-type star with an Ostrig planetary system. Full recycling must be employed on the journey. Upon arrival, a pinnace landing party will locate and refine two hundred kilos of silver-109. Following a return to the main ship, the cores of the Mattin Drive must be rebuilt. The Drive may then be re-initiated and the journey resumed.

Nothing can go wrong with the Drive, apart from a possible failure of the solenoid cores. No, that must be stated another way. Core failure is the only thing that can occur and still leave any hope of *repair,* without access to the biggest workshops of a Level Five technology.

James Parker gloomily contemplated that thought, and the confusion about him. He cracked his knuckles moodily, while forty passengers shouted at one another and at the crew. What were the other factors? Well, if the trip to an Ostrig system lasted more than a year (say, it were half a light-year's distance) then full recycling would merely permit a slow and messy death, as toxic fractions built in the life-support systems. As ship's doctor, Parker knew just how that would go—and he didn't care for it. Add the fact that the chance of being within half a light-year of a suitable system was depressingly small. Then top it off with the final blow: the instructions offered by the Manual, detailed and precise as they were, had one major flaw—never, since interstellar jumps were first accomplished using the Mattin Drive, had any ship managed to limp back home with a repaired drive unit, though a fair number of vessels had vanished without trace.

James Parker's thoughts were interrupted by the double klaxon of the *Rorqual*'s main computer, calling for attention. The group about him fell silent at once. They all knew that if there had been enough notice of drive failure, the computer would have used its dying gasp of engine power to aim for a Link-exit point somewhere near a suitable G-type star. It knew the Manual better than any of them.

The tension grew past bearing. Parker tried to swallow his own fears and looked over at Dial Senta, the ship's captain. He thought he could see a faint crease of worry on her brow, an indented V of concern above the prominent nose. It was the first sign of emotion he had seen on her guarded countenance since the crisis began.

The central screen lit up, and a collective sigh greeted the brief message. The *Rorqual* had emerged three light-days from a G-type sun—spitting distance. It was the first good news since the onset of crippling nausea had signalled the malfunctioning of the Mattin Drive.

Parker smiled sourly to himself at the buzz of relieved talk that greeted the computer read-out. One small piece of good news, and already half the group was behaving as if they had reached the safety of a galactic node. He found it hard to share their optimism. Perhaps as a doctor he had seen too many records of failure, and too few of success, to allow him to think of life as anything more than a short and dangerous affair.

The screen lit up and again interrupted his thoughts. Parker raised his eyebrows at the message. Perhaps he was being too pessimistic this time. The star they were headed for showed eight planets, and from the preliminary data at least one of them should be habitable. It was a ninety-nine-percent Ostrig match. So much for his first fear, that they would have to hunt for silver deep in a gas giant, or on a ball of molten iron in dizzy orbit close to the star.

"Jim. Join us here, would you."

Senta's words were quiet but authoritative. Twenty minutes earlier, off-duty, she had been following his lead without question through a tricky *cablana* hand. Parker was easily the best player on the ship, and Senta knew when to trust her partner's devious strategies. They had been winning comfortably. All that had vanished at the first nauseating twist. Senta had resumed the role of ship's captain so quickly and unconsciously that she still held cards in her left hand.

"Which one, Jim? Any preference from a medical point of view?"

He took the LCD output from her and scanned the physical descriptors of the planets. It was a moot point, in his mind, whether he could offer any better evaluation than the least qualified of the passengers, but Dial Senta's logic was clear. It was better to have a doubtful decision, firmly made, by someone she trusted to keep quiet about any misgivings he might have, than to scare the passengers out of their minds by involving them in the decision-making process.

Parker put his first and second fingers against two of the planets and shrugged.

"Both of these are in the right temperature range for the support of life. We could probably get by on either of them. Can you give me a double swing-by orbit, so we can get a close look at both? No point in committing ourselves before we have to."

"Sure." Senta called out another display on the computer console, and frowned. "We can do it, but we'll be too short of fuel to land on both of them. We'll still have to make the final decision from orbit."

"Then the outcome probably depends whether we would rather be hot or cold." Parker pointed at the LCD display he held. "Planet Three will be a little on the hot side, I'd judge, given that solar absolute magnitude and the planet's semi-major axis—but the high orbital eccentricity complicates that a bit. Four may be chilly. I'd expect to see big polar caps, unless the planet happens to have an unusually dense atmosphere."

"Land on Four, then." The words came from one of the passengers, Olaf Siegmund, a big swarthy man with graying hair and enormous hands festooned with heavy gold rings. "I'm a mining engineer. I know how to work cold planets. I ran operations on GC-3 and on Centaur."

Senta frowned. Apparently Siegmund knew they would have to replace the Mattin Drive cores. "Maybe you did, but you won't have mining equipment to help you here. I'm not sure how useful your experience will be to us."

"Equipment?" Siegmund laughed, a deep rumble in his barrel chest. "The only equipment I had on Centaur was a pack of half-trained natives. We shifted more ore with picks and shovels than most operators could manage with an antigrav lift and a bunch of mining lasers."

"You may not have natives, either," Parker said mildly. "I know that's the logic that goes into the Ostrig system choice, but only one planet in ten will support higher life-forms, most of which we'd find it hard to communicate with."

"Then we could be in deep trouble." Siegmund turned to Senta. "Captain, how long before we get close enough to have a look?"

Senta looked again at the computer displays. "Ten days, maybe." She glanced quickly at the other passengers, easily reading their concern at Parker's comment. "Does it require brains, Siegmund, for the heavy mining work? I mean, couldn't we dig out and process silver-109 using work animals? Ninety percent of the planets that *do* have advanced life-forms still haven't got real intelligence."

"I don't ask much intelligence. Just an opposable thumb." Siegmund smiled. "You'll be horrified when I tell you how much dirt-digging I expect to do to get two hundred kilos of silver-109 out of it." He rubbed his hands together, opened them, and looked at the old calluses there. "We're still a long way from home, I can tell you that."

He winked at a couple of the other passengers cheerfully. Parker nodded his head. Senta didn't know the big engineer that well, and she had no reason to expect that his reaction would fit so well with her own desire to keep up the spirits of the passengers. But the man had clearly done far more than Parker to restore a general confidence that their problems could be tackled with some hope of success.

Which only goes to show, thought Parker, that the little learning I have, of man's early days of civilization and exploration, can be a very dangerous thing. He winked at Dial Senta as she fed in the computer request for a double swing-by orbit of Planets Three and Four.

"That's it, then. I don't think Siegmund will be too happy with it." Senta looked up from the display, and cancelled the output. "Agreed, Marco?"

The ship's navigator nodded firmly. Lasse Polo, known to all the crew as Marco Polo, unrolled part of the tape output. "There's no doubt as far as I am concerned, Captain. The multispectral scanner data from Planet Four says there's not much sign of life there. The Polar caps extend down to latitude twenty degrees, and there are no geological faults and fracture patterns that I can correlate with abundant metals in the outer crust. Even Siegmund agreed that Four wasn't too promising, when I showed him the imagery and the spectral analysis—and he hates working on hot planets."

"And how does Three look?" Senta asked.

"Much better, Captain. It's a close Earth homolog. Even so, it will be really hot on the equator. Maybe three-ten Kelvin. We can stand it there, but we'll certainly swelter. The temperate zones would be more comfortable for us. No other problems that I can see, atmosphere all right, gravity fine."

"Then why consider landing at the equator? We have enough fuel for a landing at a higher latitude."

Polo looked dubious. "I know that, Captain. But I'm pretty sure I've been able to pick out some promising areas for silver exploration. Siegmund and I analyzed the fracture patterns and the multispectral signatures of the rock types—and the best areas are in the temperate and cold zones, all of them."

"So?"

"Well, Siegmund has been stressing to me the need for native labor to help with the digging. He says that we'll be here for twenty years if we have to do it all ourselves."

"He told me that, too," said Senta. "But damn it, Marco, if it takes that long, it takes that long."

"Hold it a moment, Captain," Parker said quietly. "I think you're missing Marco's point." He turned to the navigator. "Could it be, Marco, that you've omitted telling us something of interest? Such as—that you've found evidence of a civilization in the equatorial region of Three?"

"Of course I have." The tall navigator frowned, obviously perplexed. "Look, I just spent the last ten minutes reviewing all the output from the thematic mapper." He waved an impatient hand at the complex display on the screens in front of them. "That shows, quite clearly, that there is evidence of agricultural and cultural features in just one place on the surface of Three. In one of the valleys, a couple of degrees north of the equator."

Senta sighed. "Sorry, Marco. You actually have to spell it out for dummies like us." She looked closely at the screen. "One civilized area, you think. And it's not near the places where you would hope to find silver?"

"At least five hundred kilometers away from the nearest hot prospect. Look, this is a photomosaic of the area, made from the scanner images." He pulled out a color photomosaic. "It's got no geodetic control points, of course, so it's an uncontrolled mosaic, but it gives relative positions pretty well. Now, see here." He placed his grubby index finger on the image. "This is the place we think we see the agricultural patterns. And over here—see the circle?—we've marked the spots where we hope to find silver. Surface deposits, too, according to Siegmund. It's five hundred kilometers, great circle distance, from the cultural features."

"That's not the way we'd be travelling, though," said Senta as she leaned over the mosaic, full lips compressed and dark eyes thoughtful. "We don't have enough fuel for the pinnace to make regular runs between the two. Is that a navigable river, there, running north out of the valley?"

"I can't really tell from this distance. It might be carrying a lot of sediment, and I can't separate the sediment from the bottom topography of the river. I took an image using a visible wavelength sensor, but it gives a rotten picture because there's so much atmospheric scattering."

"How about an image at a longer wavelength? You'd get less scattering if you tried it in the infrared."

"I would, Captain, but the longer wavelengths don't penetrate water nearly as well. Microwave imaging is no good either. So we're stuck with this."

Senta looked over at James Parker. "Should it make any difference, from a medical point of view, whether we land at the equator, or at a higher latitude?"

"It might." Parker shrugged. "Unlike Marco here, I can't really tell you anything from this distance. I need to get out on the ground and take samples of the soil and the life-forms. As a general rule, there are more diseases in hot, tropical regions. That's true on most planets—but it could prove quite untrue for this one."

"But the natives, whatever they are, seem to be on the equator. And we must have local assistance, or we'll spend the rest of our lives digging." She chewed thoughtfully at a loose fragment of skin on her lower lip. "I think that has to be the deciding factor. Marco, compute the entry trajectory for the pinnace. Land us near the place where you think you see signs of civilization."

"Right, Captain. How many people will we be taking down? I need that information for the mass calculations."

Parker looked quickly from Polo to Senta and back again. That was one of the key questions, one that would reveal Senta's inner thoughts.

"All crew and passengers, and most of the supplies," she said at last. "Leave enough here for a three-week trip. That will get us comfortably to a galactic node."

Parker drew in a deep breath. So, there would be no skeleton crew and few supplies left on the *Rorqual*. Dial Senta, though she might refuse to admit it, didn't really think they would be coming up again. The pinnace had enough fuel for *one* round trip, fully loaded, to the surface of the planet. Senta preferred to let everyone take a chance on surviving in a colony on the surface, rather than condemning any of them to a possible slow death on the *Rorqual*. The surface of the planet would be quite visible to anyone who was left behind on the ship—but it would be completely inaccessible without the use of the pinnace.

Senta caught his look. "We'd better get ready for the landing," she said. "I would like to be down there in two days, at the outside. Dr. Parker, I want you to stay here for a few minutes when the rest leave. I need to go over the passenger physical condition reports with you."

The navigator and first mate departed on the double. Preparations for landing would be a nightmare. Everything had to be graded in terms of its potential use on the surface—and there would be no second chance to pick up something that was forgotten and left behind on the *Rorqual*.

After they had left, Senta sagged back in her chair. "Here, Jim, come and take a good look at me. Tell me if I'm well enough to travel." She laughed at his horrified expression. "Don't worry, I'm only joking. Look, ninety-nine percent of the time I have to pretend I'm the super-confident, super-competent captain, in full control of everything—and we both know we're all in a real mess. I have to relax a bit with *somebody.*"

"Indeed." Parker pinched the bridge of his nose between thumb and forefinger. "Dial, did you ask me to stay on just now for light entertainment?"

"Of course not." She sighed. "Jim, you're a puritan, kill-joy medic. Oh well, back to business. I've been pulling biographical background information out of the computer on all the passengers and crew. We have to know our resources, before we get down there." She reached into her jacket and pulled out a folded packet of papers. "There are forty-six of us, altogether. Twenty-nine men, seventeen women. We both already know the crew pretty well, so I concentrated on the passengers—how they will be useful when we're down there on the surface."

Senta jerked her thumb at the blue-white planet, filling the sky outside the port. The *Rorqual* was still in a circular polar orbit, seven hundred kilometers above the surface. They watched the globe in silence for a moment, both aware that it might become home for the rest of their lives. At last, Senta sighed and shook her head.

"We have to think of a better name for it than Planet Three, Jim. I've read the Manual, and so have you and most of the passengers. We all know that no ship has ever made it back with a rebuilt Mattin Drive. We may be here to stay. Any ideas?"

Parker hesitated. He doubted that they would be able to set up a colony, but it didn't seem fair to burden Senta with yet another problem—especially one that might never materialize. He decided to wait and see.

"How about calling the planet *Rorqual?*" Senta continued. "That way it will at least seem familiar to us."

Parker shook his head firmly. "I don't like that,

Dial. We have to think of the planet as just our temporary repair station. We *must* assume that we'll somehow get back to a galactic node—otherwise, we won't. It will be a perfect example of the self-fulfilling prophecy. Come on, let's take a look at your list of passengers. But let's do it in terms of *leaving* this system, not settling here permanently."

Senta unfolded her papers. "Then we've already seen the cream. Siegmund should be worth his weight in gold—better than that, in silver. Then we have one other man who might really be useful if we do find a civilization. Mulligan. He's a professor of linguistics, on his way to set up a university language department on Capella Five. He speaks nine languages, and reads another five. Best of all, he's carrying with him a trillion-word memory cube of cognates and common language structures that he compiled for all the languages in the planetary index. He can link it into the *Rorqual*'s computer, and leave it in the primary memory when we go down to the surface. As long as we maintain a decent telemetry link from the surface, Mulligan hopes that he can crack any native language —if we find anything down there that speaks."

"Don't forget we'll be stuck in one place on the surface, Dial. We'll lose contact when the ship is on the far side of the planet."

"No problem. After we leave, the *Rorqual* will boost herself to a synchronous orbit. She'll always be sitting above the same point on the planetary equator.

"Now, about these other passengers. We have two more engineers, on their way to a terraforming project on Capella Three. They don't know much about mining, but they'll still be useful when we get around to digging out silver. They'll be key men when we want to build new solenoid cores. Then there are—thank the Master of Auriga's gluttony—two staff chefs, Green Ribbon winners. They didn't announce it when they came aboard, probably because they wanted a holiday from cooking. Funny thing, they haven't complained once about the *Rorqual's* autochef. Anyway, if we find anything remotely edible down there, they'll be able to make it taste better than it ought to."

She folded the papers and tucked them away again in her pocket. "That's the end of the good news. Now for the bad news. Fifteen of the passengers are New Beginners. They were on their way to spread The Word on Menkalinan Six. The spiritual leader is Agakwe—you've seen him, the big, black man with the emerald earrings. He came to see me a couple of hours ago and explained that the failure of the Drive is a punishment for not living up to the True Teachings. According to him, we will find that Three is really Hell and that the best that we can hope to find there is either devils or damned souls."

Parker reached out his hand. "Here, let me take my own look at that list. I'm not interested in Agakwe and the New Beginners, but I'd like to see what everybody's genetic background is."

Dial Senta pulled the papers from her pocket and gave Parker a sideways glance. "And you accuse me of looking on the black side. But here you go, planning gene combinations to optimize the breeding pool before we even set foot on the surface. All right, take the papers—but I warn you, I know how my mating will go, regardless of the gene mix."

Parker smiled at her as he took the listing. "Now then, Dial. Trust the nice kind doctor. I wouldn't propose anything that would annoy you—yet. I just want to look at the passengers' hereditary tendencies to deficiency diseases. That may be a problem. I don't know what we'll find to eat on Three, but it won't be anything like the foods on a colonized planet—otherwise Three would have been colonized already." He leered. "There'll be plenty of time for your mating studies when we get down there. Polo tells me that the rotation period is thirty-two hours long. Where we'll be landing that means sixteen-hour nights."

The agricultural settlements were spread along both sides of the broad river, beginning in the south where the rapids of the foothills entered the valley. They continued near the banks until the river merged in the north with another major tributary. From there, the combined stream wound its way sluggishly onward for another few hundred kilometers before it reached a silted estuary. Three's small moons produced gentle tides in the great salt marshes that bounded the estuary's union with the northern sea. The *Rorqual*'s most powerful telescope, under highest magnification, could find no signs of settlement past the point where the tributaries merged. Polo had fretted over the electronic noise in the amplified image, trying every enhancement program in the library, but it was no good. Small settlements, if there were any near the northern estuary, remained obstinately invisible. West of the salt marshes, the ground rose sharply to a substantial range of hills, two thousand meters above sea level.

"That's where we'll find silver," Siegmund said, leaning over Polo's shoulder to take a last look before they went off to the pinnace. "Other metals, too. Tin, lead, zinc—not that we have much use for them. Makes me sick, to think that all we need is two hundred kilos of silver-109. I threw away more than that when I got through on my last job. Why didn't you carry it with you on the *Rorqual?* Come to think of it, why don't you carry spare solenoid cores?"

"Doesn't work like that," Polo absently said. He switched off the electronic magnifier and sighed in disgust. "Can't get a clearer picture. We won't know any more about those settlements until we get down there. I can't resolve anything north of the fork in the main river, and I've tried every trick in the book. Solenoid cores?" He sniffed, and spread his hands. "If that would work, do you think we'd have been too stupid to think of it? The problem is, the cores have to be completely shielded from the Mattin Drive. Otherwise, the Drive itself produces resonant changes. Then the cores won't work right. Somehow, the shielding on this Drive must have been defective, and that's why the Drive failed. Anyway, it's nice to know that it *was* the cores—if we can rebuild them, we should be off and running again. The point is, silver-109 degrades once it's been exposed to the Drive. You can't use it to build new solenoid cores. That's why we'll be on our way down to the surface in another hour, to try and dig up a new batch."

He selected another photomap from the display catalog and did an electronic zoom to a region about twenty kilometers west of the estuary. "There's where we'll be soon, Siegmund. Better get your shovel ready."

"No. That's not where we'll be for a while yet." Siegmund frowned. "First, we have to look for our labor pool, then head north to those hills. We need diggers. I wonder if that river is navigable both ways? I'd hate to get the silver, then be unable to carry it back to the pinnace."

"No problem there. We have enough fuel for one hop each way with the pinnace, if all we have to do is pick up the silver. Well, no point in speculating much more. Let's get ready for the landing. I've picked a nice, gentle entry orbit—won't be more than a couple of gee most of the way, and I'll bet money on that. I don't think Parker believes me. He's insisting on gee-shots all round, before anyone gets on the pinnace."

Polo stood up. He rubbed his rear thoughtfully, in unconscious anticipation of the coming injection, then switched off the displays with an air of finality.

"No good, Jim. We're still running into a solid wall."

Parker looked up from the stereo microscope as Dial Senta stepped under the awning and flopped down into the chair next to him. Like him, she was wearing a brief, pocketed shirt and white shorts. The temperature was enough to fog the eye-pieces of the microscope with sweat, and he had to wipe at them with a cloth every couple of minutes. He switched off the enhancer and put down his notebook.

"I assume you've just had another session with the Elders. What did you try on them this time?"

"We told them we are making a trip in the ground

flier to the northern lands and asked them what we should say to the Old Ones there. They were as polite as ever, but they wouldn't cooperate. They simply assure us that the Old Ones are dead. The only time they recognize their existence is when the Old Ones come in the summer, to take the next group of Elders away from the valley with them. Have you decided what they are yet, Jim?"

"The natives?" Parker grinned as he looked admiringly at Senta's brown legs, stretched out in front of her as she sprawled in the seat. "They're themselves. I mean, they don't really correspond to anything on Earth. I've been making a lot of analogies when I talk about them, but that's for my own convenience. I might have a real taxonomy of the local flora and fauna in a few more weeks. Meanwhile, I've been pigeon-holing mentally into Earth-based categories. There are a number of familiar features, at least for the natives. They're vertebrate, furred, warm-blooded, with a four-chambered heart—mammals, near enough."

"Siegmund says they're bears."

"He's oversimplifying, too. I'd have expected them to be carnivores, from their teeth, but they're actually omnivores, same as us. That's one way they're like bears. I would place them, from their general anatomy and habits, somewhere between *Ursidae* and *Procyonidae* in the Earth-based classification."

"Where does that put them? I don't remember much zoology."

"Roughly a cross between a bear and a panda or raccoon. The diet is similar, but the natives have much better equipment for handling objects in their forepaws, and for walking upright. And of course, they're a lot more intelligent. Did any of them stay around here after your meeting, by the way?"

"Elder Tiki is still here. The others returned to their lodges."

Parker stood up. "I'd like to see him again. It's time I had a break here anyway, and I want to ask if I can take a few more tissue samples. There were so many microorganisms in the first one, it's awkward to make a count on all of them from a single sample."

Senta led the way out from under the awning. "Any conclusions yet? You seem to have been working that microscope non-stop."

"A few. *Phew!* It feels even hotter than it was this morning."

They fell into step together and walked from the landing site to the clearing that the Elders had selected as a meeting place. Blue and purple vegetation was abundant, and the straggling undergrowth was alive with small animals and the big, clumsy native insects. The heat and humidity were stifling, but the prospect around them was pleasant enough, with the alien landscape unfolding in gentle billows down to the yellow river.

"To use one of your lines, Dial," Parker continued. "I have some good news and some bad news. Good news first. Although the natives are riddled with every parasitic disease you can think of, none of their parasites seems to fancy us as a host. That should be a relief to everybody, even if it's no great surprise. Our chemistry is quite a bit different."

"It's very good news, to me at any rate. The natives are walking wrecks. I can't imagine a piece of bad news that would cancel that one out."

"Try this. We won't catch their diseases, but we'll all be dead if we have to stay here more than a couple of years. I've analyzed the food supply that we could get from native sources, and it's missing a bunch of essential trace elements and compounds. Easy enough to synthesize, but not with the equipment we're carrying with us."

He paused and picked a serrated blue leaf from one of the shrubs. "The supplies we're carrying will supplement what we can get from these plants for a while, but we'll all begin to feel sick in a year. Then we will just get steadily worse. Remember how I wanted to check our genetic resistance to deficiency diseases, back on the *Rorqual?* Things are much worse than I thought. We're *all* going to be victims, not just a few of us."

Senta had stopped walking forward. She looked around her at the fronded plants. "It's hard to believe. None of this is poisonous, and apart from the color it looks like Earth-grown vegetation. But it will kill us. That clinches it. There'll be no settling down here for a primitive Paradise. We *have* to get away—and quickly. Jim, we've got to obtain cooperation from the natives. If persuasion won't do it, we'll have to resort to force."

"Is Mulligan convinced that he's getting through to them correctly? Maybe they just don't understand us."

"He admits he may be losing some of the subtleties, but he swears he has the basics. There's no doubt that the Elders would die rather than leave the valley here, until they become Old Ones and it is time for them to leave. Elder Tiki and Elder Bori are adamant: human life—they mean themselves—is not possible outside this valley."

"But Marco thinks he saw other settlements." Parker wiped at his forehead with a square of brown cloth, and turned to face Senta. "He was taking aerial photographs during the descent, and he's sure there are some small villages north of here, on the plains near the sea. He and Siegmund are hoping to use the natives there as their labor pool, when we begin the silver mining."

"I know. Elder Tiki says that all we will find in those settlements are Old Ones—natives too old and weak to work. They go there when they are expelled from the valley, to die in the northern sea-plains." She grimaced. "It sounds heartless, but that's what Elder Tiki said—as Mulligan's programs translated it."

They had almost arrived at the meeting place, a cleared area bounded by tall, purple sugar-ferns. The natives of the valley, young and old, came to it to meet the strangers from the sky. Parker watched as the dark figure of Elder Tiki rose laboriously from the ground to greet them. It seemed a miracle the native could stand or walk. The stocky body, less than five feet tall, was a mass of lesions and tumorous growths. They showed inflamed through the thin body fur. The upper and lower limbs were twisted and crippled and scantily covered by his discolored, molting pelt. On the fore-limbs, bone-deep ulcers showed their ugly marks through the eroded skin. The forepaws that gripped the support cane had both lost digits, and the rheumy, deep-set eyes were filmed and mucus-coated. The Elder stood with effort, body swaying, but he nodded calmly at the visitors as if unaware of his ailments.

"Greetings, Elder Parker." The guttural native welcome was transmitted through the microphone to the *Rorqual,* orbiting unseen thirty thousand miles above them, and the translation came back, half a second later, through the companion speaker. "May your years be long in the Valley."

"Less, I hope, than your own," Parker replied formally. "Elder Tiki, I am still studying the ways of the bodies of the People. If you will permit, I would like more samples of tissue from you."

"My body is yours. Do as you wish."

The native stood impassively, broad head bowed forward, as Parker again took tissue from the thin paws and scarred torso, and swabs from the corners of the patient eyes. If Elder Tiki felt pain, he permitted no sign of it to show.

"That's all I need." Parker tucked the vials away in his pockets. "Elder Tiki, last time we met I told you that I can make medicines to help your sicknesses. Let me ask you again, will you try them?"

The Elder stood motionless until the translation came, then opened his mouth to reveal the long, black tongue and the stubs of decaying teeth. He was showing polite amusement. "Thank you; but as we told you already, that is forbidden. Medicine must not be used. Next year, in any case, I will die."

"He means he expects to be sent out, to join the Old Ones in the north." Senta spoke quickly and softly, so that the microphone would not catch her words.

"Also," continued the Elder, "although I am sure that you are trying to help, you know we must remain human. What use is life at all, if we are not human?"

"What's he getting at, Dial?" Parker asked quietly. "He said that last time, but I assumed that Mulligan's programs were having trouble with some of the translations. How can he *not* remain *human?*"

She shrugged. "It must be a cultural referent that won't translate. Perhaps it's a concept that's unique to this culture." Then, to the native, "Dr. Parker would also like to take a sample of your tissue later in the day. Can that be arranged?"

The Elder nodded his broad head, waving a crippled paw to clear the cloud of gnats that flew about him. "It is against our customs, but we will make an exception. Come to my lodge tonight, Elder Parker, after the big moon has risen, and you may take what you need. Now I must go, or the evening meal will be over before Elder Tiki has taken his share."

He nodded in a dignified way, turned, and began the slow walk back to the river. The twisted, shambling figure somehow preserved a presence through all the physical deformities. Dial Senta shook her head.

"If those diseases had happened to one of us, we'd be able to think of nothing else. Jim, could you really cure them?"

"I think so. Of course, they have grossly different metabolisms and body chemistry from our own, but there are enough similarities. I believe I can find extracts from native plants that would help a lot, if only they'd let me try. I've never before heard of a case of a native population that was friendly but completely refused medical help. It's not as if we were competing with their own medicine man."

He swatted at the cloud of insects floating around his head, as if he was seeking another outlet for his frustration. "Damn these bugs. If we can't do anything for the natives, we can at least do something for ourselves. If you'll assign a couple of passengers to track down the breeding grounds for these pests, I'll fix up a spray that should wipe out the worst of them. I took specimens the other evening. Just two or three species cause most of the annoyance. Those black gnats sting like the devil."

"I'll detail a couple of people to look for habitats."

Senta was sitting cross-legged on the floor, rubbing her brown thighs. They glistened with a faint sheen of perspiration. She seemed to steam in the heat. "Jim, I'm wondering if I made a big mistake, settling us here in the valley. Marco may have been right, the only sizeable settlements may be here. But what use is that to us, if the natives won't consider leaving? They keep on saying you can't be 'human' anywhere except in this valley—and that means their own parents, the Old Ones, aren't human."

"I think I can explain that." Parker squatted down by her side. "It's a matter of conscience. They don't have the resources here to support a native who can't work—at least, they may have the natural resources, but everyone is so sick that it's all they can do to support themselves when they are young. So when a native gets to an age where he's too old even to do the work the others can manage, he has to go. Nobody likes the idea of killing his own parents. So they came up with a neat solution. When a native becomes an Old One, he or she is considered dead. He isn't 'human' any more; he's dead before he even leaves the valley, so the natives back here don't have it on their conscience. Besides, they know they'll be going the same way themselves when the time comes, so the whole system seems quite fair to them."

Senta was looking dejected. She bowed her dark head forward. "You're telling me that any natives we find on the trip north will be even older and weaker than Elder Tiki and Elder Bori."

Parker nodded. He didn't like the despairing edge in her voice. "I'm afraid so. Remember, Dial, we knew our mission wouldn't be easy—it couldn't be. We have to press on, and hope that we'll find other aliens up north in better physical condition. Siegmund says there is just no way the natives here in the valley could handle the labor needed for the mining. He can do a lot with a weak crew by using light work schedules, but everyone here is too sick to work. We have to find another answer."

He helped her to her feet and put his arm around her shoulder. They began to walk slowly up the hill toward the camp. The sun was setting in front of them, and a faint singing came from the bright camp ahead.

"You can hear my other problem," said Senta. "I can't get any work at all out of Agakwe's group. All the New Beginners want to do is hold their religious services. Did I tell you that Agakwe is now even more convinced than ever that we are all in Hell?"

Parker looked around at the peaceful landscape. "Hot enough for it. But if it weren't for the heat, this place looks more like Heaven—or it should to Agakwe. I've not told him about the problems we'll have eating native food. This place ought to seem like Paradise to him. We don't catch any of the native diseases, and even the insects don't bite us as much as they do the natives—I guess we taste wrong to them."

"It's the natives that upset Agakwe so much. He can't stand the sight of them. The New Beginners hate disease and deformity, they think it's evidence of sin. The natives have to be devils, or at the very least lost souls."

They had arrived at the pinnace. On the other side of it, Agakwe stood before a group of New Beginners, reading to them from a gold-bound book. Parker and Senta listened in silence for a few minutes before entering the landing craft.

"Sounds like the old Christian Bible," Senta remarked.

"More or less." Parker went over to the desk, pulled out the vials containing the new tissue samples, and reached for the staining compounds. "I listened to some of Agakwe's readings last night. That book is a strange mixture of most of the old Earth religions, put into the same kind of wording used in the early English Bibles. I must say, the words sound wonderful, even though they often don't make much sense. Somebody had a marvelous feeling for language."

He sat down at the desk and began to prepare microscope slides from the new blood and tissue samples. Senta stood by the lock watching the New Beginners' service. Agakwe looked like an obsidian idol, motionless in the deepening twilight. His voice, deep and velvet-smooth, carried into the pinnace: ". . . formed man of the dust of the ground, and breathed into his nostrils the breath of life; and man became a living soul . . ." Finally, nothing could be seen in the darkness outside. Only the voice went on, steady and soothing.

At last, Senta roused herself and walked over to the desk. She looked over Parker's shoulder, her dark hair touching his ear, and finally laid her hand lightly on the back of his neck.

"Jim, you're working all the time. Don't overdo it. Where are you heading? You've already convinced yourself that we can't catch any of the local diseases, and the natives won't let us treat them, not even their young ones. What are you struggling with now?"

Parker leaned back, turning his head so that Senta's hand caressed the nape of his neck. "That feels good." He sat in silence for a few moments, then sighed. "I'm not sure myself. I'm catching up on something that I haven't needed to look at for fifteen years—parasitic diseases. The natives are riddled with them. It's not something that we ever run across in a controlled environment like the *Rorqual*. Here, take a look at this."

He switched on the stereo display unit. After a second of flickering colors, the screen steadied to show a three-dimensional view of a thin, segmented serpentine form. It looked about four feet long, with a double crown of tiny hooks around the head.

"I doubt if you've ever seen one of those before. That's one of the common parasites that plague the natives. It's a cousin of the cestodes—a tapeworm, just like the ones that used to live in the mammals back on Earth. The invertebrates here parallel the Earth forms quite well—this one is a very close analog."

The blind head moved slowly from one side to the other, as if sluggishly looking for its host. Senta stared at it in revulsion.

"It's disgusting. Are you saying things like that are living inside the natives?" She leaned closer to the screen. "How big is it really? If you don't magnify the image?"

Parker looked at her quizzically. "You won't want to hear this, Dial, but that isn't magnified—it's actually shown there at *half*-scale. Tapeworms like that, in the human alimentary canal, grow pretty long. There are recorded cases of *Taenia saginatum,* the beef tapeworm, that were over twenty meters. Pretty unpleasant, right, to have one of those inside you?"

Senta's silence was an eloquent answer.

"If the Elders would only let me," Parker went on, "I could get rid of all those in a couple of weeks, with a simple treatment. That isn't the worst, though, by any means. Tapeworms cause diarrhea and weight loss, and that's a nuisance to the natives. But take a look at this one—it's much more of a real problem."

A second image flashed onto the screen, another serpentine shape, this time smooth-bodied and uniform. The soft yellow body ended in a bladelike flattened tail.

Parker adjusted the focus. "This one *is* under magnification. It's really less than two millimeters long—but I found hundreds of them in one blood sample that I took from Elder Tiki. It's very similar to a microfilarial worm—*nematoda*—that we had on Earth, and it causes really serious disease. Judging from the way that most of them look, the natives must be absolutely infested with them."

Senta leaned forward for a closer inspection, conquering her disgust at the smooth pale worm. "It's hard to believe that the natives can go on living the way they do. How can you be sure this causes their diseases?"

"It doesn't cause all of them. But the tumors and the filmy look about the eyes—they are almost certainly the result of this parasite. I checked with the *Rorqual*'s central data bank this morning, and the telemetry link spat back a whole list of things that organisms like this used to cause, before they were eradicated back on Earth. The best match that the computer could find in Earth analogs was a chronic disease called *onchocerciasis*—it caused blindness, tumors, and general debilitation, for people living in the equatorial regions of Africa. The villain of the piece was a little worm, just like this one, called *Onchocerca volvulus*."

The animal on the screen moved suddenly, a contractile ripple along its length. Senta shuddered. "Ugh. Jim, I think it heard its name. Could you cure them of this one, too?"

"If they would let me. It wouldn't be as easy to get rid of as the cestodes, but a systematic course of chemotherapy would provide an effective cure in a few months. Mind you, there would be some side effects of the treatment—nausea, upset digestive system, that sort of thing. Small price to pay, I'd have thought, to get rid of these beauties. Then there's this one."

Parker keyed another sequence into the display. Another snakelike form, this one shorter and thicker, appeared on the screen. He leaned forward to look at it, totally absorbed in examining the image. Senta took her hand away from the back of Parker's neck.

"Jim! I don't want to see the whole catalog. How many more of them? Surely this isn't another one that infests the natives here?"

"I'm afraid so. I'll stop with this one—though I could show you many more. This is analogous to *trematoda*, the trematode worms. I haven't figured out what disease it causes here, but back on Earth a parasite similar to this caused *schistosomiasis*. That's another debilitating ailment, and a bad one. Ever hear of liver flukes? No wonder the natives here are all so weak and frail. If only they would let me treat them, they'd feel so much better they wouldn't recognize themselves."

He leaned back in his chair, shaking his head in a puzzled way. "But there's a mystery about this one. It's a good deal different from the Earth-based parasite, and it doesn't seem to live mainly in the liver and the mesentery the way that the Earth variety does. I have to find out where it concentrates in the natives' bodies."

Parker switched off the display and keyed up the overhead lights. "There's something else I don't understand. When I take blood samples, there seems to be a circadian rhythm in the number of trematodes that I find, depending on the time of day that I take the sample. In the morning, I find very few of them, but late in the day the samples are teeming. The sample I just took from Elder Tiki is swarming with trematodes."

Parker stood up. "I could go on for a long time. This is fascinating work, something I never meet in ship-board practice. You know, there's a whole class of protozoan parasites that I didn't even mention. They cause the ulcers that you see on the natives, and—"

"Jim," said Senta firmly. "I have had more than enough parasites for one night. You think they are fascinating. Fine. I find them disgusting. You know, I'm beginning to agree with Agakwe's view. This *is* Hell. I never imagined such a place could exist, swarming with these *loathsome* animals."

Parker looked briefly apologetic, then smiled. "Good thing you didn't live on Earth in the old days. Look, don't judge the whole planet by the conditions in this valley. See here."

Parker moved to the far end of the room, where a photomosaic of the area was displayed.

"You can see, we're in an unusually hot and

swampy region, the worst on the planet. If this is like Earth, most of the parasitic diseases will have much higher incidence here. I would expect to see far fewer parasites away from the equator, either north or south. We just happen to be in a bad spot for them. At least, I *assume* this is a bad spot. But this isn't Earth, or any planet we really understand. There could be a danger in pushing any of these analogies too far, for diseases or treatments."

Senta had risen to her feet also and begun to pace up and down the long, narrow work-room. She brushed her hair back from her forehead with a brown forearm, glancing at her wrist-monitor as she did so.

"Damn it, Jim I *did* make the wrong decision. We should have looked further north, closer to the place where Siegmund hopes to mine the silver-109. I'm really impatient now to hear what they find in the ground-flier trip north. I'm sure we'd all be a lot more comfortable out of this valley, where we wouldn't be surrounded by all these ghastly diseases."

"Relax, Dial." Parker stood in front of Senta as she paced the room, forcing her to halt. "You just accused me of overdoing things, but you've been pushing yourself twice as hard as I have. Look at things logically."

He took her by the shoulders and pushed her gently back to a chair by the desk. "First." He checked off the point on Senta's forefinger, holding her right hand in both of his. "We must have native help to mine the silver—otherwise we'll all be dead of deficiency diseases long before we could get the amount of metal we need. Second, the diseases are unpleasant to look at, but they don't infect us—we're too alien. Third, there is no guarantee that we will find the silver in the first place we look for it. It's much more important to get that labor pool we need, while the exploration for silver is still proceeding. Until Siegmund returns, we have no idea where the best place would have been to land the pinnace—but I'm betting it is right here, where we can work at persuading the natives to leave this area and help us with the mining."

Senta squeezed his hand in hers. "All right, Jim. You can let me go now. I'm all right. I was just reacting to those awful worms, and thinking about them crawling around inside us. I'm going to plan a second camp anyway, outside this valley. We'll need it wherever the silver deposits are located, for communication back with the valley here—and I'm sure it will be more pleasant to live there. Come on, let's get some fresh air. It should be getting cooler outside by now."

They left the pinnace together. Outside, the New Beginners had finished their services and dispersed. The evening was still warm and totally quiet, except for the mournful croaking of the lizard-birds that hid in the fronded branches of the bushes flanking the path to the native settlement. Senta took a deep breath and looked about her in the scented dusk. The first stars had appeared, in their unfamiliar constellations, and Three's larger moon was above the horizon. The purple plants of the valley looked black in the pale silver light.

They watched in silence for a while, as the moon continued its slow ascent, reflecting a yellow glow from the distant river. Senta laid her head on Parker's shoulder.

"You help me a lot, Jim. You're quite right, too. Everything here in the valley is peaceful. If it weren't for the wretched condition of the natives, this really would be a good place for them to live."

"It would." He put his arm around her shoulder and caressed her warm cheek. "The ground is fertile, and it's easy to grow crops. I don't think the area in the north would be as good—the rains there, if Polo is right, will have leached most of the nutrients from the soil. This could be an easy life, but the price that the natives pay to be here is impossibly high. Logically, they'd be better off outside the valley."

They had moved slowly closer together in the darkness, their bodies quietly accommodating to a familiar pattern as Parker was talking. After a few minutes, Senta pulled herself gently away from him.

"Jim, remember what you said. Elder Tiki will be waiting for you in the above-water part of his lodge, now that the moon is up."

"Damnation!" Parker released her and began to fasten his shirt. "And you accuse me of being celibate. I was all set to forget about my appointment. I'll be back in an hour or so. Are you going to bed now?"

"Not yet. I'll go and see Agakwe again and try to persuade him that the New Beginners have to work harder and be more useful to the rest of us. I'll be waiting here when you get back."

There was enough light for him to see her smile, a glimpse of light through the dark background.

"Good hunting, Jim—catch a good haul of trematodes or whatever-they-are-here. But *don't* bring them back alive, mighty hunter."

Parker gave her a quick kiss and set out along the path to the settlement on the river. The route twisted to and fro following the contours of the land, but there was just enough light from the rising moon for him to follow the track. The tall bushes along the way were night-scented, and their heavy, alien perfume weighed on the night air. After a few minutes, Parker heard hurrying footsteps behind him. He turned and waited. It was Mulligan, the linguistics professor, puffing along after him.

"Steady on, Dr. Parker. Walk a little slower, and I'll keep you company."

"Heading into the native lodge area?"

Mulligan nodded. With his long neck and skinny frame, he looked like an erudite stork.

"I'm going to see Rosi, the village Recorder, again. She has been telling me some of the history of the natives of the valley—whenever she's not feeling too weak and sick to talk. Then she stays in the underwater part of her lodge, and I wonder if she will ever come out again. She's so thin and frail."

"I could help her on that, if only they'd let me try. Professor, we're getting nowhere with them. They live in the hottest, most disease-ridden part of the planet, and they won't leave under any persuasion. Do you have any idea why, from their description of their history?"

Mulligan folded his long arms across his chest and paced slowly forward. "They believe that this is the only place on the planet where a 'human' can live. According to their legends, they will become animals should they attempt to leave. It's really very odd. Some of their legends are like those of Earth, but they are inside-out."

"I never heard of any Earth legend that said we'd become animals if we left a certain place."

"Nor I. As I said, they have the legend inside-out. We have the story of the Garden of Eden, where humanity lived before the Fall, without guilt and sin. The Elders here have a similar story that they pass down, but in their version the natives lived without *disease*. Then Knowledge came, and with it sin and sickness. After that, the natives were 'human,' but they could never return to the old places any more."

Parker thought of Agakwe's reading, earlier in the evening. He wondered if there was a time in human development at which self-knowledge had suddenly come, crushing and irrevocable, to his own distant forebears? In which sensation and immediate gratification had given way to a world of self-consciousness, memory and foreboding for the future?

"Do the natives here say when all this happened—or indicate where their 'Garden of Eden' was located?" he asked.

"That's another mystery," replied Mulligan. "If Rosi's records are correct, they achieved Knowledge very recently—less than ten thousand Earth-years ago. If that's true, they've come along unbelievably fast. They've gone through many thousands of years of development in a few generations—and they've done it all while they were so sick they could hardly walk. Now, here's the inside-out part. According to their oral history, it was all the rest of the world—*except for this particular valley*—that served as their Garden of

Eden, before Knowledge came to them. Now, they cannot return there, even though they would be innocent there. They must remain in this valley, enduring all the sickness that goes along with it."

"But what about the Old Ones? Aren't they intelligent, and self-aware?"

"Of course." Mulligan smiled ruefully. "But you see, according to the Elders the Old Ones are dead—so that doesn't count."

"A nice logical trap." Parker brooded on the other's words, trying vainly to see a pattern that he could understand. "You know, the senior Elders will be 'dying' and leaving the valley themselves at the end of this year. Medically speaking, that might be the best thing that could happen to them. At least they'll stop acquiring new diseases, even if they can't get rid of the ones they already have."

Mulligan inclined his head and clasped his bony hands behind his back. "Perhaps so. Certainly, it is a hard life for them here. I wish we could do something to help, but the more I discuss it with them, the less likely it seems that we can persuade any of the younger natives to move from the valley. Did I tell you of Rosi's comment to me, and Agakwe's reaction to it? She quoted an old tribal saying to me: 'For we are created to suffer disease, even as the smoke goes up from a cooking stone.' I thought that was poetic, and I told it to Agakwe—we share an interest in poetry. He looked astonished, then he said to me, 'Man is born unto trouble, as the sparks fly upward.' After that, he scratched his head, and said, 'That's too close for coincidence; I'll have to keep a closer eye on the natives in the settlement here.' And he left me, muttering to himself in that deep bass voice of his. What do you make of that, Dr. Parker?"

Parker shrugged. "I don't recognize his quotation, but it's good to know that Agakwe may be getting interested in something more than holding services for the New Beginners." He paused, as they came to the widening of the path that indicated the river lodges were just ahead. "We separate here, I think. I hope you find Rosi well enough to talk to you."

"She's always ailing, but she loves to talk about their history," said Mulligan. " 'Rosi, thou art sick. The invisible worm, that flies in the night, in the howling storm . . .' " He tittered self-consciously. "William Blake, you know—but not wholly inappropriate, after what you told me yesterday of their parasitic diseases. Good luck with your work, Doctor. Try and stay in the dry part of the lodge. I'm sure the damp must be bad for them too."

"Not at all, they evolved near the rivers. It's much harder on us."

"Then it is fortunate that the conversations are so interesting—I expect a pleasant session tonight, exploring triliteral and quadriliteral roots of their spoken language. It is curious how intelligence drives communication along common paths."

But it's the *differences* between us and the natives that cause the trouble, thought Parker, as the two men separated. How do you persuade a native to violate a taboo against leaving this area and come with you to seek others who could help with the mining? That's the problem. In my experience, there is *no way* we will get them to do it; and yet we must, or we are all dead.

Perhaps it was time to forget the valley, and start from scratch in the search further north. Suddenly, Parker shared Senta's impatience to hear how Siegmund and the ground-flier expedition were faring.

The yellow river widened as it flowed north out of the valley. The flier had followed it through a narrowing gorge, steep-sided and rocky, out to a series of meanders that wound their way slowly toward the great tidal estuary. Their elevation was steadily decreasing, and the temperature dropped slowly as the tempering effect of on-shore winds made itself felt. Both men breathed easier as the colder air blew through the open side-windows of the flier.

"I'll sleep better tonight, Marco," Siegmund said, switching the controls to the autopilot and turning back into the cramped cabin. "Pity we're not going all the way to the poles. You can keep your hot planets."

"Don't think you'd like it too well," Polo remarked absently. "The thermal I/R sensor logged the north pole at two hundred Kelvin when I took a reading from the *Rorqual*. That's seventy-five degrees of frost. You'd freeze to your shovel."

He was stooped over the aerial photographs he had taken on the way down from orbit. They were mainly color infrared obliques, and he was painstakingly correlating them with the scanner imagery taken at higher altitude, then attempting to match both sources with the ground features he could see from the flier. He looked up, and out of the front windshield.

"If I'm right about our location," he said, "we should be able to see our first settlement in another few kilometers. It's really small—I couldn't see it at all on the orbital imagery, and it's just a dot on the aerial stuff. Keep west of the river. The place we want is right on the bank, where one of the small streams from the western foothills runs into the main branch."

Siegmund grunted and returned to the pilot's seat. The two men were crowded into the small flier with little room to spare. It was intended as a one-man craft, but Senta had insisted on squeezing two men into it. In case of danger, Polo was to stay with the flier at all times. 'Expendable, am I,' Siegmund had grumbled, but both men were delighted with Senta's order—each had feared that a one-man expedition would exclude him in favor of the other. For two loners in cramped surroundings, they had managed an amazingly harmonious journey.

The small flier lacked the K-band microwave transmitter that would permit video communicatioms with the pinnace through a communications link via the orbiting *Rorqual*. Reporting back to Senta had to be by voice-link only. So far, there was little to relate except the gradual improvement in personal comfort as they descended to the cooler air of the coastal plains.

"Something up ahead there, Marco. Think that's it?" Siegmund asked.

In front of them, a small group of primitive structures hugged the bank of the river. They were even rougher than the reed-and-mud lodges of the valley they had left. The agriculture surrounding them on the landward side was so feeble and so haphazard that its absence on the orbital imagery was no surprise. The wonder was that Polo could have picked it out on the oblique aerial photography, even with his trained eyes.

"I'll set us down right there, so we're shielded from the village by the horsetail trees," said Siegmund. "See the clearing in the bristle-cones? I'll position us for a rapid take-off. I doubt if we'll need it. If the Old Ones are anything like the Elders, I'll be able to outrun them even if they bind me hand and foot."

"Let me check the elevation before you land us," said Polo. "I want to keep a direct channel open to the pinnace, even if the link to the *Rorqual* fails. Let's hope that Mulligan's portable transmitter works with these natives."

"It ought to. The Elders assured Mulligan that there is only one language, and all the natives here are Old Ones, who came out of the valley. The Elders and the Old Ones meet when it's time for the next batch of Elders to get kicked out of the valley, so they must be able to talk to each other."

Siegmund drifted the flier in for a landing, then turned it ready for take-off. He picked up the portable translation unit that contained Mulligan's latest programs, then made a careful note of the best direction for a rapid run back through the trees.

"Be back here in four hours," said Polo, as Siegmund prepared to leave. "If you're not, I'll take the flier up to two hundred meters and make a pass over the top of the settlement. I'm sure they'll have no way of touching us at that height."

Siegmund grunted. "I like that 'us' you use there, Marco. I'll think of it when they stick a spear down my gullet. Listen for my beep—and be ready to go if you hear it. See you later."

He walked off quietly through the trees. Polo settled his seat so that he could watch the path. He followed Siegmund's bulky form until it was out of sight, then began to check the radio link back to the pinnace. Static interference was unusually bad. He tried a couple of different wavelengths, homing in on the pinnace's reference beacon. The signal-to-noise ratio was still poor. Polo frowned to himself and began to apply selected frequency filters. That made a big improvement. He nodded in satisfaction, decided on what seemed like the optimum set, and finally looked up from the receiver. The sun was high in the sky, the breeze pleasant, and the blue shrubs gave off a rich, resinous aroma. The only sound he could hear was the rustling of brittle leaves, and he could see no sign of Siegmund or anything else on the path that led to the settlement.

Polo stretched, yawned, and bent again to fiddle with the radio—more for something to do, than with any hope of improving the reception much. As he did so, he saw a movement off to the left of the flier out of the corner of his eye. He had no particular fear or presentiment of danger as he turned his head. Thus far they had not observed any dangerous animal life on the planet, and the Elders had confirmed that the only big carnivores were the large water-wolves that lived in the rivers.

At the edge of the trees, poised ready for flight or attack, stood a native. It was a male, naked, and holding a bunch of leaves in one grimy paw. Behind it, peeping from the canopy of vegetation at the edge of the clearing, was a female holding a small baby.

Polo swore softly to himself as he looked closely at the newcomers, waiting to see if they would offer any sign of greeting. Their faces were blank and placid, and none of them wore more clothing or ornament than a substantial layer of grime and grease. The baby clung to the female's matted hair with one tiny paw, and sucked peacefully at a full breast.

Polo looked around the cabin of the flier. Who would ever have foreseen a need for two portable translators? Siegmund had the only one, and the best video-recorder as well.

Polo reached for a camera, noting as he did so that the visitors to the clearing had smooth, glossy pelts, with no signs of the diseases that disfigured the natives of the southern valley. At Polo's movement, the male gave an animal grunt of fear. He turned and pushed at the female, and they hurried from the clearing and disappeared in a few seconds into the dense undergrowth.

Polo swore again, and looked at the camera he was holding. Despite his instructions to remain inside the flier, he stepped outside and made his way to the place where the three natives had appeared. They had left no traces behind them except for the spoor of one bare pad in a patch of mud. He went back to the flier, wondering if he should call back at once to the main camp in the valley. But what could he report to Senta? Only that he had seen three wild-looking natives, and failed to make either a visual or sound recording of their visit.

He sat down in the flier and tried to recall every detail of their appearance. One thing was certain: the three visitors were not suffering from the crippling diseases that afflicted the other natives. They had run away through the woods at a rate that the others could never have equalled, no matter what the emergency. He thought again of the blank, animal look of the strangers, contrasting it with the calm intelligence of Elder Tiki and the other dwellers in the southern valley. Finally, he resigned himself to the inevitable and prepared to call back to the pinnace. Despite his failure to record the visit, he would have to call in and report it. It cast suspicion on all the words of the Elders. There *were* natives outside the valley, and they were certainly not the dying Old Ones that had been described to him.

As he picked up the microphone, he again saw signs of movement in the undergrowth and he reached for the camera again and raised it ready for action. Then he lowered it. The new arrival was Siegmund, hurrying through the woods with a perplexed expression on his swarthy face. He paused by the door of the flier.

"You don't seem too thrilled to see me," he said to Polo. "Going to take my picture?"

Polo put down the camera again and shook his head. "Come in, quickly. You'll never believe what I've just seen."

"Fair enough," said Siegmund. "Because you'll never believe what I've seen, either. Get this thing in the air, and fly us over the settlement. I want to show you something, then we have to get back to the pinnace. The Elders owe us a few explanations."

In the main computer room of the pinnace, James Parker leaned back in his chair and rubbed at his tired eyes. He had been working late the previous night, and Dial had kept her word and waited for his return. He was feeling exhausted, and having trouble concentrating on the job at hand. The heat didn't help.

With more samples to work on, the statistical evidence was strong. Fits to the data now showed an unmistakable trend. The number of trematodes in the blood of the natives reached a low point soon after dawn. The number began to increase at noon, mounted steadily for the rest of the day, and peaked at dusk. After that it slowly diminished until morning.

That much was clear, but everything else was a mystery. Where were the termatodes during the early morning hours? They still had to be somewhere in the natives' bodies. Somewhere.

Parker snapped on the display again and called out an image showing the main circulatory systems of the natives. He overlaid the locations of the trematode counts. Was he missing the obvious? He looked for correlation with the major organs, then changed the display to look at an image of the worm itself. The parasite appeared quite a bit different from the stylized reproduction offered by the *Rorqual*'s central data bank, but that wasn't surprising. The latter was based on the Earth species as a model, and this one was merely an analogous form.

Outside, the sun stood at its height, burning down almost vertically on the camp. The heat inside the pinnace was stifling, even though Parker had opened every port in an attempt to catch any trace of a breeze. Unfortunately, sound carried in also. Parker swore. Agakwe and his followers had gathered for a noon ceremony, and Agakwe's voice seemed to carry for miles, even when he spoke at normal volume. Parker could not ignore the distraction, try as he might. The heat and high humidity made concentration a super human effort. He fought an increasing drowsiness, and listened to the ceremony outside as he looked at the display screen.

Agakwe's reading was from the same venerable sources. The New Beginners chanted unison responses at points of the reading, like a hypnotic plainsong: "*. . . the tree of life also in the middle of the garden, and the tree of knowledge of good and evil . . . and the gold of the land is good: there is bdellium and the onyx stone . . . but of the tree of knowledge of good and evil, thou shalt not eat of it . . .*"

Parker's attention wandered, drifting randomly between the ancient words and the glowing screen. He seemed to see the yellow blood flowing around the bodies of the natives, carrying its cargo of trematodes. Agakwe's voice lulled through the open ports; "*. . . now the serpent was more subtle than any beast of the field . . . and the eyes of both of them were opened, and they knew that they were naked . . .*"

Parker jerked upright. He gazed open-mouthed at the screen, all his fatigue instantly banished. His hands felt clammy, cold in the heat of noon. "*. . . and the eyes of both of them were opened . . .*"

Working quickly, he re-entered the compute mode and again began to analyze the sample data. At last he had something tangible to test, a hypothesis that was more than mere data fitting. As the calculation proceeded, the new points fell into position, as precise and satisfying as the elements of a geometrical theorem. He checked and calibrated, re-checked and recalibrated, oblivious now to the ceremonies of the New Beginners outside the vessel. He did not notice the sudden interruption of their ceremony, nor the excited hubbub of voices that followed. The world contained nothing but the new insight, moving restlessly through his mind.

After two hours his search was finished. He would need additional facts to fill out the complete picture, but first he wanted to tell Dial what he had found.

He left the pinnace just as the ground-flier was landing at the edge of the clearing. Siegmund and Polo jumped out, and he waved his papers and hurried across to them.

"What the devil is going on here?" Polo was flushed and furious, totally different from his usual calm self. "What are you people playing at?"

"Playing at?" Parker was bewildered. "It's business as usual here."

"Then why isn't the radio operating? We've been trying to reach you for the last four hours, and there was no reply from your end. Just the damned test beacon. You can guess the sort of things we were thinking as we flew back. Such behavior is inexcusable."

Parker was too excited by his discovery to take in Polo's complaint fully. He waved a hand vaguely back at the pinnace. "I don't know what happened. There's a continous duty roster to man the radio equipment in there. Look, never mind that now. I've got really big news. It could be just the thing that will get us all off this planet and on our way back to civilization."

"What do you mean, *you've* got big news?" Siegmund yelled. He and Polo looked outraged. "Why do you think we were so keen to get in touch with you back here? Wait until you hear what we've found, then you'll know what big news really is."

As they argued, the three men hurried off to the screened awnings that made up Dial Senta's daytime quarters. They reached the edge of the clearing and ducked in through the canopy that helped the tall ferns above to shield the area from the direct rays of the sun.

Dial Senta was not alone. Inside the big tent stood Agakwe, massive and unflinching. He was flanked by two women of the New Beginners. His expression was grim, but he stood impassively under Senta's tirade.

"No *possible* justification," she said, standing directly in front of Agakwe. Her brown face looked unusually pale, and her voice was furious. *"Nothing* could justify countermanding my orders. You two were supposed to be on radio duty. I am the captain of the *Rorqual,* and the commander of this landing party. You, Agakwe, have no authority to re-assign these people to duties of your own choosing—and you two should have refused to accept such assignment. Don't you realize what you did could have meant the lives of the ground-flier party, if they needed us and couldn't get through here?"

"What we have found is more important than any two lives," Agakwe responded. His eyes, a pale and startling blue in his ebony face, looked swiftly at Polo and Siegmund as they entered the tent. There was a momentary flicker of embarrassment that was swiftly gone. "I have found proof that the natives of this valley are embodiments of evil. Our lives are less important than our immortal souls." He stood erect, towering above Senta. "The natives here are an abomination, an unclean thing. We should destroy them totally, or leave this planet at once and return to the *Rorqual.*"

The two women standing by Agakwe began to speak together as he fell silent. At the same time, Parker, Polo and Siegmund broke into excited comment. Senta listened to the unintelligible babble for a few seconds, then stepped forward to the table in the center of the tent. She slapped her hand down hard upon it.

"Quiet. All of you." Her voice rang out above the confused din. There was a sudden silence. She looked around the tent, meeting each pair of eyes in turn. "I would like to remind you that I am still in command here. We have not descended to anarchy. If you object to the present set-up, the ways in which I can be replaced are quite specific and known to all of you."

She waited for a few seconds, letting the silence establish itself. Finally she took a deep breath and continued in quieter tones. "You all believe that you have something important to tell me. Fine. We have plenty of time. We'll proceed in an orderly fashion, one at a time. You will each have your turn, but there will be no arguments and no noisy interruptions." She turned to Polo and Siegmund. "First, let me welcome you back, and say that I am glad you managed a safe return even without the radio link. Navigator Polo, please make your report first. Did you contact the Old Ones outside the valley—and did you find any source of silver for the cores?"

Polo hesitated. "We believe we know where to get the silver. It's there all right, in the hills where we thought it would be. And it's on the surface, as Siegmund predicted it would be. And we saw the Old Ones, too, although I only got a look from high up, above their settlement. Maybe we should let Siegmund describe how it was on the ground . . ."

Twenty yards inside the woods, Siegmund had turned and looked back. The flier was already almost invisible through the dense undergrowth. He took out a vibroknife and began to mark the woody ferns every few yards. A rapid escape in the wrong direction would be worse than useless.

The agriculture around the settlement was pathetic. Ineffectual scraping with a shallow plow ran in crooked furrows across the ground. Siegmund paused and looked at the crops. They seemed healthy enough, but sparse and weed-infested. The Old Ones seemed to be even worse farmers than the natives back in the valley. The same root crops were being cultivated, with the addition of a ground creeper that bore a large red bean-like fruit. Midway between the settlement and the edge of the brush, a shrunken figure was bent over the vines, picking the ripe pods.

Siegmund switched on the portable translator and looked at it with some misgivings. It seemed too small and light for the job. He walked slowly forward, careful not to make any threatening movements. The Old One stood up at the sound of the footsteps and turned slowly to face the stranger.

If the Elders were like withered branches, with their twisted and knotted limbs, the Old One was a dried leaf. The fur of its body and limbs was patched and molted. Beneath it, the flesh was dried and shrivelled, peppered with the scars and puckers of healed ulcers. The rib cage stood out like a picked carcass. At first glance, Siegmund dropped any remaining hope that the Old Ones might perform useful manual labor. The miracle was their continued life, as a relic of crippling infirmities bound into conscious form.

The deep-set eyes of the Old One regarded Siegmund curiously, the look level and intelligent. The wrinkled maw opened to speak.

"Greetings to you." The portable translator came into sudden sound. "We did not expect your coming, although we knew of your arrival to our world. I am Old One Koti. Do you have news of my first-born, Elder Bori?"

"Elder Bori is well." Siegmund's words came automatically, before he had time to consider them. One word that could not be applied to any Elder—to any native—was "well." He hoped the translator would offer something that made sense to the Old One. Then the rest of the other's greeting registered. *We knew of your arrival to our world*. How was that possible?

Siegmund could think of only one answer. Communication between the Old Ones and the Elders of the valley must be regular, more than the once-a-year arrival of the latest group of expelled Elders.

"Come to the lodge." Old One Koti picked up the bag of ripe bean-pods in a deformed paw, leaned on a staff as bent and twisted as his own body, and slowly led the way toward the group of lodges. "Why do you visit us here? It will be many days before the new ones are ready for the river journey."

Siegmund considered the words carefully before he replied. Either the translator was not working correctly, or there was a major mystery here.

"We have come here to look for silver." He realized that the natives had no forms of precious metal. "For metals. In the rocks of the hills west of here. Old One Koti, I do not understand your words. What are the 'new ones' that you speak of?"

The native stopped suddenly. He turned to face Siegmund, and his half-shut eyes held a shifting look of surprise and calculation. "Indeed." The broad face was impassive. "It was nothing, just words." He waved his sinewy forelimb in the air as though carrying the thought away on the wind. "Why then do you visit us here? We are the Old Ones, we have no part to play in finding metal."

Many years ago, in a fetishist colony on the mining world of Gamma Velorum Six, Siegmund had inadvertently asked the unforgivable—the meaning of the magenta ribbon on a young girl's arm. Luck, strength and youthful reflexes had allowed him to escape with minor injuries. But he had never forgotten the way that the masks had come on after that question. It was as if shutters had closed in the minds of the hearers, protecting sacred thoughts from public view. He recognized that look now, across the years, in Old One Koti's eyes. Although he could have snapped the native's limb between finger and thumb, the settlement suddenly seemed a dangerous place, a source of hidden perils. He walked cautiously after the Old One, scanning around him as they went.

They stopped at the first lodge, down on the river brink, and went inside. A level floor about three meters deep was followed by a steep ramp that led to the under-water part of the lodge, where the natives had their sleeping quarters. The furnishings were simple, pathetically crude and unfinished. At the Old One's invitation, Siegmund seated himself on a mat of leaves next to the cooking stones. They looked at each other warily. Old One Koti, squatted on his hindlimbs, pointed with his paw at the clay jars by the wall.

"There is refreshment, if you need it. For me, it is not the time for strong waters."

Siegmund shook his head, a gesture that was common with the natives. "Thank you, but not for me. I must soon be on my way again. I came here only to ask you what you know of the country west of here, and to see what we might find there."

"We know very little. We stay close to the streams and rivers, and have no strength to roam the hills. Age is a hardship that all must bear, long before we die the second death."

Siegmund realized that the whole conversation was strangely formal, the words of two strangers who exchange polite platitudes only until they can reasonably separate. He rose to his feet.

"Then I must proceed with my journey." Siegmund realized how ridiculous the words sounded as soon as he had uttered them. To come so far and leave after a few meaningless phrases made no sense. Even if Koti knew nothing of the western hills, he certainly knew the local flora and fauna, and many other things important to a traveler through the area.

If the Old One was surprised by Siegmund's actions, he showed no sign of it. He rose to his feet slowly, showing no curiosity about the stranger from the sky. "Good fortune with your search," he said, then stood in silence, clearly waiting. Siegmund picked up the portable translator, left the hut, and started back across the makeshift fields. Near the edge of the brush he turned and looked back. Old One Koti was standing, leaning on his staff and watching closely. Siegmund waved, turned, and went on into the woods.

As soon as he was hidden from the settlement, Siegmund ran laterally as fast as possible for about forty meters, then crept back to the edge of the cleared area. He peered cautiously out of the undergrowth and saw the Old One hobbling toward the river, as fast as his crippled hind-limbs would carry him. He turned from time to time to look back in the direction Siegmund had taken into the woods. He was joined by two other Old Ones, a male and a female, and the three of them were soon hidden behind the further lodges.

Siegmund began to move in a wide semicircle, remaining in the protection of the shrubs and marking his progress every few yards for the return trip. When he came to the stream, he followed it cautiously in toward the settlement. The woods came to an end about fifty meters from the nearest lodge. Siegmund moved slowly to the edge, careful to remain out of sight, and looked out through the screen of vegetation.

The natives were standing together by the stream, talking animatedly. On the bank were three large cages, made of straight reed-wood stems tied with plant fiber. A square log raft was close to the bank, secured with two stout timbers. A rough mast was mounted on one side of the raft.

Siegmund quietly took out his telescope and the video recorder. He set the gain in the middle range and pointed the telescope at the scene by the stream. Then he whistled softly under his breath. His eyes had not deceived him. There were native young ones in the cage, two in each. He estimated their ages at between two and three years, little more than infants. They were sitting docilely on the floor, taking no notice of the Old Ones who stood by them. Siegmund attached the recorder to the telescope and operated the combination for a few minutes, then removed it and set the telescope to high gain.

At first sight the young ones were naked and dirty but otherwise normal. Their pelts were smooth and glossy, with no signs of the lesions and sores that disfigured the young natives he had seen in the valley. Siegmund zoomed in on the faces and studied them closely. All appeared vacant and uncomprehending, without the animation that he expected to see in a three-year-old. After a few seconds he again made a video-recording of the scene at high magnification, taking records of both the young and of the Old Ones standing by them.

The scene by the stream did not change. The Old Ones showed no signs of leaving, and from time to time they looked nervously around them, back toward the woods where he lay hidden. Siegmund waited. Finally, when it was apparent that the Old Ones might stay there indefinitely, Siegmund put away his instruments and quietly worked his way back, deep into the undergrowth.

Siegmund was an optimist. He had seen many things on many worlds, and somehow he had survived them all. There were few things that could throw more than a brief shadow on his spirit; but as he made his way back to the ground-flier even he would have admitted that he was uneasy. His plump face was furrowed with worry and he gradually accelerated as he drew closer to where the flier waited. By the time he reached it he was running, eager to have Polo's perspective on what he had just seen.

The group watched the video records in silence. The pictures taken at highest magnification when the flier had made a pass over the Old Ones' settlement were of poor quality, but everything they could see on them confirmed Siegmund's statements.

Senta looked closely at a still shot of the cages, then bit thoughtfully on her lower lip. She shook her head in perplexity.

"And you think the caged young ones are like the wild natives you saw, Marco?" she said.

"Definitely. Same features, same healthy look. Same dirty look, too, they all needed a wash. They were the same."

Senta sighed. She looked about her. Parker was sitting perfectly still, an absorbed concentration holding him silent. Agakwe and the New Beginners looked sullen and stubborn.

"All right." Senta shrugged. "I don't know where that leaves us. I'll admit that what you saw may be very important—but how? Agakwe, why don't you tell me what's on your mind—and try and keep it factual. I'm not interested at the moment in the religious interpretations."

Agakwe returned her look calmly. "Very well. But none are so blind as those who refuse to see the truth when it is offered to them." He ran a long-nailed hand over the short black stubble that covered his scalp. "After hearing Professor Mulligan talk of the legends of the natives of this valley, I began to suspect we were in a trap. Their tribal sayings are too like our own sacred writings. That might suggest that they are divinely created, with immortal souls like ours—but we know well that the Devil can cite scripture for his own purposes." He smiled. "So, you may say, can I."

He looked across at Polo and Siegmund. "For instance, 'why seek ye the living among the dead?' Why travel north, looking at the Old Ones, the 'dead' ones, when we have not understood the ways of the natives here in this valley? I decided that we needed to look at them more closely. Maria and Akhtar volunteered to watch the settlement for me."

He turned to Senta and shrugged. "It is unfortunate that doing so interfered with the duty you had assigned on the radio station. But our research proved worthwhile. This afternoon, when our service was over, Maria went to the native lodges and found that a fence had been built around one of the cleared areas. She and Akhtar went to one of the giant ferns that overlook the area. Working together, they managed to reach the higher fronds. Maria, what did you see?"

The taller of the New Beginners looked uncertainly at Senta, who smiled encouragingly. "Go ahead."

"Well, I saw . . . we saw." She stopped. Suddenly the words came out in a rush. "I saw Molochites, tying the young ones to wooden posts."

"Molochites?" Senta frowned. "What are they?"

"Slaves of the devil," said Agakwe. "Followers of Moloch, 'horrid King, besmeared with blood of human sacrifice and parents' tears.' Maria and Akhtar saw native young ones being prepared for sacrifice in the village."

"Being tied to stakes," said Maria. "In the clearing, inside the fence, where they thought we could not see it. Little ones, only two or three years old. Too small to understand what was being done to them. They did not cry out or try to run away."

"You saw them actually being sacrificed?" James Parker had come out of his trance and was leaning forward intently.

"No, but we saw them being led in, and then tied."

"Yes, that would be the way to do it." Parker leaned back and nodded to himself in satisfaction. He returned to his thoughtful trance.

"Jim!" Senta was looking at him with an expression of disbelief. "Do you believe all this? Are you saying that you know why they are doing it?"

"Yes. I told you I had big news." He looked around at the others in the tent, then smiled a personal smile at Senta. "But nobody asked me what it was. I know what the Old Ones were doing. I know what the Elders were doing—and I understand all their legends, and why they are here in this valley. And"—he turned to Agakwe—" "None of it has anything to do with religious sacrifice."

He leaned back in his seat and pressed the tips of his fingers together, enjoying the rapt attention of the others. "Siegmund, what's your main impression of the natives here in this valley?"

The big engineer rubbed the side of his nose. "Why, I guess it's their diseases. They're all three-quarters dead."

"Right," said Parker. "No doubt about it, this valley is a terrible place for a native to live. There isn't one of them that doesn't have three or four major parasitic diseases. Now, how did the wild natives that you saw in the north look? Sick, or healthy?"

"Healthy, the ones in the cages."

"And the ones that I saw in the woods," added Polo. "I saw them close up, even though I didn't get a picture of them, and they looked fine."

"All right." Parker nodded in satisfaction. "So here we have a peculiar situation. Sick, civilized natives in the valley, and healthy, wild ones outside it—I don't consider the Old Ones, because they all came from here. Now, let me tell you about the work I've been doing—and remember, I didn't know anything about what you were finding up in the north.

"I've been looking at the individual parasites that cause the diseases in the natives. Most of them are straightforward, and I could trace useful analogies with the old situation back in the equatorial regions of Earth. But there was one big exception, an animal rather like a trematode worm. On Earth, the nearest equivalent would have made its home in the liver, and caused a disease called *schistosomiasis*. Here it was different. I couldn't decide where the trematodes were being concentrated in the natives, even though I took a lot of samples from different parts of their bodies."

He paused. Outside, the sun was setting, and the inside of the tent was becoming very dark. Senta stood up and switched on a fluorescent lamp tied to the main support beam. She looked around apologetically.

"I know that's going to attract the insects, but it's this or sit here in the dark. I'll get some netting later. Sorry to interrupt you, Jim. What did you decide about the place where the trematodes are concentrated?"

"I didn't. I couldn't find out." Parker cracked his knuckles meditatively. "I seemed to be stuck. Then today, while I was in the pinnace looking at a picture of a microfiliarial worm, I heard you"—he nodded toward Agakwe—"reading aloud, telling how the serpent brought knowledge to man and woman. I wondered. Suppose that the parasite I was looking for inhabited the central nervous system of the natives—and suppose that it was the stimulus that somehow-or-other had changed a wild, unthinking animal to a reasoning, self-aware being. Far-fetched, maybe, but not impossible."

The others were looking at him wide-eyed. "But Doctor," said Polo. "I thought you said those worms, the trematodes or whatever you called them, were *parasites*. A parasite couldn't do anything like that."

"I wasn't precise enough," said Parker. "You see, I was using the word parasite as a general expression, for anything that lives inside another animal. Most of the things inside the natives are true parasites—they harm the host they live in. But biologically there are really three different situations. There's *parasitism*, where the animal does harm to the host, and that's the one we usually think about. But there's also *commensalism*, where the host provides a habitat for another animal but isn't harmed by it. We have protozoa in our own alimentary canals that fall into that category—they neither harm nor help us. And finally there's *mutualism*, where the host and the animal that live inside it are somehow dependent on each other, with a relationship that benefits both of them."

"That last sounds like symbiosis," said Siegmund. "Like the things that live inside cattle and help them digest cellulose."

"Exactly. Most people mean mutualism when they talk about symbiosis."

"And you're trying to tell us that those diseases are *good* for the natives?" said Senta, looking very skeptical.

"Not good for them *physically*. None of the parasites help them in that way. Look, here's the whole development as I imagine it. A hundred thousand years ago, the natives were pretty widespread on this planet. They were just animals, plantigrades rather like Earth bears, living along the rivers. They were smart enough to get by, but they couldn't think. They wandered around most of the pleasant parts of the world, but didn't populate the equatorial regions. If they came here at all, the parasitic diseases they got were so bad that evolution took its usual course and they died out. Then a group of them found this valley, just ten or fifteen thousand years ago. This particular place was different from the rest of the equatorial zone—there were the trematodes here, the valley was infested with them."

"But how could they be here?" asked Siegmund. "I thought you said that they needed to live in the natives."

"It doesn't have to be only the natives. The trematodes must have lived in a different host, probably one of the other small animals that live in the valley. But here's the difference. When the trematodes infected the natives, their preferred site was the spinal column and the brain."

"Jim," said Senta. "You'll have a hard time persuading me that the way to improve your intelligence is to have worms eating away at your brain. That would make you more stupid, not less."

Parker sighed. "Senta, the microfilarial worms don't *eat away* at the host. They get their nourishment from the blood stream."

"So how do they affect the host's intelligence?" She looked at Parker, eyebrows raised.

"I can think of three probable ways—and I have no idea which one is correct. The worms may be releasing a substance into the central nervous system that alters the rate of transmission of nerve signals. Or the worms may be producing an enzyme that permits reproduction of brain cells—our brain cells never increase in numbers, but theirs may. Or there may be an enzyme that *damps* some areas of brain activity. That one would be quite different, no intrinsic change in brain power, but a sort of re-ordering of mental priorities. You know, reduced aggression, or reduced sex drive. Maybe the real process was a combination of all three of these.

"Anyway, the natives became smarter. The valley here became habitable for them. They still had the other diseases, but they were intelligent enough to survive, even given their poor physical condition. Now, the Old Ones—"

"Excuse me, Captain." The interruption came from Mulligan, craning his long neck into the tent. "I didn't know you had a meeting here, and I don't want to disturb you. But something very odd is going on in the village. It's a big ceremony, and they wouldn't let me stay there to watch it. They said I could come back tomorrow."

Senta frowned. "Come in, Professor, and join us." She looked at Parker, who was nodding his head in a satisfied way. "Jim, do you know what's going on there?"

"Sure. It's perfectly logical. Let me go on. Once the natives here became intelligent, they tried to go back out of the valley and colonize the rest of the planet. They couldn't do it. You see, *the parasites can not be passed on from mother to child.* Each new generation must be re-infected. Outside the valley, the natives found that they were producing young ones who had no intelligence—children who were not 'human,' as they put it. They were simple animals, with no self-awareness or powers of reasoning."

"Hold it right there, Doctor," said Siegmund. "You have contradicted yourself. If the worms can't be passed on from one generation to the next, then how can they work at all?"

Parker looked at him, briefly confused by the question. Then his expression cleared, and he nodded. "Sorry, Siegmund. I was assuming that you all know something about parasites. You see, they have a complicated life-cycle. In addition to growing in the host—in this case, the natives—they may spend a different part of their life in another animal. The other one is called the *alternate host*. For the disease to pass on, both hosts must be present."

He paused. Siegmund shrugged. "I still don't get it. Who is the alternate host, another native?"

"No. It has to be a different species completely. The other animal is the *vector*, the agent that spreads the disease among the natives, and so that other species is unique to this valley—which isn't all that surprising. This is the only place we know of with such a hot and humid climate. There may be other habitats, I suppose, but they haven't been reached by the natives."

"And you know what the other animal is, do you?" asked Siegmund.

"I think so. It's the insect like a black gnat, the one that has such a painful bite. The situation here parallels one that used to exist back on Earth. There was a disease there called malaria, caused by a protozoan parasite. It was carried from one person to another by an insect called a mosquito. The sexual phase of the parasite—formation of gametes, and fertilization—took place in the stomach of the mosquito. Without mosquitoes, there was no spreading of malaria. Other diseases on Earth were carried by flies and gnats as vectors. So I suspected that the gnats here might be the transmission agents."

He stopped. The sound of piping music and singing was coming from far off. It carried clearly through the still night air, quite different from the usual guttural bark and evening drums of the natives.

"See," he went on. "The ceremony is beginning. Agakwe, the natives weren't preparing their young ones for sacrifice—they were preparing to make them human. You see, infection by the gnats is a chancy business. To make it as certain as possible, the natives leave their young out all night, in the open air—to let the insects get at them. You remember how painful those gnat bites become after an hour or two? That's why they tie the young, to stop them from interfering with the infection process. The young ones can't understand that it's being done for their own good—remember, this is *before* they're infected, so they're not at all intelligent. I doubt if the natives really understand the process by which the infection works—they probably think it's necessary to have *all* the parasitic diseases to gain intelligence. After all, they have no way of separating out the effects of the different parasites that infect them. They just have to take all of them, and different insects carry different diseases."

He paused, and several of the others began to talk at once.

"But how do you know which insect produces the infection from the trematodes?" asked Polo.

"I still don't see what all that has to do with what we saw up in the north," said Siegmund, shaking his head.

"Maybe that's what the tribal Recorder meant when she said that the young aren't human until they are three years old," said Mulligan. "I thought she was just making a joke."

"Jim!" said Senta loudly. She cut through the others' words with the urgency of her voice. "Are you quite *sure* it's the black gnats?"

"All the evidence points to it. You see, I noticed that the number of trematodes in the natives' blood was different at different times of the day. I tried to correlate that with the number of different insects that we found at different times. All the insects have their own cycles, but the frequency of occurrence of the gnats exactly matched the circadian variation of the trematodes. It's evolution at work again. The worms are in the blood at the right time of day to be taken into the gnats when they bite. That's in the early evening—and the natives must have found that out too by trial and error. That's why their young ones are tied up now."

He stopped. Senta had grunted as though in pain. Her face was tormented.

"Jim" she said. "Look up there. *Look at the lamp.*"

They all turned their heads to the fluorescent light that Senta had hung from the tent support.

"Don't you see it?" she said. *"The gnats are gone.* Usually at this hour they would be all around the lamps. Remember that you asked me to detail somebody to spray the habitats? I did, and we started to work this morning. If you're right, we've destroyed an essential host in the life cycle—and the natives don't become intelligent without that symbiotic parasite. Jim, we may have committed genocide!"

"My God." Parker sagged back in his seat. "I've been so busy with the analysis, I forgot all about the spraying. Dial, how far did they get? If all the habitats in the valley are gone, the natives will become animals again in one generation. We'll die with them."

"Let me check." Senta hurried out.

The others stared at Parker uncomprehendingly. "Why should it affect us?" asked Mulligan. "We can still live here."

"We need that intelligence," replied Parker. He took a deep breath and sat up straighter in his chair. "Well, if we've destroyed all the gnat habitats the rest of this may be academic, but let me finish the story for you anyway. Professor Mulligan, you said the Recorder told you the young ones do not become human until they are three, correct?"

"That's right. 'We become human when we are three years,' she said. What is special about three years?"

"I think she was telling you more than you realized," said Parker. "It's not just that the natives become intelligent at three—if they *don't* become infected by the time that they are three years old, they will never achieve full intelligence. Some process has to get started when they are very young."

Mulligan nodded. "We have the same thing ourselves. If language learning does not begin very young, it can never be learned at all."

"Exactly. It's young, or never. The natives found out that the young born outside this valley didn't develop intelligence. *Unless* they could be brought back here while they were still very young. Not only that, they found that the young of the wild ones in the north *would* also become intelligent, if they were brought to the valley in time."

He turned to Siegmund and Polo. "Now does what you saw on your trip north begin to make sense? The natives here are all deathly sick. Their fertility rate is low, and they have trouble keeping the population steady, never mind increasing it. They can't go and live outside the valley, or the children will not develop intelligence. But that becomes irrelevant *when they are past child-bearing age."* . . . . . .

"The Old Ones," said Polo softly. "When they can't produce offspring, they can leave the valley. They go north. And they *steal* the offspring of the wild natives, when they are very young, to send back here as new stock. Siegmund, what was it that Old One in the village said to you? 'The new ones are not ready for the river journey.' Then as soon as he realized that you didn't understand what was going on, he wouldn't talk any more about it."

"Not surprising," said Siegmund. "If it's the way Dr. Parker describes it, I would expect all this to be covered by the highest taboo. It's the center of life itself to the natives, the whole definition of their humanity. They would never talk about it to people who weren't already in the know."

He turned to Parker. "Doctor, I don't want to sound negative, but if you are hoping to cure the natives here of their parasitic diseases except for the effects of the trematodes, then persuade them to go north and work for us, you're too naive about taboo. These natives would never change their system, just because we say they can. The risks to them are impossibly high—the loss of humanity, the only thing that they care about."

"I wouldn't even try that. I'm putting my hopes on the wild ones in the north. I believe that the natives are right, after a young one is three years old it cannot achieve *full* intelligence. I'll bet, though, that it can reach *partial* intelligence if it is infected much later than that. My plan is to take some of the older wild ones, and infect them with the trematodes. That way, they won't suffer the crippling diseases that come from the other parasites, but they should develop enough intelligence to help with the work that Siegmund will have. For that they don't need to be too bright, right?"

Siegmund nodded. "If they're physically fit, too many brains can even be a disadvantage. The best workers are ones who don't find their jobs too routine and boring. What are the chances that your plan will work, Doctor?"

Parker shrugged. "You tell me. Pretty good, I'm hoping, but I don't know. On the other hand, I don't think we have too many choices. If we want to get off this planet before we're all old, we have to try it."

"And to do that, Doctor, you are willing to try and play God." Agakwe spoke for the first time since Parker had begun his explanation. "You would take an innocent people, living lives without sin and without guilt, and destroy their peace? If there is anywhere that we can make a New Beginning, surely this is the place."

Parker looked at him in surprise. The natives had apparently gone from devils of Moloch to innocents in the Garden of Eden in just a few minutes. Even Maria and Akhtar seemed puzzled by Agakwe's rapid change of views. They stared at him in confusion.

"I might agree with you," said Parker finally. "But for one thing. We kept it as quiet as possible, but we can't settle peacefully on this planet. We will all die in a few years of deficiency diseases if we stay here. Our digestive systems need a few extra intestinal flora—parasites, if you want to think of them that way—before we can sustain ourselves indefinitely on the food from this world. We could develop the things we need in the labs at any one of the galactic nodes, but we can't do it with the equipment on the *Rorqual*. This is not the place for your New Beginning."

Agakwe nodded slowly, his blue eyes solemn. "I see. That puts a different complexion on our problem. Self-slaughter is mortal sin in our beliefs—and it would be just that to remain here if we can get away. And yet—" He shook his dark head and sighed. "The end must never justify the means."

He was ready to speak further, but Senta's return claimed their attention. She did not need to say anything, relief was evident on her face.

"They had picked out all the habitats—and they had sprayed three-quarters of them. The rest were scheduled for tomorrow morning."

"Just in time." Parker leaned forward and put his hands to his head. "No thanks to me. There must be a special providence that looks after pregnant women and incompetent ships' doctors. Do you realize that we nearly destroyed a whole intelligent race?"

"We did," said Siegmund. "And if we don't do something more than sit and talk, we'll lose part of another one—us. What do we do next?"

"First we have to isolate forms of the trematodes that can infect the natives in the north," replied Parker. "That means getting specimens from the gnats. Then we need to go on a bigger, better-equipped expedition to the north. We'll try and infect wild natives of different ages, and see how they respond. I feel sure the Old Ones won't interfere provided we don't touch the infants—it will seem inconceivable to them that what we are doing will have any real effect. Perhaps they'll adopt a more rational attitude to their taboos, when they see that what we are doing really works."

"Particularly if we can show them that we can make a young one more intelligent, without all the diseases that they expect to go with it," said Senta. "It won't be easy, though. Come on. We have a lot to do. I'll make up the workplans, but I'll need all the assistance that I can get from all of you."

The others hurried from the tent, but Agakwe remained there alone, deep in thought. At last he took out his gold-bound book and read in silence for many minutes. Outside, the camp gradually became a whirl of excitement and renewed hope.

"And this letter?" said Siegmund.

The young native looked at it, broad face frowning with effort. "D?" he suggested hopefully.

Siegmund nodded. "That's right. Why were you so doubtful? That's all for today."

He gathered up the letters as the young native hurried away. "Still improving," he said to the watching Parker. "He'll never be as smart as the natives in the valley, but he'll do. How old was he when you began?"

"I'm not sure. We don't know how old any of the wild ones are. But I'd guess that he was about ten years old when we caught him, three months ago. They learn fast."

"They do. I really think we may be on our way home. We already have the first production chain rolling for silver extraction, and I'll be able to go ten times as fast when the native assistants come on-line."

The camp was set on the shores of the great northern sea, near the mouth of the estuary. The salt flats provided a good source of the seaweeds and shellfish that Parker had decided offered the least problem to an Earth-trained digestive system. A separate camp, staffed by the New Beginners, stood nearby, ready for the increasing number of wild ones who were appearing for training. Parker looked at the wall, where a moving tally of silver mined versus latest possible departure date was hung. They were gaining steadily, day by day.

"We should have all we need in another three months," he said. "I thought when we started completion would take three times that long."

"It would have, with the usual troop of diggers," said Siegmund. "Doctor, these natives are as good workers as I've seen anywhere. You should have seen the morons I had to use on Centaur."

He sounded very cheerful. Parker looked at him slyly. "So hot planets aren't so bad after all, eh?"

"Not bad at all. In fact—" Siegmund shrugged. "Might as well settle it now. You said that we could get new intestinal flora, once we're back near a big biolab, that would let us live here indefinitely. Are you sure of that?"

"Quite sure. It wouldn't be any problem at all, especially with the specimens we'll take back from here."

Siegmund nodded in satisfaction. "That's all I wanted to know."

"Are you thinking of coming back here, then?"

"Looks that way. Marco and I have been reviewing the imagery he took of the polar regions. We think there are mineral deposits there that you wouldn't believe. I'll handle the ground-hogging with native help for the field work. All we need is a good name for the company. Got any ideas?"

Parker thought for a moment, then shook his head. "Words aren't my line. You should ask Professor Mulligan. He'll suggest fifty names for you."

"That's what I'm afraid of. Well, I'll ask him anyway."

Dial Senta came in as he was leaving. Siegmund looked her up and down and clicked his tongue admiringly. "Nice outfit—and nice perfume. What's the occasion?"

"We're having a little celebration later, in the big tent, to honor the first new core for the Mattin Drive. See you there."

Parker looked after Siegmund ruefully. "You know, Dial, I never could click my tongue like that. No wonder I'm a failure with women."

"With some women." She came and stood close to him. "Jim, there's another reason why I'm wearing this outfit. It's a morale-builder. I finally became convinced today that we're going to get away from here, and now I've got to tell you something. I'm giving up my job on the *Rorqual*. There, that's put it out in the open."

Parker looked at her. They were standing very close, but she could not read the expression in his eyes.

"Dial," he said slowly, "I thought that job was everything to you. You're a top captain, with the best reputation in the business—and that will be doubled, when you bring the *Rorqual* home with a rebuilt drive. Why give it up?"

"I'm beginning to realize what we miss on board the ship—all of that."

She pointed out at the sweep of the sea, gray-green in the setting sun. Wading lizards were bright splashes of red and orange against the salt shallows, and the foothills in the distance were a dusky purple.

Parker nodded. "I know what you mean, Dial. I've felt it too. Have you picked out the world where you want to settle? You could have your pick, with your administrative record."

She shook her head.

"Then," he hurried on, "would you consider this planet? I mean, come back here after you get your system adjusted in a lab, so you could live here as long as you want."

"I like it here," she said, puzzled. "But Jim, what would I do here?"

"Run it. The whole place. When the anthropologists and the specialists in intelligence hear what we found here, they'll be all over the place. We'll need a special social structure to protect the natives. You could run that, Dial—people do what you tell them, without arguing. Don't ask me why."

"And what about you, Jim. You'll stay on in the *Rorqual?*"

He shook his head. "I probably would have, if it hadn't been for Agakwe—blast him. He acted as my conscience, the day we were talking about the use of the natives, back in the first camp. Remember what he said to me? 'The end must never justify the means.' After that, I began to realize just what we were doing. We were giving self-knowledge to a whole new group of beings—playing God, Agakwe called it. So . . ." He shrugged. "I decided I had to come back here. In a strange sense, I feel like the father of these wild ones. I took them from innocence to half-humanity—even though they'll never be as smart as the natives in the valley, because we get them too late. In a way that makes our responsibility to them even greater. I have to come back here."

"But Jim, you can't spend the rest of your life playing nursemaid. You have too much skill and training for that."

"Not really. I'm a fairly average doctor—a mediocre one, compared with the hot-shots who'll be coming in here. But I'll be honest. I have another reason for staying, and it's a big one."

He put his arms around her waist. "Dial, this planet may be nothing special to you, but to a doctor like me, it's the most exciting place in the universe. We are seeing intelligence evolving as we watch.

"Humans came by their intelligence the slow way, and nobody knows how we did it. The trematodes can't live in our systems, the chemistry is too different. But some of us will be coming back here, and when we do we'll have a few changes. We'll have modified systems, so that we can live here as easily as the native animals. Suppose the trematodes can live in us then? And suppose they produce the same amount of change in our intelligence as they did for the natives? Can you imagine what we might be? We might become supermen."

Senta looked at him, worry lines on her forehead.

"Or monsters. It sounds terribly risky. Anything could happen."

"I know. But I want to be in on it. I suspect that the trematodes set up a sort of irritation in the brain—a fever, or an inflammation, so that there's a constant stimulus to ideas. There were humans in the past who were like that, with incredible levels of creativity. People like Mozart, or Leibniz, or Shakespeare. Suppose we could all be like them? Maybe we could create that condition of the mind, in controllable amounts."

Parker's voice was excited and his eyes far away. Senta looked at him and sighed. "And the other doctors who come here will feel the same way that you do, I suppose. I'd better be here, too, to make sure you get food and drink when you need it. Wasn't it Isaac Newton who became so engrossed in his thoughts that he couldn't remember whether he had eaten dinner? Come on, we have to attend the celebration for the new drive core. If we don't get away from this planet, even my limited intelligence can tell me we'll never return."

She gently disengaged his arms from her waist and turned towards the door. As she did so, the tall figure of Agakwe entered. He looked resolute and determined.

"Captain, I understand that the new cores will be ready in a few months. How long will it be before the *Rorqual* can reach a galactic node and send a ship back here?"

Senta stood for a few moments, calculating. "If a ship were to set off again a week after we got to the node, it could be back here two months after we leave.

Agakwe nodded. "And is it true, Captain, that no one has ever returned to a node with a rebuilt Mattin Drive?"

"That is true—but I think that our chances are excellent."

"I hope so. However, I must now tell you our decision. The New Beginners will not be on the *Rorqual* when it leaves. We intend to stay here."

Parker shook his head. "You can't, Agakwe. The food . . ." He stopped.

Agakwe smiled. "Exactly, Doctor. If the Drive works satisfactorily, someone will be back here in a few months, and we will have supplies to supplement our food."

"—and if the Drive fails, you will be no worse off than the rest of us." Parker smiled. "I can't disagree with that analysis."

"But that is not the reason for our choice," continued Agakwe. "We feel that we have a moral responsibility that cannot be denied. Our visit here has created a new intelligence, different from both us and the natives of the valley. Can we leave these people to an uncertain fate, without moral guidance, while we run back to the shelter of our safe planets? The assembly voted on it, and our decision is unanimous. The New Beginners will stay here, to live or to die."

He caught the surprised look in Parker's eyes. "I know, Doctor. To you, we are a bunch of eccentrics. But we cannot turn our back on humans—for these creatures *are* humans, in all the important measures—in need of help."

He turned, and the tall figure was swallowed up in the darkness. Senta and Parker looked at each other in silence. Finally Parker frowned and rubbed his chin.

"That's twice that Agakwe has taught me that lesson. I'll not be so quick to judge a man in the future. He may be an eccentric, but he's twice the man I am."

They linked arms and headed for the door. At the threshold they met Mulligan, resplendent in an elaborate native costume.

"Ah, Doctor Parker," he said. "I don't want to disturb you, but I just wanted to ask you one thing. How long will it be before I can return here?"

Parker looked at Senta. "Three or four months, if all goes well," he said.

Mulligan smiled cheerfully. "That is most satisfactory. I will send a message to that effect to Rosi." He waved a long arm at his clothing. "What do you think of this? It was made specially for me by the tribal Recorder."

"It's—striking, Professor. Are you planning another visit here?"

"I think so. Certainly, the oral history of the natives here, and their language, fascinate me. And my presence on Capella Five can be delayed, if not dispensed with. Now, let us go to the celebration. 'On with the dance, let joy be unconfined.' "

He giggled, turned to the door, and then at once turned back. Parker sighed. It began to seem that they would never get over to the other tent.

"One more thing," said Mulligan. "Earlier today I was discussing with Agakwe the story of Man's acquisition of self-knowledge, as it is taught in many Earth religions. You know"—he coughed self-consciously—"if I may quote Milton: *Of Man's first disobedience, and the fruit of that forbidden tree, whose mortal taste brought death into the world and all our woe*. Well, after we had talked it occurred to me that we and the natives of this planet had a very similar experience. In *our* tradition, Adam and Eve ate the apple and knowledge of guilt and sin came to them. But on *this* world"—he tittered—"*there was a worm in the apple!*"

He stood for a moment, gawky and beaming, then turned and left the room. There was a crash in the darkness outside and a pained oath.

"He deserved that," said Parker. Arm-in-arm, he and Senta set out for the big tent. ☆

About the Authors

Marion Zimmer Bradley is best know for her extended series of sf novels set on the imaginary world of Darkover. Though she's been a science-fiction writer for more than twenty years, Bradley's most recent novel is a rich family saga set against the background of the circus—*The Catch Trap.*

Robert Curtis is a graduate of the U.S. Naval Academy and Cornell University Medical College. He practiced medicine in San Francisco, but now writes full-time. He has had several non-fiction juvenile books published as well as stories in the various mystery magazines. His latest novel is *Pacific Hospital.*

Philip K. Dick's short stories appeared regularly in the sf magazines in the 1950s. One of the most interesting writers in the field, Dick later turned his attention to writing novels, the most famous of which, *The Man in the High Castle,* received the Hugo in 1963. A new Phil Dick story is a rare treat and a privilege to publish.

G. C. Edmondson was born in Guatemala, studied medicine in Vienna and became a translator for the U.S. Navy. One of his most popular novels, *The Ship that Sailed the Time Stream,* recounts the exploits of a navy yawl as it travels through time.

James P. Hogan is the man who has helped to put the science back into science fiction. A British-born engineer, turned computer consultant, he writes the kind of novel popular in science-fiction's Golden Age. He is currently finishing up the triology that began with *Inherit the Stars.*

Lee Killough supplements her writing income by moonlighting as a radiographer at the KSU Veterinary Hospital in the College of Veterinary Medicine at Kansas State University. Her third novel *The Monitor, The Miners and The Shree* was just published.

Charles Sheffield is Vice-President of Research and Development for Earth Satellite Corporation and President of the American Astronautical Society. His short stories and articles have been appearing regularly in the sf magazines. His most recent novel is *The Web Between the Worlds.*

L. Neil Smith, a self-defense consultant and former police reservist, has served on the Libertarian Party's national platform committee. His first novel, *The Probability Broach,* sets the stage for a long and promising future-history series set in an alternate universe in which George Washington is assassinated at the end of the Whiskey Rebellion.

About the Editor

Judy-Lynn del Rey, editor of the *Stellar* series, was the managing editor of *Galaxy* and *IF* science-fiction magazines for eight and a half years. She has been a contributor to the *World Book Encyclopedia* on science fiction. In addition she is currently a Vice-President at Ballantine Books and the Editor-in-Chief of Del Rey Books, Ballantine's enormously successful SF/Fantasy imprint. Mrs. del Rey lives in New York City with her husband Lester, who has written memorable science fiction over the last forty years and who is now Fantasy Editor for the Del Rey line.